Let it Love

A Contemporary Romance Novel

Emma Aiseman

D1596643

To my husband -
the love of my life, my best friend, and my inspiration

Contents

CHAPTER 1

Chloe

"Okay, ladies, one more stretch for the day." Chloe walks around the room, adjusting her mic and switching to "Wonderful Tonight" by Eric Clapton to lower the pace. She stops mid-room and drops to the floor to demonstrate a minimized version of a cobra stretch. "Stretching your abs is going to feel amazing after all the ab work you ladies worked so hard on today." She exhales vocally, reminding them to breathe. "You should stop where it still feels good. Rest on your elbows if you need to lower the intensity of the stretch," Chloe jumps back up to standing to make sure no one is doing more than they should. "Now back to child's pose." Chloe counts a few beats to let them recharge. "Great job, everyone." She claps cheerfully as they all rise up to standing.

"That was incredible," Louise says, rubbing Chloe's shoulder. "I love your evening classes so much, Chloe," she says.

"Thank you, Louise." Chloe smiles, taking her mic off and fixing her ponytail.

Thank you, Chloe. Voices, smiles, and hugs appear and disappear as the ladies make their way to leave. There's nothing like teaching an evening Pilates class to get a smile back on her face. Helping these ladies feel better and stronger makes her day brighter every time.

It's not very often that she wakes up with a smile, probably close to never, but this morning was different. A blow to the concrete walls she's worked so hard building around herself, yet it made her lips want to curl up all the way to her ears, and she had no idea why. Thankfully, she didn't need to spend too much time figuring it out because Jimmy was able to undo the warm and fuzzy feeling in under ten minutes. By the time she was done getting ready and out the door, a familiar drained sensation had already been snapped back into place. Who said despondency wasn't comfortable? Walls and fences are much-needed mental contraptions to allow one to go about their daily life peacefully and unpainfully. Why would she want to take them down?

Chloe shakes away the thought and packs her backpack. She turns off the lights, locks up the studio, and runs to her usual stop, barely making it to the 5 p.m. bus. Georgia Allentown's 60th birthday party is today, and Chloe promised to be there on time.

"Hey C." The bus driver smiles at her as he opens the doors. Kendrick Lamar is blasting on the radio.

"Hey Al." Chloe smiles back and plops into the seat behind him. You can trust Al to lift up your mood any day.

"Classes canceled again?" He looks at her worriedly through the mirror.

"No, big party today, Al. Had to leave early." She checks her cell phone. "On my way," she texts Jimmy, who doesn't seem to be online.

"Go dazzle them," Al says as he stops at her station.

"You're too nice to me, Al." Her laugh rolls in a trail behind her as she jumps off the bus and sprints to her old condominium complex, up the stairs to the third floor. They need to leave by 5:30 at the latest, which means she has a generous fifteen-minute window to shower, do her hair, put some makeup on, and get dressed. She jiggles her keys through the old peeling lock and storms inside. Jimmy is sitting on the couch in his boxers, feet stretched on the coffee table, watching one of his favorite TV shows that Chloe has already lost count of.

"Jimmy!" she scolds. "We need to leave in fifteen minutes! I texted you when I left work." She undresses as she runs into the shower.

"I know, I know ... stupid party," he grunts and gets up to put some clothes on. He smells like soap, his hair tousled and still damp. Chloe turns around for a small kiss before stepping in the shower, but his mind seems to be somewhere else, not unusual for Jimmy—God forbid he has to turn off the TV for a few hours. She reappears ten minutes later, dressed and ready in record time, breaking her most recent record of twelve minutes. Jimmy is now wearing his black, and only, suit and tie, looking handsome but a little out of place.

"Is this what you're wearing tonight?" he asks, looking critically at Chloe's black dress.

"Yes, you said you liked this dress," she says tentatively.

"I *liked* this dress. It was true when I said it," Jimmy says, emphasizing the past tense of his statement, "but that was last year. You gained like two pounds since." He looks at her belly. She may have gained a couple of pounds, but her abs are still visible, and objectively, based on the scale, she may have been underweight before. These two additional pounds make her breasts look a little fuller, and she's actually been pretty happy getting some curves. But seeing his disappointed eyes has a crushing effect on her confidence right now.

"Should I change to something else?" she asks, despite it being the only cocktail dress she owns that could look fancy enough for tonight.

"I don't know... Maybe stretch the top part down a bit, show more cleavage. And put on some more makeup, maybe red lipstick," he says. She knows Jimmy loves red lipstick, or anything a bit more provocative, for that matter. Seeing other men turn their heads after his girlfriend somehow makes him feel proud. But she hates how it looks on her, hates how it makes her feel. She looks at her watch. Five-thirty...

"Jimmy, we need to leave now, or we'll be late."

Jimmy grunts again and picks up his car keys from the kitchen table. "I don't understand why we always have to do everything last minute. You knew about this party like a month ago," he says, annoyed. "You should have left an hour earlier to give yourself enough time to get ready and put some effort into the way you look. Your makeup is too minimal. It makes *me* look bad."

"I went for a classy look." She tries to smile teasingly, which doesn't seem to be working for her, not tonight, not ever. "You know how much I dislike makeup on my face, plus sometimes less is more."

"Not in your case, honey." His face has gone sour.

"I was teaching a class, Jimmy," she says calmly, trying to keep her composure. "You know we need the money."

"If you spent less time at that worth-nothing college of yours, you would have more time to work and more time to spend with your boyfriend, like a normal person."

As if spending time with her has ever been on his wish list...

"Well, I am sorry I also have dreams." Her voice betrays her, not sounding as assertive as she would have liked right now. Since she re-enrolled herself in college to complete her long—but not forgotten—health science degree, she's been hearing it with increasing frequency. Why he does not consider her a normal person for trying to pursue a college degree is beyond her. "I wish you were more supportive. You know how important it is to me." She should be able to control her tone by now, having responded to this clause pretty damn often. But she can't, apparently. Her voice breaks mid-sentence, and she takes a deep breath, trying to battle that too-familiar lump in her throat.

"Dreams are okay, as long as you don't lose touch with reality," Jimmy says, also not a new phrase of his, but this one hurts the most every time. Maybe because sometimes, when things get rough, she actually believes he's right.

CHAPTER 2

A Birthday Party

M rs. Georgia Allentown lives in one of those enormous mansion-looking houses on the way to Sugarloaf Mountain. The huge front grassy area that has been turned into extra parking space for the event is now almost full. Jimmy parks his old sedan next to a red car.

"Look at this Ferrari!" is Jimmy's admiring reaction to the car as he turns the wheel. Chloe takes a quick look in the mirror. Despite the emotional ride, her makeup still looks intact.

"Do I look okay?" she asks Jimmy, winning herself a scoff of disapproval.

"I told you, Chloe, don't ask a question if you can't deal with the answer."

That bad?

She picks up the wrapped box for Georgia from the back seat and nervously shuts the door behind her. This last hour has been so draining, she just wants to turn around, go home, curl into her side of the bed, and go to sleep. But she promised Georgia she'd be there. Georgia has been nothing but supportive ever since she walked through those glass doors of the studio for the first time a little over a year ago, asking if they had room for one more without an ounce of cynicism, even though the room was completely empty. Class had been canceled that day due to snow, but Chloe showed up anyway, hoping someone would come. She really needed the money and the company. Georgia had arrived with her driver, who was waiting outside by the door, making sure his employer made it safely through the unplowed sidewalk.

"I'm Georgia," she said warmly as she approached to shake Chloe's hand.

"Pleased to meet you, Georgia. I'm Chloe. Come on in," she said as she took her hand. Georgia's strong handshake was almost a contradiction to her soft skin, her eyes earnest and kind. *"Class got canceled due to snow, but I'm here and happy to teach a class!"* Chloe said with a smile.

"I read you have the best Pilates class in town, I had to give it a try," Georgia had said, and the rest was history. Georgia became her favorite and most loyal client, taking every possible class combination Chloe would teach; reformer classes, TRX, jump board, yoga classes, private classes, group classes, bringing her positive spirit and attitude with her every time, making Chloe forget about the world outside and think ... even if just for an hour at a time ... that maybe life had more in store for her somewhere on the horizon.

Jimmy takes Chloe's hand, shaking her off her journey down memory lane and slapping on his public smirk. They walk slowly to the front entrance, then ring the doorbell. A man dressed in all black holding a tray of champagne flutes opens the massive door and welcomes them politely.

"Welcome! Welcome!" Georgia's voice appears quickly behind him. "My dear Chloe, you look glorious!" she says, pulling her into her arms for a hug.

"Oh, Georgia, you are too kind." She smiles, feeling her insecurities slowly melting away. "Please meet Jimmy Miller, my boyfriend. Jimmy, this is Mrs. Georgia Allentown, my favorite customer."

Jimmy shakes Georgia's hand politely. "Pleased to finally meet you, Mrs. Allentown," he says, gathering all his charms. He definitely knows how to be that Prince Charming when he wants.

"Oh, please, call me Georgia." She smiles and leads them to a gigantic room decorated with flowers and candles and multiple tables covered in soft golden fabrics, all perfectly placed. The center of the space has been designed as a large dance floor, giving it a fancy ballroom look, making Chloe feel somewhat out of place.

They are shown to a table with an older couple and a young woman who is introduced as the couple's daughter, draped in a bright red tube dress that reveals generous cleavage, the kind that Jimmy can never get enough of.

"I'm Jennifer." She smiles politely, giving Jimmy a quick once-over. Jimmy, of course, takes that as an invitation, introducing himself eagerly and positioning himself on the seat closest to her. Jennifer seems pleased with the attention, and the two of them carry the conversation away from Chloe, who scans the place around, desperately looking for familiar faces.

"Please, let me introduce you to my closest friends." Georgia reappears to her rescue. She links her arm with Chloe's and steals her away, an understanding look on her face. They walk together from table to table. Georgia introduces her as "the amazing Chloe," and "the most talented trainer on the planet." They each get up to greet her politely and respectfully, then go back to their conversations. "One more," Georgia squeals with excitement. "You haven't met my nephew William, have you?" She pulls Chloe excitedly across the room, making a beeline to one of the more central tables, stopping by a young man who may have been following Chloe with his eyes since she walked in – or perhaps it was her wishful imaginative self.

The man rises immediately as their steps become committed enough to show their direction, looking handsome and approachable.

"Chloe, I'd like you to meet William Allentown, my favorite nephew," Georgia says in a celebratory voice. "William, this is Chloe Barrett, the amazing," she announces, and as her nephew takes Chloe's hand, Georgia disappears, leaving them on their own.

"Pleased to meet you, Ms. Barrett," he says formally, his baritone voice wrapping itself around her. His hand is strong and warm, and the touch of it does something to the tiny hairs on her skin.

"Pleased to meet you too, Mr. Allentown," she plays along, his formality makes her smile – or maybe it's just her being shy. "Please, call me Chloe." Something in his composure and bearing makes it hard to look away.

"Please, call me Will." He smiles back, holding her gaze. His eyes are dark and captivating, his black hair carefully cut. He looks slightly too handsome to be real. His charcoal suit is tailored perfectly to his build. This guy definitely knows how to rock a suit... "Georgia talks about you all the time," Will says, and Chloe realizes he's still holding her hand. She pulls it back gently, along with her eyes, stealing a quick glimpse at her table. Jimmy is still in deep conversation with that girl. Chloe looks back at Will, who seems to follow the trail of her eyes. An understanding look appears on his face. "There's a spare seat next to me if you'd like to join our table," he offers, pulling a chair for her.

"Oh, I ... am here with my boyfriend," Chloe responds in the most polite manner she can gather, gesturing toward her table, where Jimmy clearly has his eyes fixed on Jennifer's cleavage again. The thought of returning to her spot near Jimmy for a close-up presentation of him drooling all over Jennifer makes her queasy, but she can't see any other way around it.

"I'm sorry," Will says, and from his gaze, she's not sure whether he is sorry that she has a boyfriend, sorry for assuming she didn't, or sorry for *her* that *this* is her boyfriend. *Perhaps all of the above?* She's not sure how to respond to it either. "Please don't take this the wrong way," he frowns lightly, "and it's probably none of my business ... but you deserve more than that," he says, earnest eyes looking at her carefully. "This is ... not how one should treat their—"

"Girlfriend." The word escapes her mouth before Will has a chance to finish his sentence. As if hearing it from someone else would make it any worse. Her eyes fall to the floor.

"I made you uncomfortable... I'm sorry," he says quickly, although his voice is still filled with intention. But it's Jimmy who's making her uncomfortable. The way he strips this Jennifer girl with his eyes does not leave much room for guessing.

"Can you blame him? Look how beautiful she is."

Is she actually trying to defend Jimmy, or is it the last bit of her remaining self-dignity she's guarding?

Will's lips curve up to a dimpled smile. He's about to say something, but their attention shifts when the music changes, and everyone is called into the dance floor for some slow dancing. Her eyes bounce back to her table, where Jimmy gets up and pulls Jennifer behind him. "Seriously?!" she hears herself blurt.

Oh gosh, did she just say it out loud?

"I do, in fact." Will's deep baritone voice brings her back.

"You do, in fact, what?" Her eyes meet Will's again, puzzled, tilting her head in response to him still bearing that smile.

"Blame him," he says. "He's here with you. And he is totally messing it up."

"You have to admit, she *is* beautiful," Chloe can't take her eyes off them dancing with each other, Jimmy's hands on the small of Jennifer's back. And it's true, Jennifer is beautiful, with her long-nurtured blond just-spent-hundreds-of-dollars-at-a-torturing-hair-place hair, her turquoise blue eyes, looking like a supermodel in that dress... She's probably also the proud owner of numerous sets of fancy lingerie. In fact, Chloe wouldn't be surprised if she's wearing one of those uncomfortable sets right now, a dream come true for Jimmy. Jennifer is everything Chloe is not.

"*You* are beautiful," Will says, making her snort. This brings a puzzled look to his face, as if he's surprised by Chloe's lack of awareness of her own looks.

That's what a few years with Jimmy will do to you.

"Dance with me." Will offers a rebuttal, and somehow getting back at Jimmy feels like a good idea. She takes his hand and finds herself in the spotlight as they make their way to the dance floor. Heads turn, all eyes are on them, probably wondering what a breathtaking guy like him has to do with an ordinary gal like her, but Georgia... She's there too, and her eyes look encouraging, pleased. Will stops to face Chloe. She reaches for his shoulders, noticing how broad and tall he is. His suit jacket feels nice, a sort of fabric her fingers haven't felt before.

"This okay?" he asks softly as his hands come to touch her hips, warm and reassuring. She nods, smiling to herself. No one has ever cared whether she was comfortable during a dance. She moves a tad closer to him almost reflexively. His scent wraps around her, a mix of fresh soap and some alluring bergamot cologne she can't quite recognize. She's pretty good with guessing cologne brands, but this one is probably above the Macy's price range. She takes in the scent with her inhale, relishing it secretly. He must notice that little hitch in her breath, because his smile curves upward a little more, revealing his adorable dimples and perfect teeth. His eyes are focused on her as if she's the only person in this entire huge ballroom. She must be imagining things because that's impossible with so many beautiful women surrounding them, dressed in their fancy gowns ... yet it feels like they are alone.

Something flutters in her lower belly.

Gosh! What has gotten into her?

Is it the wine? No, she hasn't even had a chance to take a single sip.

It must be hunger; she hasn't had anything to eat since lunch.

"I need to free you up, I'm sure," she offers. "There's already a line." She gestures with her head toward the bar where two meticulously groomed blondes in glamorous designer dresses are staring Will up and down from a distance, and Chloe is clearly not a worthy competition.

Not that she's trying...

"There's no one in this room I'd rather dance with," Will says simply, still holding her gaze.

Wow...

Her mind escapes for a second before she catches a glimpse of Jimmy, who is enjoying the proximity to his dance partner a tad too much. The pace of the music changes to salsa, and the scene heats up. It's her favorite kind of dancing, which Jimmy usually refuses to take part in. Will, however, seems quite well-versed with the moves – twisting and turning her, her hips swaying with the music, and she can't help the big smile that makes its way across her face.

She's actually having fun. At a rich people's party.

What. Is. Up. With. Her?

But existing in a bubble can't possibly last long for her... Chloe feels a tap on her shoulder, and it's Jimmy, claiming her back, stretching his neck, and inflating his chest to look larger ... but to no avail. Next to Will, Jimmy looks ... well ... small. Will just nods politely and lets Chloe go, leaving an imaginary imprint where he touched her. She pulls herself away from him into Jimmy's arms, and to her disappointment, they return to the table, skipping the last part of the dance. Jimmy brings his face closer to whisper something in her ear.

"You need to move your hips more when you dance," is all he has to say.

CHAPTER 3

S'mores

The music fades, and the guests are called back to their tables for dinner. Food and wine are flowing; glasses, plates, and silverware clank softly around. Jimmy is back to his spot next to Jennifer, enjoying an extreme surface-level conversation about the weather that lasts way too long.

"So what do you guys do?" Jennifer gets bored and tries to change the topic. Jimmy assumes she's talking business and brags about his last insurance sales position, which he recently lost for not being able to get to work on time on more than one occasion within the same week – but he fails to mention that minor detail. "And Chloe is a Pilates instructor," he jumps in before she has a chance to speak for herself.

"I am also studying health science at—" she tries to squeeze in, but Jimmy beats her to it.

"Yeah, that's her side gig," he says apologetically and nudges Chloe's knee under the table. *Whatever*. "How about you?" He turns his head, along with his body, to Jennifer.

"I'm studying law at Johns Hopkins. I'll be graduating next year," she says proudly. Jimmy makes sounds of being way too impressed. "Where do you go to school, Chloe?" Thankfully Jennifer's social etiquettes pull her back into the conversation.

"It's a community college," Chloe responds. Seeing how Jimmy's chest deflates, she decides to skip additional information. Why Jimmy can't be proud of her is beyond her. College is college, she goes where she can afford, and she works damn hard to pay for it. And yes, it's been an extremely long and winding journey with a lot of bumps along the road that mostly had to do with life and money, but Chloe has finally been able to move forward at a steady, albeit slow, pace. And now she's determined to get her bachelor's degree in health science, get an internship in nutrition, and sit for the accreditation exam to get her license as a nutritionist, whether Jimmy thinks she can or not. She's been secretly saving for it.

"Excuse me," Chloe says and gets up to search for the ladies' room. It takes a while to find, since Georgia Allentown's mansion is enormous. On the way back, she wanders around a bit, her chest feeling heavy. Opting for some fresh air, she steps out into the garden. Hundreds of soft little lights decorate the terrace, somehow perfectly merging into the star-dotted sky above, giving off gorgeous fairytale vibes. A few people are there, enjoying their wine, chatting away, some standing in small groups, some sitting under the lights or next to scattered cobblestone firepits, each with cushioned outdoor furniture surrounding it. Chloe walks down to one of the unattended sets and sits down with a sigh. The pleasant heat and soft light of the flames help clear her head. She isn't hungry anymore, and actually feels a little sick. Watching Jimmy interact with other women has this effect on her.

She wishes Jimmy was a tad more attuned to her feelings. The sweet atmosphere in the garden must have gone to her head, letting in all those unrealistic thoughts. In this fairytale world, Jimmy would be more in touch with his girlfriend, he would follow her outside, ask what's wrong, spend some time with her, alone. Heck, he wouldn't be ogling Jennifer to begin with. He would pay attention to Chloe, and he would definitely notice if she walked away. But as Jimmy so frequently reminds her, no one is perfect, maybe she should take his advice and stop focusing on what he can't offer. Fairytales are just not what life has in store for her, so why fight it?

"Is this seat taken?" She hears a male voice, not Jimmy's.

"Obviously not," she says, then hearing the bite in her voice, she looks up to assess the damage. Apparently, Will Allentown was the one to notice she'd walked away.

"Ouch," he says, eyebrows colliding softly. "Is everything okay?"

"Sorry, that wasn't aimed at you," she says. "Please sit down. I could use some company right now."

"Yes ma'am." He obeys and sits down next to her. They sit quietly for a while, taking in the night sky, the clean countryside air, and the slow, quiet whispers of the flames as they burn into the wood. "This is my favorite spot," Will finally says. "When I was a kid, I would come here a lot, stay with my aunt and uncle every summer. We used to make s'mores every single night."

"S'mores?!" She feels the edges of her mouth starting to curve. "That's my very favorite dessert! I haven't had it in like ... forever!" Thinking about it somehow manages to lift her spirits up a notch.

"Really?" His head turns toward her, looking pleasantly surprised.

That she likes s'mores? Or that such a simple thing can stave off her frustration?

His eyes bright, portraying the little flames' reflections dancing all around. Chloe has to force herself from staring. He smiles at that. "Wait here," he says and gets up suddenly, disappearing back into the grand brick mansion, taking away the positive air with him. Guests are going in and out, but the garden is mostly quiet, almost surreal. Chloe wonders what Jimmy is up to right now, but she doubts he's even noticed her absence. Her throat feels tight, that lump reappearing, making it harder to breathe or think properly. This has been happening too often lately, understandable given the provocation, but she hasn't had much time to prepare.

C'mon, not now ... not when there are so many people around.

She takes a deep breath, trying to control it. She blinks a few treacherous tears away, and then Will is back by her side, handing her a long wooden stick and marshmallows, brightening up the grayness with every move.

"We're making s'mores?" She looks up to face him.

"We certainly are." He smiles cheerfully. "Making your very favorite dessert and reliving a childhood memory of mine. It's been a while for me too." He slides a marshmallow onto his stick and pushes it into the flames for a few seconds. Chloe follows along. His lips arrange themselves into a childish smile, and she can't help but smile back. He pulls back his stick and deftly slides the marshmallow between two large pieces of graham cracker and chocolate. She follows his moves with her own marshmallow, which comes out of the fire looking way too burnt for human consumption. "I see you like yours well-done," he chuckles, but then breaks his into two pieces and hands her the larger half.

"Thanks," she says quietly, "I need to brush up on my s'more skills. I'm a little rusty." Jimmy resents any mention of marshmallows or sweets in general, especially if it involves her eating them. But at this very moment, thinking of Jimmy does not bring back the familiar lump in her throat, and that feels like a major relief. "Georgia was probably a fun aunt to grow up around," she says, taking a small bite of the hot marshmallow, trying to clean up the chocolate melting away on the sides of her lips.

"Yes, very much!" he says, and his eyes light up even more as he pulls up his memories. "I used to wish she and Uncle Benjamin were my parents. Being around happy, positive people is contagious. I don't think I've ever heard my parents laugh out loud. They are complete opposites."

"I love how accepting and warm Georgia is, and I have to agree, her laugh is contagious."

"She adores you, Chloe!" She likes how her name sounds when he says it. His eyes look straight into hers, saying so many things without using any words at all. "You've changed her life, you know?"

"Me?!" She can't help the surprised and somewhat humbled look that has probably lodged itself onto her face.

"Yes, you," Will says with certainty. "She suffered all kinds of pain before she started taking classes with you. I'm sure she had mentioned that." He studies her intently. "Back pain, joint pain, nothing that conventional medicine could put its finger on, no matter how much money one might throw at it. She used to say that her age had finally caught up with her."

"Yes, I remember hearing her say that, but she was determined to take the lead on that race, and when Georgia sets her mind on something … she has an amazing attitude."

"You know my aunt well." He smiles, and those dimples appear again. "And then she met you. It was almost like she was shedding layers of pain with every class."

"Nah, it's not me. Pilates and yoga can do that, you know? And Georgia has certainly been taking her training seriously. She's also completely transformed her nutrition from comfort food to a Mediterranean diet. I'm so proud of her."

"Under your guidance."

"I'm no expert. I just make suggestions based on established and proven scientific research." Talking about nutrition makes her excited. "The Mediterranean diet is rich in antioxidants, fresh produce, and healthy fats. It helps reduce inflammation and is good for the heart. I figured if it didn't help, it surely wouldn't hurt, right?" She could go hours on this topic. If Jimmy were here, he'd have said she was babbling again. But Will seems interested – tilting his head to the side, studying her, watching what must be her face lighting up.

"What made you go into teaching Pilates?"

"It's my favorite sport, and I needed a job. The studio offered a trainer certificate, and Tania, my boss, was willing to let me take the training for free if I committed to teaching there for a full year." She notices how Will's eyes follow her with enthusiasm as she speaks, encouraging her to continue. "Helping others feel more comfortable in their own skin has always been a passion of mine." As the words leave her mouth, it dawns on Chloe that she voluntarily lets Jimmy do the exact opposite to her on a daily basis. "I'm also working on getting my health science degree," she dares. Jimmy's voice jumps into her head, reminding her how she shouldn't start a conversation about her no-good college and the forever-taking degree. "I hope to one day get my license in nutrition and open my own business for Pilates, yoga, and nutrition consultation, all in one place. The information out there is so confusing. I want to make it simple for people to take their health into their own hands. And I've seen what incredible impact nutrition and exercise can have on people's health and well-being. I want to help make a difference, even if it's a small one."

"I like your idea! And you already have Georgia's health transformation as testimony," he says, not an ounce of skepticism or criticism in his voice. It feels ... refreshing. "Where do you go to school?" Of course, that's always the follow-up question.

"It's a local community college," she answers reflexively, not both-

ering with the details of her probably anonymous community college, hearing Jimmy's voice in her head. "The only place I can afford
right now, and it's close to where I live ... and they let you take classes
at your own pace so I can keep my day jobs," she blurts out, expecting
a disappointing or degrading look, like the one Jimmy always has
when she brings her schoolwork up. But that look does not appear,
not with Will.

"Wow! I'm impressed," he says supportively.

Is he for real?

"Thanks," she says, genuinely surprised. She's just poured some of
her heart on an almost complete stranger, and he didn't try to break
her or shatter her dreams. Her eyes look up, admiring all those stars
one can spot in the countryside. She can never see that many under
the city lights. "But I'm starting to doubt whether this dream will
ever..."

"Dreams can come true, you know, if you dream hard enough."
His childish smile still hasn't gone away since the s'mores. "And
there are scholarships and grants." He puts two more marshmallows
into the flames.

"Maybe, one day." She allows herself to get carried away with what
if, but really just for a second.

"So, you said day jobs ... as in more than one? That's tough.
Where?"

Chloe nods. "A Pilates studio and a restaurant called Claudia's,"
she huffs. "They're very flexible with my shifts, so I can juggle Pilates
teaching, school work, and ... life."

"That's a lot." This somehow makes him look even more impressed.

"It's not too bad, and it pays the bills."

"I think being a waiter is the hardest job I've ever done," he says
suddenly.

"You ... worked as a waiter?" She doesn't mean the prejudiced voice, but she just can't help wondering how someone coming from a wealthy family like him would end up as a waiter.

"Yes, I tried to make a point." He laughs at the sound of her surprise. "My parents wanted me to take over the family business after college, and real estate is not ... *was* not what my young, bold self wanted to do."

"You still look young and bold to me."

"Thank you. Maybe, but I've wanted to become a writer ever since I can remember. My parents weren't very supportive of this idea, to put it gently." He halts for a second to examine her face, she gives him an encouraging smile to proceed. "They said writing was not profitable. Obviously, they were not familiar with Stephen King or J. K. Rowling. Not that I had any thought of measuring up... So, I took a job as a waiter and kept at it for a year to show them I could make a living *and* write books. My parents hated this experiment. Making a living is definitely not enough for them. But believe it or not, this has been my proudest accomplishment, and I didn't even finish the book." Will slides the marshmallows off the stick and into the graham crackers and hands her another s'more. Their fingers touch lightly, sending a gentle current into her.

Did he feel it too?

"Why did you stop?" she asks, her fingers still lingering on that brief touch.

"I realized that, as their son, there are certain expectations of me... I could see why they'd want me to continue their legacy, and I respect that. We settled on me going into business school for my graduate degree." His eyes have a shade of sadness to them as he says it.

"What do you like to write?"

"*Liked* to write," he says wistfully. "Fiction mostly, suspense, sometimes romance."

"*Liked?* As in you're not writing anymore?" she says. "Because I would love to read." Will's eyes beam at the sound of that.

"Inspiration, I guess... Lost it along the way." He shifts in his seat like he's trying to shove that thought away and, with that, changes the subject. "Would it be too daring if I joined one of your classes?"

She laughs, planning to explain that it might be an issue in a women-only studio. Something from this morning's unfamiliar warmth and fuzziness reemerges for a brief second. But the moment dissipates, and her smile turns serious as Jimmy makes his appearance at the front of the terrace, signaling with a sullen expression and a nervous motion of his head that it's time to leave.

"What the fuck was that all about?" Jimmy scolds as he slams the car door behind him, starting his car.

"What was *what* all about?" Chloe asks, struggling to get into the passenger seat with her dress. She should be the one asking him.

"Spending the entire evening with this guy? Didn't know you were into rich boys now."

"Seriously? You were ogling that Jennifer girl the entire night." She buckles her seatbelt and crosses her arms.

"You see how important it is to put some effort into the way you look? When a woman looks hot and sexy, you can't really blame me for wanting to be around her," he says admonishingly. As if openly displaying his lust toward other women in social events, whether or not his girlfriend is around, is a perfectly acceptable thing to do.

"That's not the point, Jimmy!"

"So, what exactly *is* the point, Chloe?" He says it slowly, as if she has issues understanding social cues.

"The point is that you were there with *me*, yet you made me feel like I was the last person in there you wanted to be around. You didn't even let me get a single word out in the conversation."

"All you want to talk about is your failed college studies and your unrealistic dreams. You keep embarrassing me over and over again."

"It's not unrealistic, and you can't say I've failed if I haven't stopped trying." Okay, so it's taking her longer than typical to graduate, but that doesn't make it a failed attempt. She's still pursuing it, still attending those classes, submitting her assignments, studying for her exams, and not failing them. "Slow and steady wins the race, no?"

"Fuck Chloe, you're so naive. Winning races is not up your alley. The sooner you understand it, the better." His mansplaining tone makes her stomach churn.

Who died and made him the tyrant king?

"So, what were you doing outside anyway?"

"Making s'mores," she says simply. Trying to control a sudden urge to smile despite Jimmy's toxic propaganda. "I needed some fresh air, went to sit outside. You could have followed me if your eyes weren't so attached to Jennifer's cleavage."

"Maybe I didn't want to."

CHAPTER 4

The Panelist

C hloe rushes into the building, already late. Her class started five minutes ago. In an ideal world, she would always be on time. But working two jobs and using public transportation to shuffle herself around has its limitations and certainly requires some degree of prioritization. Which unfortunately means not leaving the Pilates studio until the very last client is out the door so she can lock up before sprinting to the bus stop. She slows her pace down to catch a breath, walking through the doorway and plopping herself in an empty seat in the corner, trying to pull out her notebook and pen from her backpack without making too much fuss, the instructor already in full swing.

"I'm glad you decided to join us," he says under his breath. The semester just started, and he's new, so hasn't had a chance to be brought up to speed on Chloe's life situation. She was kind of hoping she won't have to, but with the second late appearance out of two classes they've had so far ... she should probably get to it sooner than later.

"I'm sorry, I—" On second thought, there's no guarantee it would do any good, plus most of her peers are probably in similar situations. She decides to hold back for now and try harder next time, maybe change her Pilates class schedule so that she doesn't have to cut it so short every time. Perhaps even give herself a few extra minutes to punch in a sandwich. She's starving to the point that her stomach is loudly grumbling. Niki gives her a quick but empathic smile from the front row, a friendly face in the crowd. This is the second class they've been in together. They've never actually exchanged more than a few words on the way to and from class. It's a limited class-buddies kind of friendship, someone to walk the hallways with, but that's more than enough to help Chloe not feel so anonymous. The other students seem to have closer friends around, but that's how it is when you're taking only one or two classes each semester. Not really being part of the cohort, never having time to attend any of the after-school events ... it's better than nothing, but still far from ideal. Even if she did have time for that, Jimmy would not want to be her plus one in any of these events. He already hates the time she spends in college with a passion.

The rumbling in her stomach and her impending headache are telling her that getting some food and water into her system is necessary, but Chloe manages to keep her focus and even take some notes. The new chemistry instructor is making sense, and things are clicking into place, finally.

"I'll let you all go five minutes early," he says, "in case you want to catch the business panel tonight." Business panel? How come she's only hearing about it now? While some people may not be interested in listening to a business panel when majoring in health science, for Chloe, fantasizing about opening her own health and nutrition clinic and studio, that's an opportunity. Most of her classmates, though, seem pleased and chatter away about the coming session.

"What is it about?" Chloe turns her head to Niki.

Niki gives her a shrug. "It's open to all majors – the business school invited a few established local business owners and entrepreneurs to talk about their career paths. I have no idea who's coming to speak, but there's free dinner, so I'm in." She smiles and throws her backpack over her shoulder, ready to leave. "Are you coming?" This is already more words than they've exchanged so far.

Chloe considers her options: taking a bus home, finding Jimmy on the couch flipping through channels, scolding her because there's nothing to eat. It could take a couple of hours before she can get dinner ready. Or, a few-minute walk to the adjacent building, listening to some business experts talk, quieting her stomach, watering down her now very prominent headache, and learning about owning a business – that's a no-brainer. "Sure," Chloe responds, flashing a quick text to Jimmy that she's staying for a lecture, which he clearly receives but does not bother answering.

Ugh...

They enter the room. A large table has been set up in the corner with a pile of boxed sandwiches and drinks. Chairs are spread across the room in an organized fashion. Another long table for the panel is neatly set up front, decorated with little notes with speaker names that she's too hungry to try to read. It looks like they're expecting five panelists. Chloe grabs a sandwich and a bottle of water and situates herself next to Niki, who, for some reason, has this weird preference for front rows. Chloe would feel more comfortable in the back row, primarily since this event is probably geared toward other less science-focused students. But some familiarity vs. anonymity gets the upper hand, so the front row it is. Chloe bites into her chicken salad sandwich, realizing how hungry she really is – that earlier grumbling was nothing compared to this. She could probably eat an entire chicken right now. Niki doesn't say much as they both chew in silence, except for mentioning that one of the speakers is hot, based on the headshot in the poster that's featured across campus. That could be the explanation for the acute unbalanced female-to-male ratio in the room. Chloe somehow missed every single one of these ads – running to and from class doesn't leave much time to stop by to admire campus posters or bulletin boards.

They finish chewing their food, and Chloe chugs down two water bottles on top of the one she had with her food. Niki gives her an amused look. "What? I'm thirsty," she says, winning herself a snort from her walk-the-hallway friend. Chloe glances at her watch. She still has a few minutes before the speakers are scheduled to arrive, which leaves her with more than enough time to make a run for the bathroom before her bladder explodes. "Be right back," she announces to Niki, who is busy checking out the room. Chloe gets up from her seat and literally runs.

She should really start breaking this bad habit of rushing every-where, especially in crowded hallways. Because...

Her body is met with a wall of a person's chest, covered in a suit and a tie.

A nice suit and tie.

He immediately grasps her shoulders to save her from whiplashing back. She takes a breath before looking up, planning her apology for violently crashing into the guy. After all, she was running.

"Sorry," she says, gathering a sweet apologetic tone.

An addictive scent of cologne her nose has met before wraps itself around her. Then she takes in a chuckle and a dimpled smile. "Chloe?" says a baritone voice.

Her eyes shoot up. It's been a week since Georgia Allentown's party, and although Chloe tried her best to shove that memory somewhere irretrievable, she apparently hasn't landed too much success. It's still so palpable that she's gone so far as to imagine the guy appearing right in front of her, here – at her little community college of all places. She doesn't recall hitting her head, so she lets her surprise take over.

"Will?!" She might need an MRI, though...

"Are you okay?" Will makes sure she's fully stable before letting go of her. She nods. Thankfully he has good instincts. She could have ended up on the floor.

"Sorry," she says again, but he seems pleased, smiling. "What brings you here?" She shifts in her place, clearly needing to resume the run to the bathroom.

"Volunteering for the business panel," he says bashfully. "You're here for the panel?"

"Yes," she grins, "and for the food." He chuckles. "And obviously I drank too much water, so I was..." She points in the direction of the bathrooms.

"But you're coming back?"

Is that anticipation in his eyes she sees? She's clearly been impacted by that crash...

"Wouldn't miss it," she says.

"So, I'll see you there." Will smiles, and when his head disappears into the crowd, she resumes her run into the bathroom. After she washes her hands and flushed face, she fixes her hair, then tries to get herself together. Taking a deep breath, she emerges into the hallway, this time a little more composed, and back into the room. The five panelists are already seated at the long table. Two women and a man, maybe in their sixties, then Will and another guy, who seems around the same age as Will – late twenties, maybe early thirties – but not nearly as attractive. None of them look familiar, which is not surprising as Chloe doesn't really follow any business news or websites. She mainly focuses on nutrition and physical activity research if she has any time to spare, a rare thing. Her eyes travel on their own account to Will, just in time to catch his gaze following her, a small smile playing on his face as she walks to the front row. This time, she moves slowly and carefully, too aware that she's being watched, until she finally takes her seat next to Niki, proud of herself for making it back to her chair uneventfully. Chloe tries to quiet down her breathing, not having too much success. Somehow being Will's center of attention, watching his studying eyes, is not helping. Niki shoots her a feigned scold.

Is it that obvious?

The evening is moderated by one of the business students who is holding index cards with questions. They go by order; each panelist tackles the same question before they move to the next. There are two startup company founders – one for clean energy, one in technology – one CEO of an investment company, one person has a consulting company, and then there's Will, who is presented as "the CEO of the Allentown Real estate and construction enterprise."

They all share interesting stories about their studies, career paths, aspirations, and leadership styles. Will apparently went to Yale and majored in English and creative writing before getting his graduate degree in business from Columbia University. Chloe likes his take on leadership: listening, mentoring, helping others see the big picture, inspiring. The moderator asks Will to give advice to the younger students starting out their journey.

"Make sure you don't give up on things you like, especially when you're busy building yourself up. Because that is a sure way to lose yourself in the process or lose your inspiration," he says. His eyes find Chloe. His confession by the firepit is still fresh in her mind, *Inspiration. I guess I lost it along the way.* "It's part of who you are and part of the unique set of skills in your toolbox," he goes on, "so you want to make sure you maintain it."

The evening ends with enthusiastic clapping. A trail of students lines up next to each of the speakers for additional questions. Equipped with a pen and a piece of paper, Tiffany, one of the nicer-looking girls in her class, approaches Will, trying to land his phone number, but he politely and admirably refuses. He patiently answers questions while Chloe packs up her stuff, his eyes signaling for her to stick around.

Niki gives her a sneaky look. "You could have mentioned you know William Allentown." She frowns.

"I didn't know he was one of the speakers, I swear." Chloe shrugs, spreading her hands in confusion.

"Are you guys ... together?" Niki asks with a sly smile.

"No, I have a boyfriend."

Why would she think that?

"Oh, well then, can you introduce us?" She grins.

"Sure," Chloe says, but something about it makes her uneasy.

Will is done chatting with the crowd and makes his way toward them. "Will, meet my friend Niki," Chloe says, and they shake hands. Niki gives him an unmistakable flirtatious smile, looking him up and down. Chloe's stomach churns.

Is she ... jealous?

"Nice to meet you, Niki," Will says politely, completely immune to Niki's attempt, his body language, his eyes, his smile, all focused on Chloe.

WHAT???

Niki seems pretty good at reading the room and gives out a quick "Getting late, gotta run," sending a side wink to Chloe, and disappears into the last of the crowd.

"That was an interesting session," Chloe says. "You did well. I learned a lot."

"Thanks." He offers a humble smile. "Glad you stayed after the sandwiches?" He smirks.

"I am," she admits.

"Do you need a ride home?" he asks.

It sounds like a bad idea, given everything going inside her head now. "Uh ... no ... thanks, I have the bus."

"I have a car," he chuckles. "It's not a problem at all. I can drop you off."

"It's a great bus. Drops me off right at home," she blurts.

"Alright, I'll walk with you to the stop then." He doesn't wait for an answer and just walks alongside her with his business suit, transmitting those CEO vibes while she's wearing her too-ripped jeans, one of her older sweaters, and her Dr. Martens boots, feeling underdressed for the occasion. Will doesn't seem to mind. He also doesn't seem to be in a rush to get home, offering to wait with her until the bus arrives. And given that it's dark out and by now the campus is completely empty, and perhaps she's also enjoying Will's company, she accepts.

"I was thinking about what you said in there." For some reason, she can't let go of that thought. "Do you feel that you had lost yourself when you were too busy building your career?"

Will nods. "I think that settling for too many things I didn't like made me forget what I love and lose my inspiration," he says.

"But you also said that these things are part of one's unique tool-box and should be maintained."

"That was the advice I wish I had been given," he says wistfully.

"It's never too late," Chloe hears herself say, and he nods. "So, how do you fix it?" she asks, her eyes shoot up to his, still under the impression of the mentoring atmosphere injected by the panel.

"Stop settling, I suppose," he answers honestly, "and find what it is in life that I'm missing."

She wants to ask what that may be. What could Will Allentown possibly be missing? But the bus pulls over at the station, and she has to jump on it before the driver leaves. She gives Will a small reflexive hug, stealing some of that scent with her into the bus. She can feel his gaze following her as she steps on, finds a seat, and plops into it, pulling her backpack to her lap.

Did she just hug him?

Chloe looks through the window to find Will still standing there, his glamorous face lit by the streetlight, and when her eyes meet his again, he lets out this shy little smile.

CHAPTER 5

An All-Women's Pilates

T he following week seems unremarkable. That is, no different than any other week, with Chloe's leisure activities consisting of:

1. About 90% arguing or taking thought-provoking insults or condescending remarks from Jimmy

2. 5% wondering whether that's how it's supposed to be, sometimes saying it out loud, intentionally or unintentionally, but mostly intentionally

3. 2.5% Jimmy making lame attempts at apologizing (the kind of apologies that start with "but" or "if")

4. About 2.5% of makeup sex, that although good, has slowly but surely lost its novelty and no longer justifies the other 97.5%

Had it ever?

Chloe can't quite bring herself to remember anymore. It seems that they may have hit that point of no return a while ago, longer than she can allow herself to admit. But unlike her biological mother, whoever that person was, Chloe doesn't just get up and leave when things get rough.

"You should dress more like her," Jimmy says mindlessly, pointing at a half-naked girl in a video clip on TV.

"I can't walk down the street dressed like that," Chloe exclaims.

"You can if you're with me. I like it when other men turn their heads after you." Yes, she is well-aware of that. Somehow, in a twisted way, it makes him proud.

"Not happening."

"Or maybe look more like Jennifer, you know, with the makeup and hair."

"Seriously?! We've been there already." It was a highlight of the past week's fight.

"Yes, but nothing has changed. You still go to work with sports outfits and a ponytail," Jimmy's disappointed look is unmistakable.

"Obviously, Jimmy, I'm a Pilates instructor. I am sure that even Jennifer doesn't wear revealing tight dresses and that amount of makeup to the gym ... gosh!" She sighs.

"You could wear *some* makeup."

"I do when we go out, but you know how I hate makeup. It feels like I'm dressed up as someone else. Besides, working out with makeup on your face is bad for the pores."

"Of course." He rolls his eyes. "Just don't be surprised if I can't get my eyes off other women." While Jimmy may think his last remark was sarcastic, it is, unfortunately, her daily reality.

"Do we have to do this now? I need to go to work." She has five minutes to spare before leaving for work, which would have been much better spent on grabbing something to eat, but these kinds of conversations tend to drain her appetite, not to mention her mood. "Why can't you like me for who I am? Why do you always want me to be someone I'm not?"

Just throwing a rhetorical question out there...

She grabs her bag and her keys, ready to leave.

"I'm just trying to help you become the best version of yourself," he says like he genuinely believes this is for the greater good.

"Seriously, Jimmy?!" It's always the same response.

The ladies stroll in and take their spots on the mats around the studio. Chloe hits play on her favorite playlist – her *happy songs*. She breathes away, letting the music wash some of the earlier frustrations. She is in her safe place now, surrounded by yoga mats, music, and familiar friendly faces who put their trust in her and come here regularly to relax and recharge. "Do you have room for one more?" She hears a baritone voice that provokes a strange sensation through her bones.

Why does it feel familiar?

"Sorry," she responds under her breath, too busy messing with her mic to turn around. The cable leading the mic to the amplifier, clipped as it is to the waistband of her leggings, gets tangled around her stomach. "This is a ladies-only gym," she says while still trying to untie herself. She turns her head slightly to make her point.

She must be going crazy because there's a handsome guy standing in front of her, clad in gym shorts and a sleeveless T-shirt, the kind that only looks casual but isn't really, staring at her through his deep dark eyes. And for a moment there, she could swear he looks like William Allentown, minus the suit and tie.

What are the odds? Her imagination has now officially reached a new level of unbelievable. Congrats ... and back to booking that MRI.

When their eyes meet, his lips curve upward almost instantly, these gorgeous dimples appear, and there's no mistaking now...

"Will?"

"Chloe." His smile broadens as he steps closer. "Need help with that?" He points to the cable that, in her distracted state, Chloe has somehow managed to get even more tangled. Multitasking does not always lead to the ideal outcome. She is well-aware of that.

"I think I got it." She gives it a last desperate attempt and fails miserably. "Okay, I lied."

"I got you." He tries to suppress a smile and takes another step to help her out. His knuckles graze the skin of her belly ever so slightly, creating a light tingle. His hands are warm, and he smells like fresh shower and that out-of-Macy's-price-range cologne. He must have a talent for disentangling, because his rescue mission lands a success within seconds, setting the mic and her rib cage free, which does not explain why she's left a little out of breath.

"What are you doing here?" she asks, sounding slightly too pleased, but she can't help herself.

"I was hoping to catch a yoga class." He runs a hand through his black hair, making it fall back perfectly on his forehead. "Didn't think I'd be the only guy here, though," he says apologetically.

"Yes, it's a ladies-only studio. I'm sorry," Chloe says, realizing they never actually got to finish that s'mores conversation. "But there's a gym across the street that—"

Joan, equipped with a jolly smile, jumps into their two-person bubble. "We could make a one-time exception," she chirps, sounding like Will showing up there may very well be the most exciting thing this studio has seen ... well ... ever. "He's already here. We wouldn't want to turn him away." She looks at Chloe, then around at the other women, who all seem to be nodding in unison.

"I want to make sure I'm respectful of your wishes." Chloe scans the room thoroughly with her gaze, preparing herself to turn Will away.

"No objection from me," Louise says, pleased.

"A nice guy like him? Please come every week," Naomi, the oldest (just turned 85 in June!) and yet the most energetic client in the studio, approves as well. Everyone else seems to either smile or nod in agreement.

"Guess you got yourself a class, William Allentown." She gestures to the last free mat at the back of the room, and Will smiles smugly and takes his spot.

The ladies seem to enjoy his presence, and he doesn't seem to mind being the only guy in a women-only yoga class, participating in their jokes and throwing out a few of his own, which land him raving laughs. To top that off, he's able to keep up throughout the entire class, quite unusual for a newbie. He's a natural.

"Back to down dog," Chloe commands, "and stay there for a few breaths." She stands up and walks around the room, switching the music for the more calming part of the class. Will glimpses at her through his attempted yoga posture, smiling when their eyes meet. Reflexively, she smiles back, her pulse picks up.

Wait ... what...?

She guides them through the last combination until the final savasana. The class ends, Will gets high-fives and compliments from the ladies.

"So, coach," he makes his way to her, "what did you think about your new, very not flexible student?" His dimples show again.

"You were actually keeping up. I'm impressed," Chloe says, and he looks pleased. "But there's no way Tania, the owner, would agree to make it a permanent exception," she powers through, and he nods in understanding. "But I do recommend yoga to improve flexibility. It helps prevent injuries."

"Yes, ma'am." Will salutes, still with a smile. He definitely looks like someone who spends extra hours at the gym. Chloe may have taken a peek or two when his shirt slid over his abdomen during the inverted yoga poses ... but she will absolutely deny it if anyone asks.

"So ... yeah," she just says as she starts organizing the room for the next class, noting that he's observing her.

"Are you okay?" Will's content look takes on a worried expression quite quickly.

"Me? Yeah ... why?"

Did he notice her blushing?

"Your hands." He reaches closer, taking her hands. "They're shaking." His palms are large and warm, and only when her fingers rest against them does she notice it too.

"Must be low blood pressure. I may have skipped breakfast this morning," Chloe mumbles almost apologetically. Not a new thing and definitely not unusual, especially after getting trapped in those endless arguments with Jimmy.

"That's easy to fix," he says. "What's your favorite food? I'll go get you something to eat and some coffee."

"I ... no ... thanks." She takes her hands back. "You don't need to buy me food," she says, "and there's free coffee here." She points at the little table in the corner of the room, that old Keurig machine hasn't worked for like a couple of months, but Will doesn't have to know that.

"I want to," he says, still worried. "When is your next class?"

"In one hour."

"Then join me. I was going to get something to eat anyway."

"I really shouldn't," she says, thousands of thoughts spinning through her head at once, her brain reasoning and contemplating, making it impossible to form a single coherent idea or decision. She has a feeling that this clouded judgement has nothing to do with her possible hypotension. But the gray dots are starting to appear, gradually shrinking her field of vision. She is severely caffeine deficient and is also ... for some obscured reason...

Speechless.

So, she eventually concedes. Will insists on helping her lock up the studio after her few failed attempts at getting the key to fit inside the stupid lock.

Why do they make these so small...

She may need to reconsider her habit of skipping her morning coffee post-fights with Jimmy, or perhaps just the fighting part. It's obviously not working well for her.

"You choose." She hears Will's voice. "What do you want to eat?"

"I'm just going to get coffee," she says, trying to minimize the financial damage. He studies her for a second, and whatever it is he sees seems to increase his sense of urgency. The next thing she knows, she's seated at a Starbucks corner table. Her best friend in the entire world, Valerie, says she can guess when Chloe is hungry, hypotensive or not, based on the silence, and it's probably true. She feels her vocabulary has taken an unscheduled leave.

"What can I get you to eat?" Will asks, but Chloe is too checked out to answer. She also can't bring herself to protest when he picks up sandwiches and pulls out his wallet at the cash register. Despite her strict rule of not letting anyone pay for her or buy her stuff, even if they make a few, or a lot, more figures than she does, she remains silent, mentally playing connect-the-dot with those gray spots that are reappearing, clouding her vision.

She blinks, and he's back at the table, pushing a coffee cup toward her. "Drink," he says, and she obeys, sipping a sweet liquid into her mouth. After a few moments of silence, maybe a bit more, she can finally see him clearly. It should be illegal for a man to be this handsome.

"What is this ridiculously delicious thing?!" Her vocabulary is slowly catching up with her.

"Caramel macchiato," he chuckles. "That's my favorite drink. I had to take a guess. Hope I wasn't too far off. It has enough caffeine and sugar to get your blood pressure up in no time."

"That was a good guess. I love it!" She grins as if she has just been handed a bowl of candy. Jimmy never lets her drink sweet stuff. Certainly not sweetened coffee. In his playbook, coffee ought to be bitter. He's just no fun.

"What do you usually order?" He pushes a warm sandwich toward her, reminding her to eat.

"I don't usually..." she falters, "eat or drink out ... just at Claudia's, before shifts, maybe just coffee with a lot of milk."

"Pilates studio, Claudia's, college." His left eyebrow creases a tad. "You keep yourself busy. Got to make sure you eat."

"Yes." She takes a bite from her sandwich, trying to characterize the sudden burst of flavors.

"Pesto mozzarella."

He can read minds now?

"I like it! Another one of your favorites?" She smiles, and he nods, chewing on what looks like the exact same sandwich.

"Does it happen a lot?" He points to her hands.

"Not too often, only sometimes when I forget to eat, which happens if I'm in a rush or too busy or too angry..."

"What is it today?"

"Probably all of the above." She takes another delicious bite.

"Who is making you angry?" he demands.

"Not who, probably what – my poor choice of relationship." She tries to keep the joke light, but it comes out more bitter than intended. For all she knows, it may be like that in most long-term relationships.

"Ah, that guy from the party?" Will asks, his brows crushing together, his fingers clenching to a fist at his side.

"Jimmy, my boyfriend for the past five years," she says. Speaking with her mouth full is not a good habit, she knows, but what's a girl to do when she has a lot to say, very little time to spare, and happens to be very hungry?

"He doesn't deserve you," Will offers, fist still clenched.

"Well, trust me, I'm no picnic either."

Defending Jimmy much?

Chloe lowers her hand gently to Will's, making his fist relax. The touch stirs an unexpected swarm of butterflies in her stomach, and she quickly pulls her hand away.

What was that?

"I beg to differ here," Will says, his dark eyes following her hand.

Did he feel that too?

"That's nice of you, but you just don't know me well enough," she says matter-of-factly. "If you did, you wouldn't think that."

"Sounds like a challenge," he says, a lopsided smile on his face.

"No, just stating the obvious."

"It's not obvious to me." He seems surprised.

"Says the guy who doesn't really know me," Chloe chuckles.

"Okay, we can change that, and then I can let you know," he smirks.

And having a boyfriend – it should probably spell trouble, yet it doesn't. Wanting to get to know her better is not something Jimmy has ever taken an interest in, and until this moment, Chloe has accepted it as ... normal. But then again, Jimmy *is* her boyfriend, and she probably shouldn't be strengthening her relationship with another guy. Especially given the tendency of this particular guy's touch feel like a new ... first.

She takes a quick peek at her watch. Ten more minutes until her next class.

"Feeling better?" Will takes her hands again as he did earlier, observing them intently. "No longer shaking," he confirms. Although if he keeps holding her hands like that, she will start shaking again, and this time not from hypotension.

"I do feel better, thank you." Her cheeks feel warm despite the air conditioning blasting above them. "Never thought I'd have a Starbucks favorite, a new first and best." Her laugh comes out a little louder than intended, and she has a feeling she wasn't talking about the food or the coffee.

At this, Will's smile grows wider, those dimples show up again, and he says smugly, "glad to be part of a pivotal moment."

CHAPTER 6

Hamburger, Fries, and A Surprise

The last class at the studio ends, and Chloe gets to her evening shift at Claudia's with an unexplained source of renewed energy. Something she can't quite fathom given her perpetual sleep deprivation since she's gone back to school. Teaching Pilates and yoga is indeed energizing, but this bout of energy now... This is unmatched. She puts on her brown apron with the green Claudia's logo, whistling some song – she can't remember where it came from, but it somehow got itself stuck in her head.

"Someone's happy today." Claudia smiles at her as she walks by, adding her know-all wink.

"Hey Claudia." Chloe smiles, noticing her own face in the open kitchen top mirrors. She doesn't recall her cheeks being such a shade of pink. Is this a new thing?

"There's someone waiting at table four for you," her boss announces jovially.

"Waiting for me?" Chloe blushes. She's worked in this restaurant for almost a year now. The vast majority of customers here come with their families, with their kids. She's never had a customer showing up just for her.

"He came about an hour ago, asked if you're on the schedule today, ordered iced tea, and said he'd wait."

He...?

"Sorry about that," Chloe says, knowing Claudia doesn't like camping at her restaurant, trying to fight those smiling muscles curving her lips.

"Are you kidding me? He's welcome any day!" Claudia gleams. "He's like a magnet. Ever since he walked through the door, people keep on coming."

Chloe straightens her ponytail, takes her notepad, and walks over to table four. Her heart beats a little harder as she's trying to hypothesize – or is it *fantasize?* – who the mysterious person might be. Those faster heartbeats turn into pounding palpitations at the confirmation of this.

"Will? Are you stalking me?" It comes out a little more enthusiastic than she planned, but there's only so much she can do to control her tone when gasping for air. He's back in a suit and tie, giving off authoritative, big-boss vibes.

"Sorry, didn't mean to be stalking you." His baritone voice is unfazed by the accusation. "I wanted to make sure you were okay. You got me a little worried this morning," he admits, holding her gaze, his dark eyes honest, kind, and ridiculously beautiful.

"I am, thank you." She feels her cheeks warm up, and given their earlier pinkish color, she just hopes it goes unnoticed. "I'm good. Thanks for introducing me to the most delicious coffee ever."

"Ah! Caramel macchiato is my favorite," he says smugly.

"So, I guess now we share two favorites – s'mores and a Starbucks drink." She hears herself sounding like a silly teenager and already regrets it.

"I guess we do." His smile turns into a dimpled decorated grin.

"Can I get you more iced tea?" She looks at his almost empty glass. "Anything to eat?"

"Sure, any insider recommendations?"

"Are you into healthy or the good stuff?" It may not sit well with her future certified nutritionist self, but she can always deny it. Besides, taking everything to the extreme is up Jimmy's alley, not hers.

"Good stuff, of course," he says. Why does it feel like this is what Chloe was hoping to hear? It's a perfect contrast to Jimmy, who would have rubbed his forehead right now and scolded her for trying to talk him into junk food.

"Any food allergies?"

"Nope."

"The burger is incredible. It comes with homemade garlic fries and a surprise."

"What's the surprise?" Will's eyebrow curves up playfully.

"If I told you, it wouldn't be a surprise." She smirks and regrets that too. Her tone sounded ... teasing? He smiles at that, and she quickly points to the menu, clearing her throat. Her heart skips a beat ... again. She may need to get that heart of her checked.

"Ha, it does say a surprise," he chuckles. "Okay, now I'm curious."

She takes that as a yes. "Medium? Medium-well?"

"Medium, please."

"And more iced tea?"

"Sure. Can I help?"

She laughs. "This is a restaurant. You are the customer. I am the waitress." She stops for a breath. "So sit tight, and I'll go get your food."

"Right," Will tries to suppress an even bigger smile, her eyes linger a tad too long on his lips, and she has to pull herself away, disappearing into the kitchen.

Claudia's curious eyes burn a hole in her face. "Burger, medium." She states Will's order in the most nonchalant tone she can gather.

"Who's this handsome mystery guy?" Claudia says cheerfully.

"Just a guy from the studio."

"Ah yes, I thought this was a women's-only studio, no?" Claudia teases.

"Yes, he showed up to a class today and charmed his way into it."

"I see..." Claudia winks at her again. "Joe!" She calls to her husband working the grill, "Give this burger some extra love. I want to make sure this guy comes back!"

Chloe juggles between a few more tables before Will's burger is ready. He keeps himself looking busy with his phone, but she can't help noticing his eyes following her whenever she passes by, smiling to himself.

"Here you go, sir." Chloe shows up with the dish. "Hamburger, fries, and your surprise," she announces in a celebratory tone.

"Smells delicious," he says. "So what's the surprise?"

"This." She picks up a pre-filled, pre-paid lottery ticket. "Grand prize this week is ten million."

"That's a cool idea," he says, and she just nods and disappears back to work, back to all her other tables, letting him have his dinner in peace.

Claudia was spot-on – this evening was definitely busier than usual, which means more tips, so Chloe really can't complain, but it also means much more work. And about halfway through her shift, she can already feel her legs protesting. Will leaves a generous tip and a little note with his phone number. "In case you need anything," it reads, written in the tidiest handwriting. She bickers back and forth with herself on whether to keep it or ditch it. Then she notices he didn't take the lottery ticket and she has to protest, but he's already gone.

Chloe grabs her phone from her back pocket, punches the number into a message, and quickly texts, "you forgot your surprise."

"It's for you," his text appears instantly.

The family in table two is signaling for more water, so she shoves her phone and lottery ticket into her pocket and goes back to work, tucking away today's events into that place where her few happy memories live, and then gets rid of the note.

CHAPTER 7

Valerie

Fun things sometimes happen when one least expects them, and when Chloe's phone buzzes and she sees Val's name flashing on it, a big smile fills her face.

"Val!!!" She picks up and screams into the phone with excitement, only now realizing how much she missed hearing her best friend's voice and for some dumb reason couldn't figure it out on her own. She could have easily dialed her number – she was only a ring away.

"Clo!!" Valerie's voice is happy. Her ginger personality radiates through the line even at that one word. "I miss you!"

"I miss you too!" Chloe says. They haven't seen each other – outside of video calls, that is – since Valerie found out her biological mother was Jewish and went on that two-week self-discovery trip to Israel. That was six months ago. They've been FaceTiming regularly, yet when her best friend in the whole world, her person, is thousands of miles away, every call feels like a small celebration.

"What have you been up to?" Chloe asks excitedly. Her day fills up with colors in anticipation for Val's stories. She seems to really be living life to the fullest, and Chloe would not mind a piece of it, even just a crumb.

"Mmm, you know, weather is great, food is amazing. Those Israeli soldiers are so... HOT. I'm thinking of maybe joining the military."

"You what?!"

"Well, it's not a big deal; army service is mandatory in Israel, two years for females, three years for males, so I was thinking, why not? But I may need to volunteer because I'm over 21... So it's probably a shorter service, but I'll get to meet new people, make new friends, polish my Hebrew to words that are actually used in conversation, embed myself in the culture, maybe acquire some combat skills and get to contribute my part, so much in one!" Her voice sounds so liberated and determined and ... elated, *take my life into my own hands and make it what I want it to be,* kind of happy.

"Wow, Val, I'm so proud of you!"

"Thank you!" Val squeals. "I knew you would support me! But wait, let's see how it goes. I have a full day of tests and screens ahead." She lets out an excited exhale. "Now tell me what you've been up to."

"Not much, same old, you know." It's Chloe's go-to answer.

Pathetic.

"C'mon, I know for a fact it's not true," Val teases.

"For a fact? Do you mind sharing your evidence with me, please?" Chloe's heart misses one singular beat; Val knows her well.

But can she sense stuff Chloe hasn't even allowed herself to feel yet?

"Well, let's start with your voice."

"What about it?"

"It's different, happy."

"It's because of you. I am happy to hear your voice and your plans!"

Not a lie.

"Happier... Clo, are you censoring? Is the asshole there hearing our conversation?"

"No, I'm on break, at work." Maybe Val is forgetting the seven-hour time difference. "And Jimmy is not an asshole." Although this has been Valerie's nickname for him ever since she first met him, and he's definitely lived up to it.

"He *is* an asshole, but anyway, you sound different, plus TJ said he saw you at Starbucks having some intimate moments with a hot guy!" Of course. Val has eyes and ears everywhere. She knows everyone and somehow manages to keep in touch with everybody, even when she's on the other side of the globe in a different time zone, busy changing her life for the best.

"So that's what you're asking." Chloe laughs, trying to buy herself some time. Her stomach is twisting and turning.

Did they look like they were having these sorts of moments?

"YEAH... Duh!"

"Well, it's not what you think." Chloe tries to lower her expectations quickly because Val's vibe tends to be infectious.

"DO TELL!" Val says it so loud that Chloe has to move the phone away from her ear. "No, you know what? Turn on your camera, I want to see you."

Chloe obeys, pressing the little camera symbol.

"Good, now let me look at you." Valerie moves the phone so close to her face that Chloe can only see the inside of her eyes. "Yes!" Val says triumphantly. "Something is different! So, who is the *hot guy*?"

"Let's not call him the *hot guy*, okay? His name is Will."

"Full name, please."

"William, don't know his middle name, Allentown."

"As in the rich – sorry, *wealthy* Allentown family?"

"He's Georgia Allentown's nephew."

"So, he is hot *and* rich!"

"Val!" Chloe protests. She has no interest in Will and definitely no interest in money whatsoever unless she makes it herself through hard work. And even then, Chloe's motto is to only make what she needs to get by, and hopefully, one day a bit extra to save for retirement, but not a dollar more. Money has never been one of her drivers.

"I know, I know … sorry, I'm interrupting way too much."

"Jimmy and I went to Georgia's birthday party, and Georgia introduced me to Will." She pauses to hide the impending tremble in her voice with a deep breath. "Jimmy was ogling that girl and went up to dance with her, so Will offered to dance with me." Chloe halts to get her breathing in order. "Then I needed some fresh air, and he came after me."

"Will came after you? I like the sound of it."

"Val…"

"Sorry, continue please."

"So … yes, we made s'mores and chatted by a firepit outside until Jimmy wanted to go home. Then I somehow ran into Will again on a business panel at school. He was a panelist."

Then she hugged him at the bus stop, and her heart has been beating erratically ever since…

Chloe's breath hitches, and she takes another inhale before allowing her outside voice to resume. "And then he came to a Pilates class, and I had a drop in blood pressure after class because I forgot to eat breakfast. So long story short, Will noticed my hands were shaking and dragged me to get some coffee." She tries to sound as casual as possible, just two best friends talking about the usual stuff.

"O-kay," Valerie was waiting patiently for Chloe to finish her story but now can't stay quiet anymore, bursting energy in her voice. "Now, help me get my facts straight here. The asshole was being the typical dick that he is, hot guy Allentown has been very observant about your whereabouts, the asshole knows about hot guy, hot guy likes s'mores *and* came to see you at the studio, your blood pressure dropped when you saw him... Sounds like all the essential components of a true love story."

"Wait, no, he didn't come to see *me*. He came for a Pilates class."

"Right," Valerie snorts. "In a women's-only studio."

"He didn't know."

"Of course not."

"And my blood pressure dropped because I skipped breakfast." Chloe chooses not to mention the fight with Jimmy that kept her awake at night or her aggravated morning that led to her skipping breakfast. Valerie already hates Jimmy enough as it is. No need to add more fuel. "And Will noticed it and insisted on getting some caffeine and carbs into me... And then ... he came back to check on me at Claudia's when he got off work."

"Allow me to summarize here. William Allentown is observant and kind, he cares about you, and he follows up! I like him already!" Val's voice is confident and optimistic, as if nothing is impossible. "So, what's next?" A plan, Valerie always makes plans.

"There's no next, really. It is a women-only studio. I recommended the gym down the street, which he will probably skip anyway because he definitely works out regularly at a gym already."

"Why would you do that?!" Val sounds seriously disappointed.

"Because I have a boyfriend," Chloe reminds her.

"Clo, you know what I think about this boyfriend of yours. Jimmy is not good for you." Yes, Valerie has never been shy about that. "You deserve someone who actually cares about you and loves you."

"Jimmy does," Chloe tries to argue with no conviction.

In his own way.

"Well, then someone who actually shows it too. Not someone who doesn't support any of your dreams or aspirations, and lets you work two jobs in addition to going to college, while he's spending his days sleeping and sitting on the couch watching TV because he doesn't feel like going to work in the morning and can't keep any job for more than two weeks. There's a pattern here." Deep down, Chloe knows Val is right. Val's voice shifts. "I know we both had a rough start in life, but that doesn't mean we can't break that cycle. It's up to us, and us only," Val says in a dead-serious voice.

Valerie is a doer, and she definitely practices what she preaches. She proves what she's just said on a daily basis. But that's a typical Val thing. Chloe isn't sure whether this is something she could ever have the courage to do. By now, she has come to the realization that doing things she likes, although she hasn't had a chance to do so many, tends to lead to situations she enjoys, and being in those situations obviously makes life more fun.

Well, this is stating the obvious, but what about the opposite?

Chloe allows herself to go down that less-positive line of thinking for a moment. Would doing things she *doesn't* like, lead to situations she *won't* enjoy? And, as a consequence, lead her life on an unhappy trajectory? Make her miserable? Obviously, everyone has to do things they may not like as part of commitments and responsibilities, but what about things one doesn't like to do and does not have to do either? By not changing or questioning them, is she actually making a choice?

Is she leading herself to a life she doesn't want to be in?

Her brain hurts just from thinking about it.

CHAPTER 8

A Cold Cold Night

"I'm hungry. I can't believe the fridge is empty," Jimmy scolds as he wanders through the kitchen. Chloe is exhausted after a long, albeit interesting day, hoping her boyfriend for the past five years would be a little more supportive, but not overly surprised to find out he was home all day in that same spot on the couch. "Couldn't you stop by the grocery store on your way back? Or get me something from Claudia's?"

"You can go to the grocery store too, you know?" She walks past him and into the shower.

"For fuck's sake, don't give me those passive-aggressive hints." His face is sullen. "I actually did something important today. I had a job interview for a sales job," he shouts through the closed bathroom door.

"How did it go?" She can't say she's holding her breath. Jimmy has been starting and losing jobs on a monthly basis, always for the same reason – he's not willing to put in any effort, and mostly not willing to drag himself out of bed and into work in the morning.

"Starting tomorrow," he says, sounding almost excited.

"Congratulations!" she says, hopeful that this time it sticks. She opens the door to give him a hug. He doesn't hug her back at first, and when he does, his hug is cold, and rigid, like typical Jimmy – outside of sex, as far as he's concerned, affectionate displays are unnecessary. But then again, maybe that's how it is for everyone. It's not like she has much to compare to. Chloe backs up – she should know better by now – and goes into the shower, leaving the door open as Jimmy is still there.

"I have a good feeling about this," he continues.

"I'm glad," she says, although honestly, this feels like déjà vu. She's heard these exact same words at least twenty times in the past...

Gosh ... five years, has it been that long?

"Tell me more about the new job," she says, letting the hot water wash her face and hair, feeling her muscles starting to relax. "What will you be selling?"

"You're going to LOVE this! It's a supplement that makes you feel stronger, build muscle and lose weight. All at the same time! I even got you some free samples to try!"

"Thanks, Jimmy, but I'll pass." Magic powders make her wary. And losing weight while building muscles at the same time? This alone defies basic human physiology.

"You could lose some pounds, you know."

Here he goes again...

"Jimmy, I am perfectly happy with who I am. I don't see anything wrong with my weight."

"Five more pounds and you could get that supermodel body you always wanted."

"You mean *you* always wanted..."

"Same thing. It's on the kitchen table," he sneers.

"Jimmy, I'm not going to poison my body with some unproved,

untested supplement lacking any scientific evidence in order to lose weight. This stuff can kill people."

"Well, let me break it to you, Chloe, the side effect of living is dying, so pretty much everything we do kills us eventually."

"Okay." This view of his is depressing. "We can't control every-thing," she is gravely aware of that, "but there are certain steps we can take to live healthier lives and reduce, at least, some of the risks. We can also choose to avoid unnecessary perils, should at least control what we can, and this certainly falls under unnecessary and avoidable."

"Whatever." He sounds disappointed. "Suit yourself."

Chloe turns off the water and pulls the towel behind the shower curtain. "Tell me more about the role itself," she asks while rubbing the towel on her skin. The light-happy mood that surrounded her all day today swiftly reverts back into her usual gloomy state at home.

"It's this thing where there's a regional manager in charge of a few area sales managers, who are in charge of individual salespeople. The more you bring to the table, the higher your rank goes."

"Based on your sales?"

"Yes, but there's a way to expedite it." He pauses, letting her admire the idea for a beat, although she's everything but. "Because the higher up you are, the more money you make, not just from your sales, but also from the sales of the people you're in charge of."

"Okay, so how do you expedite it?" She wraps the towel around her body and steps out of the shower.

"By investing."

"Investing your profits?"

"No, Chloe," Jimmy says slowly, mansplaining. "That – would – take – too – long. Why – would – I – leave – money – on – the – table?" The audacity of this man. She takes a deep breath, trying to stop a colossal explosion.

"So, how do you speed it up?" She ignores the belittling aspect of his tone, focusing on what may be more alarming here. She's not sure she likes where this is going.

"Jesus, Chloe, do I have to explain everything to you? Good thing I'm sparing you from another semester in college. This is such a waste of money!"

"You what?!?"

"Yes, so I have a surprise for you."

"Excuse me?!"

Did he seriously just drag her college into the conversation now?

"So, I took the $6,000 we had and invested it, and guess what?" He smiles proudly, waiting for her to admire his geniusness. "I am the new regional manager!"

"You took my college money and invested it in a sketchy pyramid scheme?!" She feels the blood boiling up in her veins.

"Chloe, I don't think you're seeing the big picture here." His condescending voice grows louder and angrier.

"Without even consulting me first?!"

"Fuck it!" His glare is now mad and chastising. "I can't believe how ungrateful you are!"

"Jimmy, I've been saving this money for so long, so many extra hours of work..."

"Well, too bad, it's my money too!" At this point, he's practically shouting.

"Jimmy, I work two jobs and take care of all our expenses, and I've been doing it almost alone for the past several years." She tries to keep her voice under control, but it comes out sore and broken.

"I think you are failing to see the big picture here. This money is going to make even more money, but you, Chloe – with your lack of vision – you can't even see it! Do you really think going to college will get you anywhere? Who are you kidding?" His eyes are spiteful, almost cruel. Seeing the grave impact of his words on her seems to encourage him to proceed, "When are you going to wake up? You're nothing without me. Even your parents knew nothing good would come out of you. Fuck, Chloe, you're so ungrateful!" He sighs furiously and walks away before she has a chance to say anything else. He always has to have the last word, pulling the biological parents punch on her.

Who gave him the right?!

She puts on an old T-shirt and flannel shorts quietly, feeling nothing but defeat. She tries to make the lump in her throat go away, but really she's known Jimmy for so long, none of it should be surprising to her. Her college dream is slipping further and further away from her, making her question herself, her abilities.

Maybe that's not what life has in store for her... She's been spending too much time fighting windmills. Maybe she needs to let that dream go.

She sits down on the laminated living room floor, under the window overlooking the park she used to enjoy watching, once upon a time. Her knees are pulled tightly to her chest, her back leaning against the wall. She's spent too many long moments of reflection right here in this exact corner. It seems to have a curved spot in her shape. Tears drop along her cheeks, trailing down to her shirt and knees, and she can't make them stop. She weeps quietly until she can't hold it in anymore. Until her sobs take over completely. Until she can barely breathe. Her body is shivering, resorting to short, shaky gasps of air. At some point, late into the night, she probably falls asleep, because when she opens her eyes again, they feel swollen and heavy and burning, her entire body is sore, and it's already morning.

CHAPTER 9

A Beam of Sunlight

"The asshole did what???!!!" Valerie's voice is so loud that it can probably be heard from Chloe's phone through the entire street. Chloe just shakes her head, continuing her night stroll around the block. After a full day at the studio and half a shift at Claudia's, she needed some time to relax before going home. Her eyes are still freakishly swollen from crying last night. This habit needs to stop. Chloe feels helpless, powerless... Both Georgia and Claudia stopped her today to ask what had happened to her eyes, a question she dismissed with a bad allergy (to Georgia, which brought about having to pop one of those twenty-four-hour Zyrtec which, of course, didn't do much) and lack of sleep (to Claudia, who said something about needing to make sure her kidney function was in order; she should have used the allergy excuse again but couldn't take another Zyrtec in less than twenty-four hours).

Valerie's voice presses on, "I don't understand. Why can't you just get up and leave this son of a—"

"Val!" Chloe interrupts. No need to get Jimmy's mom into the mix. "We've been together for five years. I don't even know what life without him looks like anymore." Jimmy is far from perfect, but he has stuck around so far. Growing up as a foster kid, this is not something she takes for granted. "And besides, I don't just quit when things get rough."

"Chloe, this is not just *things getting rough*. This man is a piece of shit, and that's not new. He's constantly making you cry, trying to break your spirit, shatter your dreams, change who you are like you're some piece of clay... I know I sound like a broken record, but Clo, you're my best friend, and it breaks my heart to let you keep going back for more." Valerie pauses to take a breather, and Chloe wishes she was half as strong and determined as her best friend. "And let me tell you how life without this abusive bastard will look like – it'll look amazing! You don't need him! Sure, you'll be sad for a bit because you're not used to being without him, but I promise this will go away once you realize you are so much better without him. Getting used to something good is easier than you think."

Deep inside, Chloe knows Val is right, yet she hears herself say, "Val, he's not abusive."

Because if he was, she would know, right?

"So, Clo, this is where you have it all wrong." Valerie is on fire.

"You know he doesn't hit me. Jimmy would never—"

"Oh, that makes him such a great boyfriend, Clo! Remember we had that conversation?" And she does, of course, remember. One of many discussions they've had where Val tries to talk her out of her relationship with Jimmy, and for some reason, Chloe becomes defensive, trying to convince Val and herself that...

That what? It's not that bad? That she can swallow her pride, suppress her dreams, and go on with her life?

That being with Jimmy is better than being alone? That Jimmy needs her, and she can't just leave?

No one said life was supposed to be easy, not for people like her. She'd learned that early enough, and this is part of life.

"Clo, abuse comes in different shapes and forms. The way he talks to you, the way he treats you, the things he does – that's mental abuse. And I sure hope this motherfucker doesn't hit you because I'll kill him!"

"Val! He doesn't hit me," she says again. If he did, well ... that would be a whole different story. That would move leaving him from the *maybe-it's-something-she-should-do* category to a *must-do* category, from sitting on the fence to taking action. Or at least Chloe hopes it would. And she knows, somewhere deep inside, that he's not good for her. She knows she's better off without him. She just wishes she could be strong enough to get up and leave.

But she isn't. She's all alone. Valerie is so far away, and besides Jimmy ... she's got no one else.

An incoming text message interrupts her thoughts, then another, then another... "My boss is text-bombing me right now," Chloe announces, "got to go. What time is it there anyway?!" Valerie is a night owl, but this is probably a new record, even for her.

"Yeah, gotta go to sleep," Val says, and they end the call on the "*think about it*" note.

Chloe opens Tania's text messages, hoping nothing bad happened. She doesn't usually text her more than a single abbreviated message at a time.

"GOOD NEWS!" Chloe sighs with relief as she reads the first few words in the chain. She could really use some good news right now.

"You have a new client!"

"Just committed to 10 private Pilates/yoga sessions!"

"The 1 hr long sessions! 1-2x/ week, do you have the bandwidth?"

"Yay!" Chloe quickly texts back with a smiley emoji before the offer goes to one of the other instructors. "Of course, I do." Despite already working over twelve hours a day between the studio and Claudia's, she really needs the money. "Any day/time preference?"

"The client requested, if possible, Tuesday and Thursday mornings."

"How about 7:45 am?" Chloe's first class on both days is at 9 a.m. This could work well for full one-hour sessions plus a fifteen-minute break to organize the studio.

"Let me confirm that with the client," Tania says. Hopefully, the new client is open to early morning classes. Chloe returns the phone to her back pocket, ready to go back to her night stroll, but it buzzes again. "Looks like a match," Tania confirms.

Wow, when it works, it works.

"Perfect! Do you want to assign a backup instructor?" Chloe texts quickly. Tania likes to do that for 1:1s to avoid unplanned cancellations.

"No backup this time. The client asked for you specifically."

"Me?" This takes her by surprise. There are many more experienced instructors their studio could offer.

"Yes, you, honey." Tania sends a heart eyes emoji. "So, you're in?"

"Of course." It's probably one of the new ladies that came to her last open trial session. There were a few who said they might sign up. Chloe hopes to not disappoint. Private sessions are a big deal.

"Perfect, I'll let the client know. First class tomorrow! Congrats!" Tania adds a few thumbs up.

Chloe already feels the excitement of being able to work closely with a new client. Ten whole hours! And as small as it may be, in the backdrop of her latest storm, this feels a bit like a beam of sunlight.

Chloe shoves the phone back into her pocket. The night breeze, coupled with the good news, makes her feel significantly better. She takes the stairs back to her apartment two-by-two, ready to face Jimmy's grumpy face, who's giving her the silent treatment for not being supportive of his new endeavor. She needs to get some good night's sleep if she wants to retain her new client.

The next morning appears quickly. Chloe makes sure to not skip breakfast for a change. She is less familiar with the early-morning bus schedule, so just to be on the safe side, she doubles her estimated travel time and gets to the studio 45 minutes before her new class. She preps the studio for the day, opening the curtains to let natural light in and blasting some energizing music in the background, singing to just herself. She hears the little bell at the front, signaling that someone has entered the studio. Her new client is apparently very early. Good, they'll get to catch up before the actual class, discuss goals and plans for the coming session. Making her way toward the entrance, she can't figure out why that insane scent of bergamot – that over-the-Macy's-price-range cologne – is being summoned by her desperately-needing-MRI brain. Now of all times... And this goes beyond delusional when she turns around, envisioning that familiar reflection in the large, mirrored wall. She slaps herself mentally, because maybe she's still not fully awake?

"Good morning," the unmistakable baritone voice kicks in, forcing the rest of her senses to come to a final evidence-based conclusion.

"I promise I'm fine." She turns to face William Allentown in the flesh. "I really appreciate you coming by to check on me again, but I have a class starting in..." She glances at her watch, but there are at least thirty more minutes until her new client shows up. "Soon." Living with Jimmy is hard enough without the overwhelming feeling that she's missing out on...

Other things.

"Yes, I'm a little early," Will smiles sheepishly, lifting up his hands, and she realizes he's holding two Starbucks cups.

"*You're my new client?*" Chloe can't hide her surprise. "When Tania said a new client, she never mentioned... It's a women's-only studio, you know?"

"I do, in fact. You may have mentioned it a couple of times." He smirks.

"How did you talk Tania into it?" She fiddles with the hem of her tank top.

Why is she nervous?

Tania had been pretty adamant about taking only females into the studio. Chloe has trained men before, but Will's presence has this disorienting effect on her.

"She mentioned it but said the restriction only applies to group lessons, so I signed up for private lessons. Is that okay with you?" His gaze turns serious, searching her confirmation.

Is it?

Chloe's not sure how she feels about the idea. She would love to take on a new client, gender irrelevant, but the thought of being around Will for a whole entire ten-hour session, alone in the studio, makes something in her stomach flutter.

"Be honest, I'll understand." He takes her contemplation as reservation.

Would it be wrong of her to say yes? It sure doesn't feel wrong.

"Uh ... yes, of course it's okay." She nods, shaking off the guilt that accompanies the excitement bubbling through her. "But just to make sure you're prepared, these classes could get a bit physical." She realizes that came out wrong. "I'm used to touching when teaching and correcting, to make sure you hit the right muscle. I just don't want you to think I'm sexually harassing you," she blurts out, making it sound even worse, feeling a bit breathless.

Why is she like this around him?

"Is that so?" Will looks amused.

"It *is* so." Her heart does a little somersault in her chest.

"I think I can live with that," he announces. His mouth curves up to a full dimpled grin. He takes a few steps toward her and offers one of the cups. "Brought you some more of your *ridiculously delicious thing.*" He turns her own words against her. Or rather, to her benefit.

"You didn't need to get me coffee," she says, trying to bite down her smile.

"I wanted to."

"Thank you." She lets that smile out and takes the cup from his hand, gesturing to the bench in the corner, usually used for taking off shoes, but perfectly suitable for pre-workout coffee. Will sits down, and she joins him at a safe distance, facing him. She takes a sip.

"So, let's go over your goals and make a plan for the session. What brings you in?" She tries to sound casual, or at least hopes she does. He stalls. "Okay, don't tell me you just want to work out, because you're clearly doing that already." She allows herself a moment to admire his impressive lats and deltoid muscles. It's just impossible to ignore, with the sleeveless gym shirt he decided to wear today.

"Correct," he says, a smile playing on his lips as he notices her eyes studying him. "But I am not very flexible, and I think this could potentially be a source for injuries, especially in the long run," he says, clearly well-prepared for her mini-interrogation.

Chloe nods in agreement, pulling a new chart from the desk behind her and scribbling his name at the very top. Well, she's aware of her messy handwriting, but this one really does look like a scribble. Her hands are a bit shaky, and it's clearly showing. Not like low blood pressure shaky, just a little unstable for some unfathomable reason. This doesn't usually happen to her, but right now, the universe is probably grateful that she didn't choose surgery as her career, or any other profession that requires fine motor skills, for that matter.

"Anything else you'd like to achieve during your ten-class session?" Chloe asks, checking the little circle beside the word 'flexibility' in his chart. She usually likes to fill in the circle with her pen, but that will require more precision than she seems to be able to apply at the moment. "And maybe also tell me why you think I'm the best person for the job."

Yes, her inner self would love to know why he had explicitly asked for her, and her only, as his trainer.

"I'd like to ... well, I'm sorry if this comes off as assuming or too personal ... but you seem like you could use..." His eyes speak without words for what feels like a long moment, and it appears that somehow the conversation has shifted its focus to her.

"Listen." She quickly assesses where this is going. "Just to make it clear, I am not some charity case, and I am not into the *Pretty Woman, Cinderella* story or whatever fantasy, so if you think you're here to save me ... spare it." Her voice has a bite to it. Maybe she's too primed by Jimmy always thinking he knows what she needs that she's starting to think that everyone around her suffer the same symptom.

Despite her reaction, Will keeps his calm and just carries through with what he was going to say before she, quite aggressively, interrupted him. But he doesn't talk about money or make some condescending proposition. He simply shrugs and says, "I thought you could use a friend." His voice is almost naive, his eyes sincere, making her regret what she has just said. And the way she said it.

"Oh." Her eyes trail to the floor. "Sorry I snapped at you." She feels her cheeks burning. "I was making assumptions." She wonders if she should reiterate the fact that she has a boyfriend but decides this may be too presumptuous.

"Understandable, you don't know me – yet," he says, adding the yet in a half-question, as if trying to gauge her take on the friendship offer.

"Did your aunt put you up to this?"

"Aunt Georgia?" He laughs. "She could get pretty influential, but no, this one is all on me."

"Don't take it the wrong way, but what's in it for you?"

"Aside from Pilates classes to improve my flexibility? I really enjoyed our last few conversations, and I guess I could use a friend too. Making friends these days is not as easy as one might think." He runs a hand through his hair. "And besides, I've accepted your challenge – remember? To get to know you better."

He's clearly been paying attention during their conversations.

She has to at least consider it. Making friends has not come easy for her either. Sure, there are multiple people she's friendly with, that's easy, but friends... people she can actually trust? Who actually care? Valerie is her only true friend, her person. In her memories, they've always been friends. But she's so far away now. And Jimmy... Chloe used to think he was her friend, but she's slowly growing to understand he may actually be the opposite of that. So yes, she could definitely use a friend.

The real question is, can she really be friends with Will, given that being in his proximity does all kinds of things to her heart?

Well, he has just friend-zoned her, so he's probably not experiencing the same manifestations.

"I'll consider it." She lets out a small, shy smile. "You're right. I barely know you."

"I have ten hours to convince you to be my friend then," he announces in a celebratory tone.

"Okay." She's not absolutely sure who is really the one being challenged here.

"Just be prepared."

"For what exactly?" She frowns.

"Ten hours mean at least thirty prompts for conversation," he announces.

"Is this statistic based on solid scientific evidence?" She's not even convinced she has this many topics to fill a conversation.

"Of course." He smirks. "You go first."

"Ha ... alright. Any specific health issues, concerns, or past injuries I should know about?"

"Using questions from that chart you're holding is against the rules," Will chuckles, making something in her melt. "I have an old knee injury." He shows her a faint scar extending from his knee down to his shin. "From when I was six. My rescue mission to save a cat from a tree didn't go very well." He smiles.

"Awww. You climbed a tree to rescue a cat? That's so adorable."

"The cat didn't think so," he says, laughing.

"Oh no!" Her mouth seems to curve to a smile on its own, making his eyes glow in response.

"And this one too." He points to a small scar above his left eyebrow. Despite looking at his admittedly handsome face quite a lot in the past few days, it's the first time she actually notices this little scar.

"This one is actually se ... small," she starts but then quickly corrects herself.

Was she seriously about to say sexy? Is she losing her mind?! A foolproof way to make new friends.

Will smiles at that half-word he heard, looking again quite pleased.

"Any pain or limits to motion that I should know about?"

"Not that I can think of, but I'll be sure to let you know."

"Great, so let's get started," she says, signaling him to follow her to a back room. "This is a Pilates reformer," she says, gesturing to one of the reformers in a row of eight, backing a mirrored wall. She puts on her favorite Pilates playlist and connects to the speakers.

"This looks like a sophisticated inquisition contraption, but I'll take your word for it," he says smugly.

"Good, very brave of you," she says, her smile a tad wider. "So your head goes here," she points to the headrest of the long Pilates machine, "and your body here. Lie down on your back."

"Yes, ma'am," he obeys.

"Your feet go here." She points to the foot bar. "Let's start with feet in parallel, fist-distance apart, but take your socks off first. I don't want you to slip. Or if you want, we sell Pilates socks," she says. His eyebrow twists the tiniest degree up, just where that little scar of his. Chloe takes it as some signal of confusion and adds, "I prefer barefoot, but that's just personal preference."

"Barefoot it is," he says.

"Now, you want to keep your spine in a neutral position." She lets her palm hover over his stomach, feeling the heat radiating from his body. "That's the touching part I warned you about." She halts, awaiting signs of approval.

"Permission granted." He smiles.

"Like this." She gently lays her hand on his abs.

Note to self: these are some impressive abdominal muscles.

A weird tingling sensation travels along her fingers. "Now, straighten your legs as you exhale. This will push you all the way down, then let your body go back in a controlled motion as you inhale." He does as told. "And go slow."

"Question one," he announces between repetitions, shaking her out of her reverie. "Favorite food."

"Hmmm..." She wasn't expecting the quick shift. "My favorite food in the whole world is mashed potatoes, but only if it's made of freshly cooked potatoes, not the one made out of dried potato flakes." She scrunches her nose.

"That's awfully specific." His eyes climb, meeting hers.

"Now, I'm going to move your feet to the second position," she says, laying her hands on his toes, gently shifting their direction until his heels are connected. "How about you?"

"Eggs, preferably sunny-side-up."

"That's fitting." Chloe can't help herself.

"Oh yeah? Why is that?"

"You're a positive guy." She smiles.

"With a side of chopped salad with olive oil and lemon squeeze," he smirks.

"And my mashed potato is *awfully specific*?" She tries to pinch his arm, but his skin won't yield, and the touch feels more personal than intended. Her cheeks heat up.

"Now, these are the straps. We'll warm up your arms." She quickly shifts gears and hands him the straps hanging from each side of the headrest, switching the reformer's springs to lighter resistance under his feet. Putting her professional hat back on feels much more comfortable. "Now bring your arms up, and as you exhale, lower them down to your sides." She demonstrates the moves with her hands in the air. He follows with the straps.

"That's actually fun." His gaze is fixed on her.

"Right? Wait until we get to *feet in straps*. That's *my* personal favorite, but we'll do that in the end," she says. "Gosh! Why does it sound like a sexual innuendo? I promise I did not mean it this way." Her cheeks turn instantly crimson, earning her Will's most adorable infectious laugh. It wasn't even that funny, but it takes them a few minutes to recover. Each attempt to speak brings about another unified burst.

When he's finally able to speak again, he says, "Favorite game."

"Like sports games?"

"Whatever you like."

"I LOVE board games. My favorite is The Game of Life." Thinking about the hours and hours she's spent with Valerie playing this game brings back so many happy memories, and her mind wanders for a few seconds until their eyes meet.

"You like board games!"

Yes, even though Jimmy calls them 'bored' games.

She's bracing herself for a similar reaction from Will, but he has the sweetest smile on his face when he says: "I love the game Clue."

"Never played."

"You're joking, right?"

"Not joking," she pouts.

He shakes his head slowly in feigned disapproval. "I have to fix that."

They go through an entire class, Chloe's teaching, Will plays along, surprising her every time with his ability to follow her instructions with almost perfect form.

"Now be honest. You've done this before?"

"Pilates?" He holds her gaze again.

"Yes."

"Never, but I had no idea what I was missing."

"You're doing very well for a first-timer."

"I aspire to achieve," he smirks, "and I have the best teacher, now don't forget to show me the feet in straps. I'm curious." His words make them share a knowing smile, like those personal jokes shared by friends who've been together forever.

"Of course, I always keep my promises," Chloe says, handing him the straps again. "Now, this is tricky. Leave one foot on the bar and bring the other leg to you." He obeys, and she slides the soft part of the strap to the arch of his foot. "Now push on it a bit until you feel enough resistance to stabilize yourself, and only then bring the other leg to you and put on the other strap." Will looks a bit confused but follows along. "Great, now you can straighten both of your legs, keeping your feet in the straps," she says.

"It *is* fun!" A smile stretches across his face.

"Now lower your legs slowly and then bring them up straight. Try to keep your lower back on the carriage," she says, her hand supporting Will's legs to make sure he doesn't go too far.

"You're right. *Legs in straps* totally trump *hands in straps*."

"I know, right?"

Why does it feel so good to know Will enjoys the things she likes?

"Okay, question number three," he reminds her of the challenge. "Best and worst gifts."

"Mmm... I don't like expensive gifts. Pretty much any gift with a monetary value above $10 is unacceptable."

"You sound like a government employee."

"I wish."

"So, within the $10 range – best and worst?" he asks again, eyes lifting to hers.

"Worst is flowers."

"You don't like getting flowers?" Will seems positively surprised. "Explain."

"Because they die. Unless it's fake flowers, which I'm not sure why, but I don't like them either. Flowers always remind me of funerals or apologies – so better skip the wrongdoing and spare the apology."

"Noted," he says, suppressing a small smile.

"Best gift is stuffed animals. I love them, they're cuddly and cute, and I don't think one could have too many of them. How about you?" Her eyes meet his, and she has to pull herself away before...

Before what?!

"You can take your feet off the straps, but one by one." She helps remove one of the straps and guide his leg back to the bar, then he follows with the other leg.

"Do I have to adhere to the $10 rule?" This wins him a smile.

"No, unless you're getting *me* something."

Seriously?

"I'll keep that in mind." His eyes say too many things, she can barely keep up. "Worst gift I've ever received was a women's wedding ring - my ex-girlfriend was being passive-aggressive about getting married after we broke up, bought herself a ring, and gave it to me for my birthday."

"Wow! That's creative! And expensive."

"Yes."

"What happened?"

"We were not meant to be," he says, his face impassive. "I gave it back to her, she has since used it for someone else, and they are now married. I hope happily ever after."

"I'm sorry," she says, *feeling anything but.* "Do you regret not marrying her?"

"No, she deserves to be happy with someone who truly loves her. I didn't have it in me." He sits up. "Best gift – a notebook." He runs his hand through his hair. "My grandpa gave me an empty notebook when I was ten years old to write my ideas and my stories. He was always very supportive of my fondness for writing. I used to take that notebook with me everywhere."

"Do you still write?"

"Nah. I think I lost my inspiration somewhere along the process of becoming an adult." Something sad in his eyes flushes an appearance for a brief moment before he quickly shakes it off. Reminding her of his words by the fire.

Chloe gives him an encouraging tap on the back. Their conversations have taken a slightly deeper turn than perhaps intended. This brings back his smile.

"Time for stretches," she says, gesturing toward the mats at the center of the room. "I'll show you some stretches that could also be good after your weightlifting sessions at the gym." He lifts an eyebrow at her statement.

Has he not mentioned weightlifting? Great, now he knows she's checking him out.

"Yeah, well, that's pretty obvious. Have you looked at yourself in the mirror?" Chloe almost chokes on her own words.

What an outstanding rescue...

This makes his lips curve into a smug smile. "Stretches, sir," she reminds him, and he returns to the last position, which was a down dog, chuckling to himself. "Now cross your right knee behind your left and lower yourself down to sitting. Left leg across your right, sit up tall." Chloe takes her place next to him to demonstrate the stretch in tandem. "Now reach your right arm up and exhale, twisting over to your left," she says gently. "Don't forget to breathe."

"Any minute now," Will grunts. "I feel like a pretzel." He rumbles into the twist. "Might not be able to move tomorrow."

"Okay, grumpy," Chloe laughs and pokes him in the ribs, or at least tries to, but encounters a wall of intercostal muscles. "That's a good twist for your spine." She quickly pulls back her hand. Will shoots her a feigned suffering look, still chuckling.

She's probably had more fun in the past hour than she's had in her entire lifetime.

CHAPTER 10

Some Planks, Cobras, and Downward Dogs

"Your lottery ticket!" Chloe beams as Will enters the studio for their second class, holding her new favorite coffee. "You won! Ten thousand dollars!!!" She jumps up and down ecstatically like a five-year-old. She's been feeling this way since the moment she found out, and even though it's *Will's* lottery ticket, the thought of breaking the good news to him just made her unusually happy. Will's smile instantly turns into a grin. He puts down the two Starbucks cups, which are easily becoming their new morning routine, and without warning, sweeps Chloe up, spinning them around effortlessly, sending Chloe squealing as if nothing else matters except here and now.

"You mean *you* won!" he says happily as he puts her back down gently, his hands lingering on her hips, making sure she regains her balance before letting go. She can feel his warmth surrounding her, and for a moment, her mind plays tricks on her, showing her a glimpse of where hope seems to live. "I had a good feeling about it," he says. Her heart is working overtime, trying to catch up on the missing beats.

"So! What are you going to do with the money? Something fun, I hope," she asks, her eyes still on him, her hands still clinging to his arms for balance.

Or maybe she's not ready to let that moment fade yet.

"Me?" He looks surprised.

"Yeah, it's your ticket."

"I gave it to you," he frowns.

"Well, you couldn't have known you'd win."

"I gave it to you *hoping you'd win*, and I never take my gifts back!" he says with conviction.

"That's very generous of you, but I can't accept it." Her tone is serious.

"You already did when you accepted the ticket. There's no going back now," he refutes playfully. "If you hadn't taken that ticket, no one would have won."

"Ugh…" She's not sure how to counter his last argument. "No… I may be willing to consider splitting it."

Will shakes his head, amused. "I object."

"Overruled."

He crosses his arms across this impressive chest of his, but when she keeps her insistent face on, his mouth curves up a bit, and he says, "There's no way around it. You take the prize, but you can take me to dinner if it makes you feel better."

"Okay," she says in spite of herself, "dinner is on, but it's not a date."

They're just friends. A friend taking another friend for dinner, it's a very normal thing to do.

"Not a date, just two friends going on a friendly dinner." He joins her clarification venture. "And it has to be *your* favorite restaurant."

"Careful what you wish for, Allentown. I'm not known for my exquisite choice of restaurants," she laughs. "You choose the restaurant, but there are two rules – it has to be expensive, no discounts! And they have to have good mashed potatoes."

"Deal!" He seals it, and they formally shake hands, swallowing their chuckles and washing it off with some much-needed caffeine.

"How is college going?" Will asks, smiles still etched into their faces.

"Pretty good so far. I was planning to take just one course next semester, but now with the extra cash, I may be able to squeeze in all the leftover credits I need to graduate by the end of the year." Chloe realizes this as she says it. A moment ago she wasn't even sure she'd be able to pay for another course this year. With Jimmy dipping into her savings, her dream was slipping further away. Now she may actually be able to graduate this year! A burst of energy hits her. It's so sudden that her body shoots up, not sure what to do with her arms and legs, other than feeling like hugging someone. Will looks at her, genuine excitement written all over his face, he stands up, matching her energy. And before the reasoning part of her brain can have any say over all the other parts, she leaps into his space. Her arms and legs wrap themselves around him like a monkey. Will just laughs and cooperates, holding her effortlessly for the second time this morning.

This is not a very platonic hug. It wasn't her intention, yet here they are. She better get herself off that tree...

"Chloe, I am so happy for you!" Will's voice rumbles through her body.

It takes several unsuccessful attempts to inwardly command her treacherous body to release its hold of Will until she finally lowers herself back to the floor.

"Sorry," she says quickly. Her cheeks are burning, her heart is racing. Her eyes lift to Will's to assess the extent of damage to their newly formed alliance.

"What for?" His eyebrow lifts right under that little scar.

"The hug ... got a little too excited about the prospect of graduating." Her voice comes out a little raspy.

"Are you kidding? That was the best hug known to humankind." He grins brightly, letting his dimples prove his point.

No, no. That was a dangerous, dangerous hug, and it took an inhuman effort to pull herself away.

"Now back to work, sir," she quickly deflects, nudging Will gently toward the yoga room for some warm-ups. Nothing like putting on her trainer hat to dial down the heat. Chloe takes off her sneakers and socks, positioning herself on the mat next to Will's. They do some spine warm-ups and stretches before getting down to their routine. Will follows closely – downward dog, plank, upward dog – matching his breathing to hers.

"On your next exhale, pull your left knee forward," Chloe commands gently, "coming to a high lunge, arms reaching up, breathe." She twists her head to observe him. His sleeveless shirt stretches over his abdomen, showing a small strip of skin and impressive abs.

This was supposed to cool off the atmosphere...

Luckily Will is too busy following her commands to notice her trailing gaze. "Exhale and open your arms into warrior two. Nice!"

She was definitely referring to his ability to smoothly shift through the routine.

"On your inhale, flip your left palm up, reverse warrior, then exhale." Will follows her motions with his gaze, the intensity of it makes her feel ... good. An unfamiliar sense of confidence. Her heart rate goes off-track, and it's getting hard to keep up with moving and talking at the same time. She has to force a deep breath.

He's only trying to learn the moves.

"Set your left forearm on your thigh, reaching your right arm up. And again," she says softly, her voice wavering. Will obeys, and she gets up to correct his stance. "Straight back," she says, stepping closer. "Use your core as the stabilizing force." Will's mouth curves up when Chloe's hand touches his abs to make her point.

Gosh! she could do this all day ... what's gotten into her?

"Ran out of questions?" She tries to shake away the tension.

"Never." He turns his head toward her, challenge back on. "Okay, first question of the day – what's your favorite animal?"

"That's an interesting one." She walks back to her mat and goes through the flow they've just practiced, facing him to ensure he follows. "I like bunnies that look like cats."

"Is that a thing?"

"I don't know, but that's what I like," she says. "Don't forget to breathe. That's a central part of yoga."

"Have you ever seen one?" he asks, then inhales as instructed.

"I am sure I have. Otherwise, I wouldn't know."

"Alright, I guess I'll allow it." He smirks.

"Why, William Allentown, you are very accommodating," she chuckles. "Now you."

"Goldfish. That's the only animal my parents let me keep as a pet."

"Did you try to ask for a different pet?"

"Well, the cat thing didn't quite go my way."

They repeat the flow a couple more times and move on to planks and ab work. "Favorite book," he says, not even breaking a sweat.

"*The Love Hypothesis* by Ali Hazelwood. I'm a sucker for a good romance, and this book made me happy. That's rare," Chloe says.

"Rare for you to be happy?" He looks surprised ... concerned even. She just nods.

"Your turn."

"The Talisman, by Stephen King and Peter Straub, I like fantasy books, and this book is what made me fall in love with reading as a child."

"I remember thinking as a kid that it had an impressive page count."

"Indeed, so you've read it?" He seems content just at the thought of them sharing an experience.

"I have. I read it faster than I thought I could, I loved it."

They move on to cobra. "That's a great stretch for your abs, my favorite." She falters, hearing herself. "I meant the stretch, not your abs."

Well, both probably...

Will smothers a laugh. "We're going to stay there for a bit, don't forget to breathe." Chloe forces herself to remain quiet before she says any other embarrassing remark.

"It feels good," he admits, still smiling.

"I know, right? Now release the stretch, let your head rest on the mat for a few minutes, breathe and relax."

"This feels even better," he says, sighing loudly, closing his eyes. "First kiss," he muses, turning his head to face her.

"What?"

Is her mind playing those malicious tricks on her again?

"That's the third question for today," he says, his cheek squished against the mat, making only half of his smile visible.

"Mmm," is what Chloe manages to muster. Heat spreads through her cheeks. She can only hope it's not noticeable. "The captain of the football team in high school. He was a senior, and I was a bold and fearless freshman. We had never exchanged a single word before, but I had this crazy crush on him. I just walked up to him one day, got on my tippy toes, pulled him by the shirt, and kissed him."

"Very provocative of you." Will seems impressed. "What did he do? I'm sure he didn't mind," he says with a mischievous smile.

"Oh, *he* didn't mind. It only took him a second to recover from the shock and take the lead on what ended up as a VERY hot kiss." Chloe's cheeks burn now. One is resting on the mat, but she's pretty sure the one that isn't is visibly red at this point. "But unfortunately, *his girlfriend* did mind."

"You kissed a girlfriend-ed boy!" he says in a feigned authoritative tone as he sits up, amused. His left eyebrow shoots up under that scar, awaiting an answer.

"I'm pretty sure it's not an adjective, but yes, I was so busy admiring him that somehow the fact he had a girlfriend became a minor issue." Chloe suppresses a smile. "Anyway, enough about my first kiss, your turn now." She sits up too, wondering where her bold, fearless self had disappeared to after high school.

"It wasn't nearly as epic as yours," he admits, "and definitely not as hot." Is he blushing? Will Allentown embarrassed is straight-up adorable. "It was a girl I had a crush on in middle school. It was her first kiss too, so needless to say, we both had no idea what to do, it took a few tries to figure it out. It didn't help that we both had braces." His laugh is infectious. Yes, those perfect teeth had to be someone's hard work, although she finds it hard to imagine a time when something about Will was any less than perfect.

"This just keeps getting better." She tries to stop herself from laughing, but it's impossible. "Sorry," she says, still chortling. Somehow it seems that the number of times she's truly laughed in the past couple of weeks far exceeds the miserable number of laughs she's had in the last few years.

CHAPTER 11

Birthdays

A couple weeks go by, and Chloe is surprised by how quickly Tuesdays and Thursdays have become her favorite days. How the dread of going home every night has been replaced by anticipation for the morning. And by those growing flutters in her stomach that she hasn't been entirely willing to admit, not even to herself, so intense that it surpasses Jimmy's aggravating insults.

But when Jimmy notifies her of his plans for his 24th birthday, a little gray cloud makes its way to cover her recently formed sunshine.

"What's going on?" Will asks during what has turned into their usual coffee time before class. He studies her with his gaze, his left eyebrow pinched up right under that adorable little scar of his.

"It's Jimmy's 24th birthday tomorrow. I was hoping this year would be different, but he wants to do the same as every year."

"Which means?"

"Getting wasted with his buddies at the bar across the street from here, staying up all night wandering the streets, ending up on his friends' couch by morning, if he's lucky. Jimmy says that at least once a year he should be able to do whatever he wants. He does whatever he wants every day anyway, so I don't see..." She shrugs. "I was hoping that by now he'd be old enough to start breaking these bad habits." She lets out a tired exhale. "Anyway, I'm expected to join them, but I don't like being around his friends, especially when they're drunk."

"Have you told him?"

"I have. He likes to dismiss it, saying that I think I'm too good for them and that I should at least try to get along with them because they're his buddies." She takes a sip from her coffee, letting the sweet hot liquid wash away the knot forming in her throat. Being around Will certainly works its magic, chasing that cloud away. It's the moment they go back to their day that she's not looking forward to. "And I *have* tried, but he has this *friend*, Trevor, who likes to give me dirty looks, undress me with his eyes... And when he gets drunk, he likes to touch."

"Has he...?" Will's gaze shifts from concerned to ... protective? Jimmy's never had that kind of look, at least not with anything Chloe-related.

"He tried, but I got away and have avoided being around him since."

"And Jimmy didn't stop him?"

"He didn't see, or maybe was too drunk to see. I told him about it, but he said I was trying to make excuses to keep him away from his friends."

"I can't believe this asshole!" Will's eyes narrow, his fist clenches by his side, and a flash of anger crosses his face.

Getting himself all worked up... For her?

Chloe wraps her hand around his fist, feeling a new buzz of electricity with every finger she unwinds. "Anyway, this was a long time ago. Maybe he's changed."

"Don't go," Will's eyes shoot to her as if ... *pleading?*

"I can't. It's my boyfriend's birthday." Unease spreads across Will's face as the words leave her mouth. "I'll just Uber myself home if they start getting ... well, when I start feeling uncomfortable."

The next day arrives too quickly, to Chloe's dismay. She knows better than to pick a fight with Jimmy on his big day. He chooses a red dress for her to wear, one she wishes she never actually owned, but Jimmy got it for her a few years ago – it's too revealing for her taste, too tight on the *right* spots, and just generally too ... red. Spending the evening with drunk Trevor, she would much rather wear an oversized turtleneck sweater and a baggy pair of jeans, something she could blend in with, certainly not that dress.

It's your boyfriend's 24th birthday, she scolds herself. *Maybe Trevor will bring a plus one?* Wishful thinking would be an understatement.

Her mind is focused on her plans for tonight, repeating them like a mantra: don't drink, stay focused, look for early signs, split once she feels uncomfortable, *call me if you feel unsafe* – Will had made her promise.

Jimmy has already informed her, surprise surprise, that he'll be venturing out with his buddies later tonight and that she'll have to Uber back home. It's really just a couple of hours before she can break free of this twisted situation. She's already counting the seconds. Chloe can't ignore the fact that she needs to do some thinking. But not tonight, her brain is already too wired. She makes sure to set up the Uber app on her phone. She can't allow any unexpected issues tonight.

They Uber their way to the bar. Thankfully Jimmy agreed not

to take his car, the one he never lets her drive, but she has to make sure he doesn't get tempted to drive himself after his up-and-coming drinking session.

They get to the parking lot. Jimmy steps out of the Uber and strides toward the bar, letting Chloe stumble behind him on those vicious heels he insisted she wear. The wind on her bare back makes her shiver, reminding her of a minor technical detail that somehow slipped her mind. She was so focused on everything else that she forgot her coat. Well, just a few steps and she's inside. She can do this.

The bar is warm, inviting, actually. Soundgarden music is playing in the background. Jimmy's buddies are already seated at a booth, looking fresh and ... sober. Maybe tonight isn't going to be that bad? Maybe Jimmy was right? Perhaps she has been too focused on excuses in the past few years instead of giving them another *fair* chance. Brad has a girl wrapped around his arm, but Trevor, unfortunately, doesn't. He gets up to give Chloe a hug, of course. His eyes morph into a slow once-over, his hug a little too intimate.

She feels queasy but is able to shake it off quickly, fixing her mind on Will's words – *'Call me if you feel unsafe.'* She shoves herself between Jimmy and Brad's girl, who introduces herself as Vanessa, determined to make the most out of the evening. Pete and Tim are seated next to Trevor. They give Chloe polite head nods and go back to a heated football discussion. They order some drinks and appetizers and even make some decent conversation. Trevor's eyes wander between her cleavage to Vanessa's with increasing intensity after each beer he chugs, but he seems harmless, at least for now. Vanessa is clearly uncomfortable, shifting closer to Brad, who wraps his arm warmly around her, already half-drunk.

"How long have you guys been together?" Vanessa asks, looking at Jimmy, who's busy draining his monstrous-size beer.

"Five years," she hears herself reply.

Has it really been that long?

"Wow! That's awesome!" Vanessa clasps her hands together, doing a little excited jump in her seat. The alcohol in her system is definitely showing, but she's a cute drunk. Chloe takes a sip from her iced tea. No way she'd let a drop of alcohol into her system in this explosive forum.

"How long have you and Brad...?" Chloe's unsure whether the word 'together' would fit. Brad, although charming, hasn't been known for sticking to one girl for too long.

"A whole week," Vanessa says jovially. Well, nothing new under the sun.

"Nice!" Chloe tries to match her excitement or at least reduce her own skepticism. Being the only one sober at the table feels weird, almost like being an observer looking at them from a distance. She lets her eyes roam around; observing the comers and goers may serve as a much-needed distraction.

"What have you been up to, beautiful?" Trevor tries to make conversation, turning one of her favorite words into something cheap.

"Not much. Teaching Pilates, studying," she answers politely, which requires an enormous effort.

"Interesting." His eyes slowly creep to her chest again. She should be reciprocating the question but encouraging a conversation with drunk Trevor is the last thing she wants to do.

The door to the bar opens, and two guys dressed in business suits walk in, a wild contrast to the typical jeans-clad in-comers. And despite staying 100% sober tonight, she must be delusional because, from her angle, one of them looks so much like Will...

Stop thinking about him.

His gaze finds hers, sending the slightest little nod her way, accompanied by a small reassuring smile.

It is Will!

She nods back, trying to control the edges of her lips from climbing up her cheeks.

Has he come here just for her? Is he looking out for her?

Slow down, heart. He's probably just grabbing a drink after work with a colleague.

"So, how did you two meet?" Vanessa's sweet voice startles her.

"Huh?"

Did she notice their shared head nods? Their silent, wordless exchange? The blood gushing through her veins?

Guilt feelings quickly build their way up, her pulse on the verge of getting a speeding ticket.

"You and Jimmy," Vanessa lets out a confused look.

False alarm. Please proceed with the complex task of being.

Chloe's heart is making a heroic effort to return to baseline. "At a football game, we were seniors in high school. It was a dare. My school's team was totally killing it. Jimmy had dared me to go on a date with him if his school ended up winning, which was close to impossible." This memory of their five years younger selves makes her smile. They used to have fun together, once upon a time.

"So, his team won?" she asks expectantly.

"Actually not," Chloe laughs. "But we ended up dating anyway."

That's what happens when you go against the playbook.

"Oh." Vanessa releases a cute quizzical look and cuddles herself farther into Brad's chest.

A leg rubs at Chloe's, making her jump in her seat. She looks around the table, everyone seems busy drinking and eating, but Trevor's face is fixed on hers.

Of course.

Another leg rub.

She shoots a searching look to Jimmy, but he seems utterly oblivious at this point, or at any point in the past several years, for that matter.

"Stop," she hisses at Trevor. Cold sweat slowly covers her torso, pulse beating loudly in her ears, making the outside noises sound like she's underwater.

Another rub.

She gives Jimmy's arm a shake, leaning in. "He's doing it again," she whispers.

Jimmy is beyond the point of communicating or caring. Doesn't even bother to look in Trevor's direction. "Just go home," he says wryly, "you didn't want to be here in the first place."

"Fine," she scoffs and gets up to the bathroom, planning to call an Uber when she's out of their sight and wait there until it comes. From the far side of her visual field, Chloe can see Will's head turn after her as she walks away, his eyes following her closely. She enters the bathroom, shuts the door behind her, and presses the little Uber icon, entering her home address with shivering fingers. This requires a few attempts to get right. Then waits for what seems to be taking forever while the Uber app finds a driver nearby. She counts the seconds until one is finally found.

Fifteen minutes?!

She can literally feel her face fall. She walks out of the bathroom to wait in the little hall. Any place would be better than going back to that booth again.

A hand pulls on the back of her shoulder. Chloe turns around only to find Trevor standing too close, invading her personal space.

"Waiting for *me*, beautiful?" he asks in a deep voice. Alcohol breath fills up the distance between their faces.

"Trevor, get away from me. You're drunk!" She pushes him and turns to leave, but he grabs her arm and pulls her back to face him.

"I know what you want. I've seen the way you look at me," he says, still holding her arm, making her back up until she's trapped between his body and the wall. She gives him another shove that does nothing to his massive body, alcohol or not.

Chloe considers her options – escaping doesn't seem to be one of them now. A punch to his face? This would probably hurt her more than any impact it could have on him. A kick to his crotch? He's a bit too close for an effective kick.

"Don't touch me!" She raises her voice this time and tries for a stronger push. Considering the abundance of alcohol in him, he should be losing his balance...

But it does very little. If anything, it seems to encourage him.

"You heard her!" An angry voice appears somewhere in the distance, connected to a hand that pulls Trevor away from her in one determined motion, sending him with a thump into the wall.

"Hey! Mind your own business, man!" Trevor mumbles, a little shocked and shameful, rubbing the back of his head.

It takes Chloe a few seconds to register that those burning eyes and withering glare belong to Will. He grabs Trevor's shirt, staring him down for a long moment until Trevor looks... Shriveled.

"If you ever try to touch Chloe again, I'll know where to find you!" Will's voice is firm and protective. He lets go of Trevor's shirt and shoves him away. Trevor gives him a startled look and, with his tail behind his legs – backs up and quickly disappears.

Will turns to Chloe. His charged glare softens as his eyes meet hers, turning into concern. "Are you okay?!" he asks with a comforting touch, examining her face and arms for signs of bruises.

Chloe just nods. This rapid twist of events makes her mind switch quickly from a full-on fight-or-flight mode to some sort of... *Excitement*? But without slowing down. Breathing is not as easy a task as one might think.

"Thank you," she finally manages to speak with her outward

voice.

"Do you want to call the police? File a complaint?"

"He hasn't really done anything other than imagining I was coming on to him."

"It looked more like an escalating sexual harassment from where I was standing."

"It would have been maybe if you hadn't shown up in time. Plus, he was drunk. He wouldn't dare do it when he's sober, so I'm going to let it go for Jimmy's sake." Chloe shrugs. "Did you come here because of me?"

Will nods. "I had a bad feeling after this morning," he says, "and Avery, my business partner, wanted to get some beer after work, so ... here I am." He ruffles a hand through his hair.

"I'm glad you came." Chloe exhales, trying to sport a smile.

"Me too," Will says. "Do you want me to take you home?"

"Already called an Uber." She looks down to her phone. "It should be here in five minutes." The app reloads for an update. "Oh, ten minutes."

"Are you sure you want to be alone tonight?" His eyes are still full of concern.

She isn't at all sure, but instead just says, "I am."

"I'll wait with you," Will offers and turns to walk alongside her without waiting for an answer. One hand is nestled protectively on the small of her back, his other gesturing something to Avery, who nods in understanding, patiently waiting at their table. Her eyes drift to the booth where Jimmy and his buddies are carelessly enjoying another round of beers. Vanessa and Brad are no longer there, probably ditched the party. Chloe can't blame them. Jimmy looks so wiped he doesn't even notice them passing by.

"I'm fine, really," Chloe says when they are outside. "Although Trevor forever ruined the word 'beautiful' for me."

"That's too bad. I'll make sure not to use this adjective when expressing my thoughts around you." Will's eyes are saying something she can't quite decipher.

In what kind of dream world would he need to use that word around her?

"Much appreciated." The cold air helps her relax and blow the unpleasant Trevor images away, but also makes her shiver. She has to clench her jaw to stop her teeth from chattering. Will, being so attuned to her, seems to notice even the slightest of shivers.

"Is your coat inside?" he asks, coming closer as if to wrap his arm around her, but stopping himself midway.

Chloe shakes her head. "I forgot it at home." She lets out a self-deprecating laugh.

"You had other things to worry about today," he says quietly and takes off his suit jacket, wrapping it over her, instantly spreading a wave of warmth through her.

"You'll be cold," Chloe protests, although taking his jacket off her skin is the last thing she wants to do right now.

Luckily, Will won't take no for an answer. She takes a deep breath, letting his familiar scent surround her. The teeth chattering stops, and she gives an at-ease command to her jaw.

"You know," he turns to face her, "it doesn't have to be this way."

"What do you mean?"

Is he talking about them? About her and Jimmy?

"Relationships," he says. "Jimmy is an asshole. You deserve better." Will searches her eyes. Another wordless exchange runs slowly between them before the Uber driver pulls into the parking lot, and the moment is gone.

"Thanks for being here for me," she says, reluctantly peeling off the warmth of his suit jacket and handing it back to him, despite his insistence that she keeps it. Then quickly, before she says or feels something she may regret, she disappears into the car.

CHAPTER 12

Rain Rain...

"I hate to be the bad news bearer," beat, another beat, "but your boyfriend *is* bad news." Valerie's text stream fills up Chloe's phone screen in between taking dinner orders and serving them. Her cell phone buzzes repeatedly in her back pocket, and she has to glance at it while punching an order to the kitchen.

She doesn't usually take morning shifts at Claudia's, and on the rare occasions she does, they're usually not very busy on weekdays. Today, though, is unusual. Which is just great, considering she was hoping to go over her Principles of Genetics notes one more time before her afternoon exam. And there it is, in case she needs another distraction – Val shares a photo from Jimmy's Instagram page, dated from last night, with a blonde girl, and another one, still the same girl, his arm around her, looking drunk.

But was not too drunk to post it online.

He definitely has a weakness for blondes, another item on the endless list of deficiencies he's been finding in Chloe, and no, she refuses to dye her hair for his whims. "Please tell me you broke up with the asshole and forgot to tell me," Val demands.

"No..." Chloe types back.

At least not yet. She just doesn't have the guts.

"He's on this work training week in New York," she adds to her text.

"So that's what they call it now?" Val has always been more defensive of Chloe than Chloe herself. "Well, I guess I should congratulate him for finally finding a job then." Her sarcasm is so loud it even comes through in her typing.

"Gotta look at the bright side, right?"

"No bright side with this asshole if you ask me."

"Val!"

"Being honest."

"Got to go back to work. Tables are waiting."

There you go, change the subject.

"Say hi to Claudia for me. Call you later, babe. Let me know if you need me to send someone to break his arms or lace his tongue through his trachea." Valerie is quite the tender problem solver.

Ugh. Chloe sighs, blowing a few strands of hair off her forehead. She knows she should trust him. He says it all the time, and he's been her boyfriend for five years. But somehow, loyalty and a sense of commitment don't strike her as taking too dominant of a role when it comes to Jimmy's character. Especially considering the degree of his contempt for almost everything that makes Chloe, Chloe. The arguments and disagreements they've had lately, especially since Chloe decided to stand her ground and not give up on what she really wants, going back to school, despite Jimmy's immature vocal objections. And then adding alcohol to the mix, and voila – a one-night mistake in NYC. Or if you ask Jimmy, he may not necessarily think of it as a mistake but rather, a personal development opportunity.

Running through recent events, Chloe feels like a total fool. Last week when Jimmy came back from work and said he'd be gone for an entire week in New York for company training, Chloe was actually thrilled for him. He had finally found a job that made him want to wake up in the morning, at least for his first month on the job, and professional training was an added bonus to kick-start the new role. Unfortunately, her cheerleading role was decorated with his annoying condescending gloating on how quickly he was moving along in his new career.

More like buying his way up with her college money.

And then a reminder of her 'no-good, pointless, lame excuse of a career.' Jimmy never misses out on the opportunity to remind her how much of a visionless loser he thinks she is. Yes, when it comes to insulting her, Jimmy has quite the elaborate vocabulary.

Her shift at Claudia's ends, and Chloe rushes to her mid – although not really the middle of the semester – exam.

What could be a better place to go over her notes one last time than the bus? Got to be creative to maximize study time. The stress and rush make her hands shake. The bus comes to a sudden stop – not that stopping at a station is considered sudden, but it is when focusing on her study book – which results in dropping her bag to the floor, open side down, of course. She bends over to pick up her pen and notebook, scanning the bus's floor to make sure nothing else is rolling around somewhere, but her efforts need to come to an abrupt stop once they reach her destination. Being late for her exam is not an option. She sprints from the station to the campus building. Her phone buzzes again. She's hoping Jimmy hasn't posted new photos. The screenshots she saw earlier are still fresh enough in her brain. She looks anyway.

Nothing like an image of her boyfriend with another girl to boost that pre-exam confidence. Or any other part of her confidence, if there's any left.

But to her surprise, a heart-warming *"Good luck today"* accompanied by a flexed biceps emoji appear on her screen from an unsaved number. Chloe recognizes it right away. She never saved Will's number to her contacts that night at Claudia's when she'd texted him about the lottery ticket. Still, the digit order and combination make some sort of sense.

She may have memorized it...

"You remembered," she texts back. This definitely warrants a slight delay in her arrival time.

"Of course I did," he writes back instantly, although she can barely remember mentioning the exam, not thinking anyone cared about her stretched-out college efforts. Jimmy couldn't care less.

But Will appears to be everything Jimmy isn't.

A big smile takes over her face and stays in its place as she rushes into class, thankfully not late this time. Niki shoots her a look from the front row, signaling to the empty seat next to her. Chloe takes it, throwing her backpack to the floor at her feet, emitting a relieved sigh.

"How's the second boyfriend?" she scoffs. Chloe is not sure whether she's joking or annoyed. "You could have said you two had something going on."

"We don't." Her eyebrows stretch up. "I told you, I have a boyfriend." They haven't really had a chance to speak about it since that business panel night, since Niki missed a couple classes, and Chloe missed another.

"Well, then you are completely blind because he's totally into you," Niki says with a knowing look.

He is?

And for some reason, hearing it makes Chloe all warm and fuzzy inside.

Gosh ... is she blushing?

"And judging by the look on your face," Niki's serious tone turns teasing, "you are SO infatuated with him." Chloe coughs, almost choking on her own saliva as she swallows hard.

Go ahead, deny it. What is she waiting for?

Luckily for her, the instructor signals them to quiet down and start the exam.

"How was it?" Valerie asks with an upbeat expression over a Face-Time video.

"Went pretty good," Chloe says, hoping she aced it. Genetics is the course she's been enjoying the most so far this year.

"How's the asshole?"

"No idea." Other than the photos he's been posting for the world to see, he hasn't sent Chloe a single text since leaving for New York a few days ago. Well, he actually did send her one miserable text when he couldn't find his gym gloves. Quite upsetting on the one hand, but at the same time, not having him around, some new strange sense of calm has been taking over her. It almost feels like a...

Relief? Liberation?

Chloe opens her bag to dig out her wallet. The bus should be there any minute. "Ugh!!!" She sighs heavily as her fingers fail to retrieve it. She digs in again, holding her breath.

"What?" Valerie's concerned voice demands, trying to assess the situation through the small camera.

"I'm so clumsy."

"What happened?"

"Lost my wallet. I dropped my bag on the bus earlier, it probably fell out," she mumbles, quietly freaking out. "And my bus card... AND my home keys."

"Just take an Uber. It should have your credit card information saved to it. I'll look up a locksmith for you."

"No, Val, go to sleep. It's the middle of the night there. I got it."

"Not going to sleep. I'll call you in 30 minutes, want to make sure you're home and safe."

Chloe opens the Uber app. She used it on Jimmy's birthday. It shouldn't be too hard to do it again. She scrolls through it, and ... *of course* she deleted the payment method. Her credit card is no longer set up to her profile.

Her stupid online safety practices...

Okay, she could ask the bus driver nicely. Or better – she could walk to the stop where Al's bus line runs. Al would let her on for sure, problem solved, all under control.

Except for that drop that she's just felt on her face ... seriously? There wasn't even a forecast for rain.

Chloe starts running, looking for a big tree or anything to hide under but the rain gets stronger quickly, like getting stuck in one of those automatic car wash places. By the time she finds cover under the roof of a gas station, she's completely soaked, and rain is no longer the only issue. Thunders, of course, have to join the party. Chloe tries to call Jimmy with no success – is he ghosting her? Busy with work training? Or posting more irritating photos on Instagram? Either way, there's not much he could do now.

The rain quiets down a bit, and she's back to the street. Her phone rings. Finally, Jimmy! It was such a bad idea, but he was the only person she could call. She picks up.

"Got myself stuck in the rain, and I lost my keys ... and my wallet." Her voice comes out desperate and self-deprecating. "Go ahead, call me a loser all you want. I won't get mad this time." Knowing that this quick confession will bring about some unwelcome berating makes her wince. She waits for it, but the habitual scolding does not appear.

Instead, a warm yet worried voice floats through the speaker. "What? Why would I call you a loser?! Where are you now? I'll come get you."

Chloe looks at her phone screen, puzzled, and stops in her tracks. That unsaved number again. She didn't even bother looking before answering the phone.

"Will?! I am so sorry. I didn't mean to dump all this info on you, I was trying to let Jimmy know... I thought he was returning my call," she blurts out.

"I'm glad you did. Share your location. I'm on my way," he says, his voice laced with concern. She can hear keys clanking in the background, a door closing, a car starting. A flash of lightning bolts through the sky in front of her.

"No, I don't want to bother you. I'm almost home." Her last word is interrupted by a booming thunder, and it starts pouring again. The test might have gone well, but aside from that, this day is a total wreck.

"Still waiting on that location," Will reminds her, and she just sighs and sends it. At this point, she's feeling quite desperate, soaking wet, still a few miles away from home, with no one else she knows well enough to call for help. Will makes it so easy to just say yes.

"Will!" Chloe calls out, feeling a dash too excited when he pulls over next to her partly rain-free hiding spot. "You don't happen to have a towel in there, do you?"

"I do, actually." He exits the car, pulling out a towel from the back. "It's my used gym towel. I hope you don't mind." He smiles apologetically.

"Can't be too picky in my current state." She laughs as Will steps closer to wrap the towel around her, looking dazzling in his fresh out-of-work attire. "I could hug you right now!" She leans closer before remembering she's soaking wet and moves back.

"I would allow it," he grins, closing the distance for a hug. Water soaks into his button-down shirt and tie, but he doesn't seem to mind.

"I'm going to get your car all wet," she warns, trying to dry herself with the gym towel that smells like fresh laundry and fabric softener and ... him.

If anyone could smell that good after a workout, it would definitely be Will Allentown.

"Don't worry about it." He laughs fondly. Chloe is quite amazed by it. Jimmy would have freaked out by now. One drop of water in his car, and he'd be pissed. "Where to? Is there anyone with a spare key?" he asks, and it dawns on her, as she shakes her head, that aside from Valerie, there's no one else she would have handed over a spare key or called for help, for that matter.

"Thank you for coming to my rescue." She smiles. "My place, please. I'll call a locksmith to break the lock." Her phone rings, and she leads the way with hand gestures while scrambling through her wet clothes for her phone. The thought of briefing Jimmy on the current chain of events makes her queasy. She wipes her wet hand on her already wet jeans and looks at the screen. It's FaceTime video call from Valerie, and she lets out a relieved sigh.

"So, I called four different locksmith companies in town and also Jo-Jo, who would happily come pick your lock anytime," Val's assertive voice is definitely not impacted by the late hour in her time zone.

"Who's Jo-Jo?" Will asks in a quiet, protective voice.

"No one you need to worry about." Chloe sends a smile his way, then turns her focus back to the phone. "You're an angel Val!"

"Not quite. Hear me out first," Val rejects the credit. "So, three of them won't be able to make it tonight, only tomorrow around noon. The fourth one can do 4 a.m. with a triple charge, and Jo-Jo... I kind of regret calling him because he was completely stoned. Wait, is your ass sitting in a fancy car there?" Val's tone changes abruptly from operation commander to impressed.

"Yes, a friend of mine, Will, pulled off a heroic rescue mission here," she says, Will doesn't know she's been talking about him non-stop to Valerie for the past couple of months, and she'd like to keep it this way.

"A friend? Let me see this *friend*, I need to make sure you aren't being kidnapped," Valerie plays along.

"I'm not," Chloe chuckles, turning her head to Will. His lips curve into an adorable smile, despite seeming focused on driving in the heavy rain. Chloe turns the camera in his direction once he stops at a traffic light. "Will, meet my best friend Valerie. Val, meet my friend Will." She makes the introduction, a little embarrassed.

"Nice to meet you Valerie," he says with a smile before returning his eyes to the road.

"Damn!" Valerie's mischievous voice takes over the car. "Okay, even if you are kidnapped, I don't care!" Will chuckles at that. "So, I'm not sorry anymore to let you know that you won't be able to enter your apartment tonight," Valerie announces.

"You know he can hear you, right?" Chloe reminds her. Will cracks up in the background.

"My place then? I have a spare bedroom. You're more than welcome to stay," he says softly.

"I could never," Chloe refuses gently despite knowing her other option is to sit by the stairway of her apartment building and wait for a locksmith to come at 4 a.m. in the morning. And a triple charge... but so be it.

"I'd say go for it, Clo," Val interrupts through the speaker.

"I make a pretty good mashed potato, and we can play *Life*."

"This is an extremely specific Chloe-tailored offer." Val is taking charge again. "Chloe says yes, and thank you very much, Will," she says formally.

"It is indeed," Chloe agrees.

"So, it's a yes?"

"Mashed potatoes and a game of Life, there's really nothing more a girl could ask for." Chloe smiles contently and nods, despite being fully aware that this might bring a new kind of mess into her life. But somehow, it feels right, and there's nothing else she would rather do tonight.

Okay, tonight is not a fair comparison as her options are quite limited, but also any other night ... and any other day.

"Have fun, you guys. I think I can call it a night now," Valerie reminds them of her presence. "Love you, Clo. Call me tomorrow."

"Thanks, Val. I Love you too," she says and hangs up.

Will turns the car, and within a few minutes, they are well on their way to his place. This is probably the boldest decision she's made since the ninth grade.

CHAPTER 13

A Round of Life

W ill's penthouse downtown is tastefully and modestly decorated, which is pleasantly in line with his demeanor. Modern clean lines, warm solid colors, not the flashy rich-guy style she
was expecting to see, another point to his already-expanding score-
board. Not that she's keeping track or anything.

She takes a quick shower with his soap and shampoo, peeling off
one more layer of personal barriers, and puts on Will's clothes that
he laid out for her on the bed in the guest bedroom: sweatpants that
she has to fold a few times on the waist, a Queen T-shirt that reaches
her mid-thighs, and a hoodie of his, all share the same scent: that
mix of fresh laundry, him and some of that bergamot cologne that
by now has imprinted itself forever in Chloe's olfactory system to
be known as *Will's scent*. And once fixed, it cannot be undone. She
lets her damp hair stay loose, knowing her curls will kick in soon
enough if she doesn't pull them back tight, but somehow, far away
from Jimmy's critical look and his obsessive nitpicking, she feels
like being herself again, or better yet, free to just be. She walks out

of the bathroom, wearing all Will's stuff, finding him too, wearing sweatpants and a T-shirt, looking jovial at the sight of her.

"My clothes look good on you," he grins.

"You like Queen!" she deflects quickly. Unless he chose his least favorite shirt for her to wear.

"They're my favorite! The way they constantly questioned central music dogmas and shattered them is incredible to me."

"Agree!"

So he sacrificed a T-shirt he actually likes for her.

"How about you?"

"Huh?" Wearing another man's clothes and scent on her makes her mind drift off to uncharted territories. And the fact that they belong to Will is really not helping.

"Who's your favorite band?" Judging by the smile on his face, he's definitely on to her.

Focus.

"Aerosmith, of course!" she squeals, "because they're just ... amazing." She feels a little too befuddled, scrambling for better word choices.

And it's clearly showing.

"They've been my favorite since I was a kid and saw the 'Cryin'' video clip, got hooked, then I heard 'What it Takes,' and from there just fell in love with their music."

Will smiles and pulls out his cell phone, busies himself with the screen for a second, and the entire space instantly fills with the familiar melody coming from all directions through perfectly positioned speakers across the space. Steven Tyler's voice takes over, making her smile reach all the way to her ears.

"Let me show you around." He grabs her hand. That tingling sensation doesn't subside, completely resisting the laws of desensitization. "This is the living room." He walks to a pair of sliding doors with heavy dark metal frames. "And from here, you can see all the way to the city on a clear day." Chloe looks outside. The view is breathtaking, even in the rain, and there's a small seating area with an outdoor fireplace.

"Very cool," she says.

Articulation is beyond her at this point.

They walk back into the kitchen and through a separate corridor that opens into a lounge space that looks to be devoted to reading. The guest bedroom she's just come out of, also becoming known as Chloe's room and then Will's bedroom, share the same extra-large bathroom – significantly larger than the current living room and bedroom combined in her and Jimmy's little apartment.

There's another smaller bathroom on the other side of the apartment, connected to another room that looks like Will's library or office. "If I ever go back to writing again, this is where I'll write." He points to a seating area under the heavy shelves filled with books, even cozier than the lounge reading area. Chloe walks in, letting her fingers slide across the massive collection of books, admiring the selection. A special area is devoted to all of Stephen King's books, then suspense and fantasy books, tons of philosophy books, then leadership books, then books about writing.

"I could spend a whole week in this room," she says cheerfully, spreading her hands wide.

Will steps closer with a grin that shows off his dimples as if enjoying the attention this room is getting. "I would love that," he muses. "Hungry?"

The growls in her stomach may have given it away. "Starving!" she admits.

"Let's get you some food." He pulls her back into the kitchen, where a familiar smell is starting to emerge. The speakers keep playing Aerosmith songs, making her body sway to the rhythm happily, eliciting more content smiles from Will.

"Are you making mashed potatoes?!" Given the earlier overload, her olfactory system is probably playing tricks on her.

"I was, when you were in the shower." He opens the lid of one of the pots on the stove. "I keep my promises. And the meatballs are still cooking."

"So, you cook too!"

"*Too?* On top of other things you like about me?" he says, teasing.

"Yes, you make unbelievable s'mores," she laughs. Will's face lights up as he recalls the memory.

As it turns out, Will can make the most superior mashed potatoes. The two of them have a delicious and pleasant dinner, during which they talk about her exam.

Was that today?

Then they call the credit card company. Chloe only has to report one lost credit card – the only one in her wallet, which also equals the total number of credit cards she has anyway, which means she won't have any credit card until a new card is issued and makes it to her mailbox.

They then move to the living room for... "The Game of Life! You actually own the game!"

He was not kidding. It's just too much good for her to handle at once.

"You're not the only one into board games," he says smugly.

They set up the game on the coffee table, sitting on opposite sides on the thick cream-colored carpet. "I'm blue," Will calls out, aligning the little blue car.

"Purple," Chloe says, quickly aligning her little car next to his. Their knuckles brush, a light buzz... He must have felt it too because his gaze shifts, meeting hers halfway.

"College or career?" he asks, still holding her gaze.

"College!" At least in the game, she has the option to choose right from the get-go. She spins the dial and lands straight on graduation day.

Wouldn't that be nice?

"Wow, four years went by so quickly," Will exclaims and spins the dial, taking the college route as well. "Spring break in Florida, pay $5,000... Seriously? That's just typical."

"Can I join? Never been."

"I'd love to take you." He smiles. "Wait, actually?"

"Actually never been? Or actually join your trip to Florida?"

"Ha ha... Both?"

"Actually never been to Florida, not sure Jimmy would approve the other." She feels a flush in her cheeks. Will's gaze lingers as if he's making a mental note. So far, he's remembered her favorite food and favorite game, played her favorite band... The fact that he even bothers paying attention to these bits and pieces of info about her is striking.

"Get the cards," she commands. "I need to choose a college career."

Will lays out the cards facing down, and she picks the one that has a little fold on the side. "Looks like someone may have marked this card," she says suspiciously "A doctor! A hundred thousand a year! Did I take your favorite card? Shocking! You know they make more than that."

"Yes, and yes," he says with feigned disappointment.

"Okay, now you choose," she says on his next turn. He picks one card and gives it to her. "A vet! You'd make a great vet," she cheers.

"Thank you, you are very kind, Chloe Barrett."

"You are very welcome," she says smugly and rubs his arm, and despite touching him quite a lot during their Pilates and yoga sessions, she quickly pulls her hand away.

A full hour into the game, and they're already out of game money.

"Can I ask you a question?" Will inquires, turning his body to face her. She nods. "Earlier, when I called, and you thought I was Jimmy, you said something about calling you a loser... And then when your phone rang in the car and you thought it was him, you flinched." His face turns serious. "Has he called you a loser before?"

A beat.

How should she answer this question?

"Sorry if I was out of line," Will quickly offers, sensing her unease. "You don't have to answer if you don't want to. It's none of my business." But his eyes show it bothers him. A lot.

"He has called me a loser and other ... degrading snarky remarks," she admits quietly, her voice barely heard. Will seems genuinely concerned. Not criticizing or condescending, a friend who cares. "Quite a lot actually."

"For losing stuff?"

"For everything. For taking so long to get through all my college courses – I'm sorry, but working full time to pay for rent and food AND college takes time. And for not having too many friends – I think having one true friend is worth a million times better than having many 'convenience' friends. And maybe I could live with that, but calling me a loser for being a foster kid... Seriously, as if I had done anything to upset my biological parents the minute I was born."

Wow, that came out way too strong, way too much. Like a violent vomit of oversharing. He did ask, though.

She feels a drop on her face, and another one.

Are these tears?

Chloe tries to blink them away without landing much success. She closes her eyes for a second, trying to redirect her thoughts. And when she opens again, Will is right there, pulling her into his arms, letting her head rest on his chest, comforting her. "Sorry, I just barfed my entire life story on you," she tries to joke behind her tears, but her voice comes out broken and strained.

"I am sorry you had to go through all that. I had no idea." He runs a hand through her curls gently, then lowers his head to look at her. "Chloe, does Jimmy hit you?" His palm caps her face, lifting her chin gently to meet his eyes.

"No, he isn't violent or abusive." She shakes her head.

"I don't know Jimmy well enough to say, but, you know, people can be abusive without using physical violence. Mental or emotional forms of abuse are no better, sometimes even worse."

"I don't know. He has a big mouth, but it's just words."

Is she defending Jimmy again?

"Words that hurt you," Will reflects, and she can't counter it. Valerie has been telling her the same thing for years. "And he doesn't appreciate you. I saw you flipping through Instagram earlier. Was that him with another girl?"

"Yes, he's in NYC for work training, ignoring my calls and texts, posting all those photos with that..."

"He doesn't deserve you."

"He would probably disagree."

"It doesn't have to be this way. It truly doesn't."

"You've said that to me before. Jimmy says that all relationships have their issues and every person has their pluses and minuses. And the fact that his cons are bothering me so much – that's just because we all want what we can't have, and that his pros are what I take for granted."

"I don't think this logic applies here..." Will says gently, but his jaw is clenched. "We're talking about the bare minimum – being supportive, loyal, accepting. And you deserve much more than that – someone who sees you and loves you for who you truly are." His eyes are deep and honest, and for a second, it almost feels like a promise.

"Yeah... I'm not sure that's what life has in store for me."

"You'd be surprised." His gaze so intense that she has to break eye contact.

"Also, I'm sorry about..." he starts, as the second part of her little autobiographical monologue sinks in. "I didn't know you were..." He stumbles on the last part.

"A foster kid," she completes the sentence for him. "That's okay, I got over it many years ago." She plasters a smile back on her face. "Enough about me for one day. That's a story for another time. Now it's your turn."

Will nods, giving her an out. "Sure, what do you want to know?" He sits up straight, letting her go of his embrace. The spots on her body that were connected to his feel like open sores.

"Writing." She hangs out the word. This question has been on her mind since the day they met.

"I loved writing. It was my getaway, my happy place. I could lose myself in it for hours at a time."

"So why did you stop?" She can tell how much he misses it.

"I gave it up, went into the family business, something I wasn't too happy about but learned to live in peace with," he says, a wistful look on his face.

"But why can't you have both? Even if you made a choice for your main career, who said you have to give up what you love?"

"I didn't give it up willingly. Choosing a different career path didn't leave me with too much spare time on my hands, and I think that the more I pushed myself in the direction of doing what I needed to do on account of what I wanted to do... I started to forget how writing made me feel. And far worse than that, I couldn't write anymore even if I tried." Will shrugs. "I just lost my inspiration."

And at that, she takes his hand in hers and gives it an understanding squeeze but remains silent because finding time for important stuff is one thing, but inspiration... That's a whole different animal.

CHAPTER 14

Opening A Door

C hloe wakes up to the sweet smell of ... home-cooked breakfast? She didn't think spending a night in Will's bed would feel so ... natural. A perfect evening that started with Will's *to-die-for* mashed potatoes and meatballs, a round of Game of Life that ended with two *game money* broke players, each with more than four kids and throat-deep debts. Some profound conversations about life, love, and inspiration, topped off with funny insistence (from Will) that he'd sleep in the guest bedroom and give her his bed, claiming it was more comfortable. She tested both beds, and he was not lying. And although the guest bedroom was far better than her bed at home, and she had mentioned that to Will, he still insisted. So just like a perfect gentleman, he kissed her cheek good night, which made her blush and change colors like a chameleon, then he disappeared into the guest bedroom for the entire night. And just like that, she found herself in his bed, snuggling in his thick, fluffy comforter, between those dark blue silky sheets, trapped in that fresh laundry scent and Will's scent. She couldn't recall the last time she'd had such a sweet, restful sleep. Although she had been a little stunned by the dreams she may or may not have had during the course of the night when surrounded by all things Will (with the exception of Will himself).

But it's morning now, so she peels those thoughts off, gets out of bed, and washes her face, inspecting her hair in the mirror, now with her full-blown curls. She hasn't seen these guys for so long, after years of abusing them, pulling her hair back in a ponytail, blowing them dry or using her last resort – the flat iron. She let them loose last night, and they've happily made their comeback, bouncing on her shoulders and upper back.

"Good morning." Will grins as she appears next to him, taking her in, her curls, her smiling face, her body wrapped in his sweatpants and hoodie. His smile grows more prominent, a new kind of happiness she hasn't seen in him so far. "How did you sleep?" he asks, handing her a steaming cup of coffee. What has she done to deserve such a friend?

"Amazing," she says, and her voice makes this tiny pleasureful sigh which makes his chest rise a bit higher when he takes a breath. "This is really bad, though," she says, stepping closer. The table is set with pancakes and, of course, sunny-side-up eggs.

"How so?"

"You're spoiling me. I won't be able to go back…" Suddenly, using the word 'home' is impossible without the sentiment that should have accompanied it.

Home as in her apartment? Her regular life? Jimmy? Probably all three, and none of them feel right. Maybe to realize what's truly bad for her, she needed to be reminded of what's good?

"So just stay," Will simply says, and for a moment, her mind almost considers it. That one sip of caffeine hasn't really kick-started her common sense yet. Will leads her to the table. "I figured if you like s'mores, you might like pancakes too?" he says in a half-question, looking hopeful.

"That's very impressive logic," she chuckles, "and you're correct," she confirms. "How did you sleep in the guest room?"

"No complaints," he smiles, "but I think it's time to get a new mattress for that bed. that is, if you stay."

"No way I'm giving up your bed. Too comfy," she jokes.

"It's all yours," he says with his adorable, dimpled smile, apparently liking the sound of it.

What on earth has gotten into her? Is it Will coming to her rescue without questions asked? His hospitality? Last night's vivid dreams? Probably just the lasting effect of her sweet night's sleep in his bed combined with the lack of caffeine.

She puts her cup on the counter, then closes the gap between them and hugs him. Perhaps she overdid that closing-the-gap thing, though. Her body is pressed against his in all the right and wrong places. They've had friendly hugs before, but this...

This is not a friendly hug. What is she doing?

She can feel his body warming up to her, his heat. He's probably a whole foot taller than her, but she can feel his sweet breath on her face. His eyes shoot to hers, her heart racing against his massive chest, and from this up close, there's no way he can't sense it.

Has she gone completely crazy? Time to break this moment. But she's having a really hard time stepping back.

It requires an excruciating amount of mental effort before she eventually peels her body off Will's warmth. Bringing herself to a safe enough distance, she plops into a chair, tucked close to the table, where gravitating back to him would require more than a modicum of effort. Funny thing, her breathing is still labored, her senses still heightened at every single one of those points of touch. Her cheeks flushed. She can definitely feel it. Will seems ... content? A bit out of breath, maybe? He brings her coffee cup to the table, his eyes gleaming brightly. He sits down beside her, piling some pancakes and eggs into her plate as she's still stunned by her own actions.

"I feel like I'm being disloyal." Chloe's voice comes out low, almost whispering, as she speaks to Valerie through a transatlantic Face-Time chat. Thank God for modern technology. Chloe is sitting on the thin, musty carpet outside her apartment door, head leaning against the peeling wallpaper, legs stretched out in front of her. She left work early to meet with one of Val's recommended locksmiths, who hasn't shown up yet. Not Jo-Jo, as bringing up his name again made Will frown possessively, a sight too cute to mess with.

"Finally!" Val squeals. "When I saw your face last night, I knew you wouldn't be able to resist!" She jumps up and down, making the images on the phone move quickly in all directions.

"Stop moving. You're making me dizzy!" Chloe crosses her legs. "What do you mean *not able to resist*?"

"The hookup! Tell me everything!"

"*What?! No!* We didn't hook up, you goof. Let me remind you, I have a boyfriend." Her fingers reach out to the side of her phone to lower the volume before one of the neighbors joins their conversation.

"So, you kissed? *A hot steamy kiss?*" Val's enthusiasm is ecstatic.

"Of course not!"

"Well then, honey," she sounds disappointed, "let me break it to you, that's not cheating. Wait! *There are other things,* of course! I could see that being considered cheating." The excitement is back in her voice. "Even if you kept some of your clothes on, you naughty girl!"

"No, Val, we didn't *do* anything." Chloe sighs, trying to keep her voice down again, but her cheeks are heating up. "It's about how I *feel*. I feel guilty for how much I like being around him. About how fast my heart beats when he so much as stands close to me, or accidentally touches my hand, or looks at me... I feel guilty that my head is filled with thoughts about him. Val, am I crazy?"

Chloe blows a few strands of hair off her face, uncrosses her legs, and then crosses them again, watching how long Will's sweatpants look on her. She had to tuck them into her ankle boots. He did wash her clothes yesterday and dried them in his dryer. Yes, the man not only cooks and pulls off epic rescue missions, but he does laundry too! He had her cleaned clothes folded neatly, including her not-so-presentable underwear and bra, and ready for her this morning.

Yet she is still wearing his clothes.

She showed up to work like that, since it was much more suitable for a Pilates class than her jeans and blouse. At least that's what she was telling herself.

It was clearly hinting at the possibility of spending a night in another man's bed ... which technically was true.

She promised to return them cleaned. Will didn't seem concerned, but she should definitely do it.

Despite how comforting it feels to wear them. It might be a little hard to explain another man's sweatpants and hoodie in her closet.

"There's an obvious explanation for what you are experiencing." Val's smirky laugh awakens Chloe from her daydreaming ... partly.

"There is?" she asks, only half-focused, catching herself sniffing Will's hoodie again.

Stop!

"Yes! It even has a name!" Val pauses for a full-on dramatic effect. "It's called – falling – in – love," she says slowly as she drops each word like small explosives.

"*What?!*" Chloe jumps up to standing. "No, Val, that's insane!"

"And this, babe, is called denial," her laugh rolls playfully over the speaker, "and I don't blame you – he's handsome, charming, and cares about you, all of which are in total contradiction to your current piece-of-shit-asshole-of-a-boyfriend, pardon my French."

"Val, you're delusional," Chloe protests, not with much conviction.

"That may be correct," she laughs, "but not this time. I know when I'm right, and I'm right."

"And you know that based on what exactly, Sherlock?"

"The sound of your voice, the spark in your eyes." Her smile is mischievous. "I've been wondering about it, you know? Ever since Georgia Allentown's birthday party, you seem ... glowing! And I was wondering about it quietly, just between myself and I." She stops to laugh.

"Oh please, quietly?" Chloe cracks up.

"Yes, quietly, don't digress." She takes a second to squeeze in a breath. "And when I saw you with him in the car yesterday, everything just clicked! Mystery solved!"

"You do remember Jimmy, right?"

"Believe me, I wish I could forget. But maybe now you finally have a good reason to dump the asshole. I know you think that taking action is harder than just staying, but by not doing anything, you're actually making a choice, and it's a damn lousy choice." Valerie tries to be the voice of reason, but somehow it sounds revolutionary.

Chloe tries to defend her choices, or lack thereof, but at that moment, she can't come up with a single good argument. "I'll break his heart if I leave him," she finally says. The only time Jimmy got emotional and told her he loved her and couldn't live without her was when she tried to leave him. He had promised to treat her better, appreciate her more, stop comparing her to other women or try to bend her into these weird idealistic ideas he has about how and what she should be like. And just like that, she believed him, forgave him, turned around, dragged her rashly packed suitcase back inside, and stayed. And for a couple days, it felt like the beginning again. But then, and it didn't take too long, Jimmy snapped back to his usual stance, usual disdain, usual oppression ... and all those empty promises he had made melted away faster than snow, leaving a war zone behind.

"He'll get over it. He breaks your heart on a regular basis." Val's ironic reminder floats over her memories. "Tell me one thing you like about Jimmy," she challenges. "No, forget about it, that's useless. Tell me one thing you like about *yourself* when you're *with* Jimmy."

That's a tough one.

"Like about myself?" There are so many things she doesn't like about herself when with him. How easily he breaks her, the long nights crying, her tears-streaked face and swollen eyes in the mornings that she has to carry through the entire day, blaming it on allergies. The giving up on herself, on her dreams. But the worst part is probably believing Jimmy when he says she's a loser, that she'd get nowhere in life, that nothing good could come out of her insistence on getting that degree of hers – *just a waste of time and money,* he always says. That her biological parents had done themselves a big favor by abandoning her. She still fights his words sometimes, rebuttals his claims. But the longer time passes, the less convinced she is in her truth, and if she doesn't take a stand, she might one day forget who she is, or at least who she was. That fierce, fearless, determined kid who would fight to get her way, fight to survive.

Why does everything have to be a fight?

She had no control over her life trajectory when she was a young child.

But now she's all grown up – can't use that excuse anymore.

Has she put herself in this situation by choosing to stay with Jimmy? Probably. She's constantly remaking this lousy choice every day, apparently.

But she can still change it.

"Val, I think you're right," she finally says. "Not taking action is still choosing. This has to stop. But I'm not going to leave Jimmy for someone else. I need to do it for me." A new kind of excitement starts sizzling inside her.

"Now you're talking, girl!" Val's proud voice is unmistakable. What has she done to deserve a best friend like Valerie?

"Chloe Barrett?" A voice appears at the end of the corridor.

"It's the locksmith. Gotta go," she says.

"Good, keep me posted." Valerie blows her a kiss through the screen.

CHAPTER 15

Not A Date

"I'm in," Chloe texts Will once she regains access to her own apartment, as he made her promise when he dropped her off at work in the morning.

Will sends back a thumbs-up emoji right away, followed by, "Still on for our not-date tonight?"

This makes her smile. Tonight is her only free evening this week, and she promised Will to take him for dinner, the prize money having already secured her tuition for this entire year of college.

"Still on," she texts back. And although she clearly defined it as *not a date*, the thought of getting dressed and going out for dinner with Will makes her heart constantly flutter, which brings about some guilty feelings.

"Everything okay?" She shoots Jimmy a text, not that he deserves her concern. So much has happened in the last twenty-four hours under Jimmy's radio silence. Well, silence toward Chloe, that is. As he's definitely been oversharing his whereabouts with the rest of the world. Since leaving for NYC four days ago, he hasn't made contact, not a call, not even a text, and he hasn't been answering her calls either. Nothing. Well, nothing other than asking about his gym gloves. She opens her Instagram, trying to see if he's been active. This is honestly making her a bit worried. But there it is – a post from this morning, the same girl in his arms, this time even closer. If the last upload had his arm wrapped around her shoulder, now he's already hugging her hips, his fingers stretched on the bottom of her rib cage, almost grazing her severely oversized breast. His eyes are locked on her VERY generous cleavage.

Let her just throw up right here in the corner.

In this picture, unlike the ones from last night, he doesn't look drunk anymore, which makes it so much worse. Chloe shakes herself away from these thoughts and closes the app. If that's what he wants, she won't stand in his way, but she has to do something, because that photo is coming close to making her blood reach a boiling point.

She looks around. Their apartment seriously looks like someone broke in, which is not unusual given Jimmy lives here. If Will decided to walk up and ring her doorbell, this would be embarrassing. She rolls up her sleeves – actually Will's sleeve, as she hasn't yet come to the right state of mind to take his hoodie off – and starts the daunting task of organizing. An image of this morning's hug flashes into her mind for a second, making her anger dissipate slowly. She cleans up the kitchen and the living room, getting to the old newspapers stacked under the table. She wishes she could throw these away, but Jimmy would freak out. He has this thing with old newspapers, collecting them in boatloads as if one day he will get to read them all. Chloe doesn't quite get the story behind it. She's not sure he even knows. It's just another one of his weird habits. She pulls the never-ending stacks and shoves them behind the sofa, knowing this will put Jimmy in a total fit, but she doesn't care anymore. And although she has no intention of Will ever seeing their bedroom, it's about time to try to organize that room too. Jimmy's side of the bed is filled with stuff that he probably planned to pack and couldn't fit in his bag.

A few paper bags decorate the floor, plastic bags and wraps of stuff he probably bought and packed but could not get himself to throw the wrappers away, or God forbid, put the junk he didn't take back in its place. Chloe sighs, picking up the empty boxes of travel-size toothpaste, travel-size shaving cream, a condom box...

A what?!

Her heartbeat soars instantaneously, anger pulsing up her veins. With shaking hands, she picks up the little box of...

Flavored condoms! The motherfucker!

This is clearly a new box that was emptied out completely into his travel bag to NYC.

The guy was planning to get busy on this business trip – obviously not with her.

Chloe has been on the pill since they started dating five years ago, which was also the last time they had used one of these.

So, he went and got himself a whole box of condoms and didn't even bother to hide it!

The fuck?!

Breathe, need to breathe, she tries to remind herself. And then it suddenly strikes her – she's not even surprised, not a bit. It fits his personality so perfectly. The writing has been hanging on the wall for so long, but she chose to ignore it, refused to read those VERY bold letters.

Is that the first time? Has he been cheating on her all along? She tries to recall nights he came in late, days he'd disappear for hours on end while 'looking' for a job.

Interesting...

How blind has she been exactly? And for how long?

She snaps a picture of the box with her phone and sends it to Jimmy, accompanied by a gentle, *"What the heck?!"* text. This seems to grab his attention quite quickly. She can see the three little dots on the screen. Her heart's racing.

So now he finally decides to answer?

"The fuck you going through my stuff for?!" is unfortunately not a surprising response coming from her loving boyfriend.

"Cleaning up our bedroom, you left it on the floor. Using condoms now?" Somewhere inside, she hopes he'll come up with some sort of an intelligent excuse, that he'll say he bought it for a friend or something. It may be a lie, but at least a stomach-churn-alleviating lie, and she'll never be able to truly know.

But "Gotta stay safe," is what he chooses to write. The bastard. Not even denying it.

"Safe?! Are you fucking kidding me?!"

"Of course not."

Okay, what does that mean?!

A beat. Another beat. Then another text. "Just in case something comes up, always good to be protected, don't you think?"

He is kidding, right?

"What kind of a sick joke is that?"

"Would you prefer that I just go with whoever without protection?"

Whoever? Apparently this isn't a joke.

"I WOULD PREFER THAT YOU DON'T SCREW AROUND WITH SOMEONE ELSE!"

Gosh!

Her heart is on the verge of combustion. If this wasn't a text, she'd be screaming to the roof. Her face is burning. Flames would be coming out of her eyes if this was humanly possible. She needs to get some steam out right now. Cleaning up the apartment is just not going to cut it. She gets up, out the door, and down the stairs as quickly as her body takes her. Earphones in her ears, loud music on, and she's gone. The only way she knows is running, the only sure way to get through without getting herself in trouble. Running has always been her outlet in tough moments. And unfortunately, there have been many. Too many.

This is just one of them – she's been through worse.

She picks up the pace, replaying the past five years in her head. She should have left a long time ago. Silly her, letting Jimmy convince her to stay, believing he needed her, thinking that being with him was better than being alone. She starts sprinting now. Her breathing is labored and ragged. She focuses on the music, the breeze on her face, and the cold air that's burning her throat. Her mind is beginning to let go of the pain, the shame, the guilt, and the memories.

An hour goes by, maybe more. By the time she turns the corner back to her neighborhood and into the apartment complex, she's able to pull herself out of her own mess of thoughts. She climbs up the stairs, two at a time, out of breath from running but mostly from fussing. She can feel that sharp pain under her left rib. She thought something like that would make her sad, would break her heart. But she's had enough shattering. All she can feel is anger, resentment, disgust.

And then nothing ... nothing at all.

For the first time since Jimmy came into her life, she can finally let go without the usual guilt feeling creeping up on her at the thought of leaving him. Maybe this is exactly the wake-up call she needed? That nudge to gather the strength to get up and leave.

Is she brave enough to be alone again?

Jimmy should be back home on Wednesday. By then, she could be gone, out of his life for good. Her mind is contemplating, charting a wishful action plan. She can rent a new place, move her stuff, and never turn back.

Can she? Does she still have what it takes?

Should she at least stick around to confront him? Does he even deserve it?

Her phone buzzes from somewhere in the apartment. The thought of Jimmy trying to apologize quickly sneaks into her mind.

Will that settle her back into place?

But she wipes it away just as fast. Even if it is him, she can't give in. She can't put her common sense to sleep anymore.

Luckily she doesn't have to. A flutter-provoking "Picking you up in an hour" pops on her screen, attached to that unsaved number.

How is it possible that one single message from Will can make her entire world bright again?

Maybe it's time she added his number to her contact list.

Leaving everything behind, loud music on, Chloe strips off Will's hoodie and sweatpants and gets into the shower. An hour is plenty of time, considering her last under-fifteen-minute record. She lets the hot water wash away the latest events, the good and bad memories of Jimmy. They've had a few good memories, but weighing it all together, she can finally admit, at least to her own self, that the negative ones, even with this last one removed, far exceed the positive ones.

Why has it taken her so long to realize? If there was a statistical test for relationships, hers and Jimmy's wouldn't make the cut-off. Heck, she doesn't need a sophisticated test for it. They clearly don't.

She gets out of the shower, drying her hair, opening her curls just a tad to create waves, putting on her favorite blue dress and a touch of makeup. And for the first time in five years, she's not doing any of it for anyone but herself.

And it feels pretty darn awesome.

Chloe's phone buzzes, announcing that Will is outside. She grabs her purse and keys, puts on her only pair of heels, and lets that wave of excitement rush her through the door. Butterflies swirl in the pit of her stomach. An exhilaration she hasn't felt before. She takes a deep breath while she still can.

It's not a date, just two friends going to dinner.

Chloe steps outside her building to find Will leaning against his car, looking handsome as always, wearing dark slacks and a light blue button-down, sleeves folded halfway up his impressive set of forearms.

"You look stunning," he says as they lock eyes, stepping closer to give her a small kiss on the cheek.

A friend, her friend... Why does he have to smell so good?

"Thank you, you don't look too bad yourself," she says, warmth spreading through her face.

Is she blushing again? Better stop flirting.

"Have you picked out a restaurant?" she asks, her voice coming out a little shy.

"I have," he says and opens the door for her. His eyes follow her every move as she situates herself in the passenger seat.

"Do they have mashed potatoes?" she asks before he closes her door.

"Of course they do, it was first on the must-have list." His laugh is soft and warm, chasing away those earlier gloomy thoughts of Jimmy with another woman.

The restaurant is a short scenic drive. Aerosmith's "Jaded" is playing in the background as they take a wooded side road.

"This is another one of my favorites!" She sings along, leaning her head back into the headrest, already the third Aerosmith song in a row. "Made a playlist?"

"Maybe." A small playful smile curves its way up his face.

For her?

"Really? I like it!" she says, rubbing her hand on his forearm, which sends a tingling sensation into her fingers.

No, abort!

The restaurant looks like a combination of a rustic winery yet with a modern, classy touch, almost romantic. A perfect spot for first dates.

If this was a date, which it isn't.

They are greeted by the host and are taken to a small table by a massive window overlooking an impressively manicured garden.

"This place is gorgeous," Chloe says as Will pulls a chair for her. He waits for her to sit, then positions himself across from her, offering a smile. Her eyes follow closely, anticipating his dimples. He doesn't disappoint.

"It's the perfect spot for a first date," Will says.

They sure agree on that one.

"You mean a first not-a-date?" She corrects him with a smirk.

"Yes, not-a-date. I do remember that." He offers a polite smile. "You have a boyfriend."

"Correct."

For now.

"And apparently, my mother has set me up for a date on Wednesday," he says with an apparent lack of enthusiasm. Still, it does something weird to her stomach.

Please don't go.

"Nice," she offers, not sure what else to say. "Who's the lucky girl?"

He chuckles. "I haven't met her yet. My mother was sparse on details, afraid I'd find flaws in her plan."

"You don't sound too happy about it."

"That's because I'm not," he says. "I don't like it when my mother plays matchmaker, and I don't like blind dates either."

"Understandable, although I can't speak from personal experience, you know, being with Jimmy." Yes, that kind of chased away any remote possibility of pretty much everything, although she hasn't really felt like she was missing anything.

Up until now, that is.

"You've been together for a long time, right?"

"Yes, five years as of yesterday." *Five sad years,* she wants to add but doesn't.

"*Yesterday?!*" His eyebrows collide. "And you chose to spend that special day with me?" Not an ounce of cynicism, just pure surprise in his voice.

"Well, as you're probably aware, he's been pretty busy."

"Right... I am sorry," Will offers.

"Thanks," she says, "it's okay. Jimmy's never been big on anniversaries anyway, so I knew what to expect. I am just happy he finally has a job that he's willing to put the effort in."

Along with extra-curricular activities, and Chloe's savings.

"Where did you guys meet?"

"A football game in high school. His school was playing my school."

"Rivals. That's original."

"He dared me to date him if his team won. They didn't stand a chance." She rushes through the story, hoping to not spend the evening discussing Jimmy. He's been possessing over her life for long enough.

"Let me guess, your team lost, and he won you over?"

"Actually, no. My team won."

But somehow Jimmy did win her over. At least for a while.

"So, you ignored that one little sign," he chuckles, "and decided to date him anyway." His voice comes out a little...

Wistful? Longing?

"Yes."

Ignored that one little sign and then all the other signs that followed.

"And somehow, we ended up together, and you know ... life... Before I knew it - five years had gone by."

Did she intentionally use past tense on that last part?

Will's eyebrow creases under his little scar. His eyes search hers. "Are you happy with Jimmy?"

He noticed, of course, he noticed. Nothing escapes his studying gaze. A single syllable, a hand gesture, a smile, a sigh. Is he like that with everyone? Chloe would sure like to know.

"Being happy is a decision. It's what we make for ourselves." Her voice is firm, insistent.

"I agree, but are you – happy?" he demands.

"I'm still working on it." The waiter steps in to take their orders and fill up their wine glasses, breaking that eye contact. Chloe looks down at the menu, and Will follows. She's happy to see they have mashed potatoes coupled with several of their dishes.

"Do you love him?" Will persists once the waiter leaves. He's asking an awful lot of questions for someone who's about to go on a date in a few days.

"Not everything is about love." Her voice wavers. She hasn't tried to piece things together in such a way.

Will's eyes shoot to hers. "I think *everything* is about love," he says softly.

"Well then, William Allentown, I think you know something that I don't," she says, liking how his name rolls on her tongue.

"I think you're avoiding the question." He smirks, making his dimples appear again.

"I used to think I loved Jimmy." The words escape her before she can weigh in, sounding regretful. "But there are too many things I don't love about him, too many things I don't think I can live with. And I used to think he loved *me,* but I can't come up with a single thing he likes *about me,* not a single thing he hasn't tried to change. Maybe he just likes the *idea* of loving me."

"He's a fool." Will reaches for her hand and takes it, squeezing gently. This time he doesn't let go. He's about to say something else but stops himself.

What's going through his mind? What is he not saying?

His touch is warm, and although meant to comfort her, it makes her heart race again. She wants to tell him about her new revelation, her bickering about leaving Jimmy, but she's afraid it would make her look desperate and pitiful. So she decides against it.

The waiter returns with some bread and spreads that smell and look delicious.

"Tell me about your parents." She shifts the conversation.

"My parents?" He takes a sip from his wine before responding. His eyebrows shoot up. "What would you like to know?"

"Anything you'd like to tell."

"My mother, Aline, and my father, Maxwell, are both managing the family business," he says with such humbleness that anyone not familiar with the Allentown multi-billion-dollar real estate and construction empire would think they manage a tiny little diner. "I'm an only child. They're tough and strict but loving in their own way. I wish they had more love for each other, but I'm grateful nonetheless."

"How did your parents meet? Something romantic?"

Must be if he's such a firm believer in love.

"Arranged marriage, sorry to disappoint. Georgia told me once that my father was in love with another girl who his parents disapproved of, so they stepped in and put an end to it. Then they introduced him to my mother. Marrying within their social class was apparently very important to my grandmother."

"Did your mom know? How did she feel about it?"

"For her, it seemed like the natural thing to do. She still lives in that era of social class adherence, unfortunately. She may agree with your statement that it's not all about love."

Her very sad statement. The one she doesn't truly believe in but had to adopt in order to be able to live in peace with herself.

"She doesn't think love should have a say in who we choose to spend our lives with. My theory is that she's never actually been in love."

"You may be right." Chloe considers it.

Is she speaking about his mom? Or her past self?

"May I ask about *your* parents?" He searches her eyes for approval. "You don't have to say yes."

"You may," she nods. "I can't remember my biological parents. I have no idea who they were or how they looked. I was a foster kid." She takes a sip of her water, studying Will's eyes, too afraid to let that side of her show.

Would sharing these not-so-fun facts about her make him see her in a less favorable light? Like it did with Jimmy?

Will takes her hand again, encouraging her to proceed. No pity, no judgment.

Why is she finding it so surprising?

"I was a sick kid, in and out of hospitals, thanks to what the doctors thought was related to the reckless behavior of my biological parents – drugs, alcohol, you name it. You know, most people are wary of adopting a sick child. It took almost ten years for my guardian angels to find me – the sweetest, kindest couple, Joseph and Susie Barrett. They were older and had lost their own children.

It's a really sad story; both their kids had a genetic disease called Tay Sachs and died before they were three years old. So, Susie and Joseph decided to adopt *me*, of all kids – I was extremely lucky," she says. And the more she tells him about herself, the more he seems to want to hear.

The food is served, but Will is so focused on her that he asks her to continue, while they eat slowly. She tells him how Joseph died of a heart attack when she was fourteen and how she lost Susie to cancer when she was sixteen. She tells him about the money they had left for her and how she took it all and donated it to the Tay Sachs Foundation in memory of Joseph and Susie's deceased biological children. And how she still feels that this was the best decision she's ever made.

And Will is listening intently to her story, supporting and encouraging. "I know your adoptive parents would have been proud. What happened after they passed? You were still a minor," he asks, still holding her hand, comforting and protecting, and she wishes, just for a moment, that he would be there forever.

"I ended up in another foster home. That's where I met my best friend, my person, my non-biological twin Valerie!" Chloe insists on ending her autobiographical confession with a positive twist. Because something good had to come out of all the bad. That's the only thing that helped her accept her fate.

"Valerie!" Her name brings a smile to Will's face, throwing both of them back to the night before, when Val convinced her over FaceTime that it was a good idea to spend the night at Will's. "She's funny," he says, "and cares a great deal about you, I can tell."

"She's relentless!" Chloe laughs. "By the way, you were correct. The mashed potatoes are delicious!"

They finish their food, too stuffed for a dessert. The waiter hands Will the little leather case with the bill – so assuming. Will opens it up and reaches for his wallet.

"Mine," Chloe snatches it from his hand. "A deal is a deal," she insists.

"The deal was about you taking me to dinner. I never agreed to let you pay for it," Will says playfully.

"That's what taking someone to dinner means. This is more like *you* taking *me* to dinner, not part of the deal," Chloe protests, still with a smile.

"Alright, I'll let you take me to dinner next time," he says smugly. She considers it for a few seconds, finding it hard to resist.

"Okay, I'll allow it." She nods with a feigned serious look. "A second not-date?"

"Precisely."

"A busy week for you, Allentown. A not-date with me today, a blind date on Wednesday." The thought of Will going on an actual date with someone else makes her queasy.

Or maybe it's the wine talking?

It must be the wine because her legs feel wobbly on the way to the car. She has to hold on to Will to ensure she doesn't trip. It's also the only plausible explanation for why her hands grab onto his collar and pull him closer when he stops to open the car door for her. Since she's wearing her heels, she only needs to stretch her head up to press a small kiss into his lips. And they're so soft and warm.

What is she doing? She has no right claiming him, not now that he's about to go on a date with someone else, and she has a boyfriend.

She lets go of his collar, folding it back in place, giving herself a chance to reason, giving him a chance to protest.

Will opens his mouth to say something but doesn't. She can feel his warm breath on her face, his cologne wrapping her in. He looks to be contemplating for a second but then closes the gap between them, trapping her gently against his car, returning her kiss, gentle at first, slow, devouring. He stops to look at her, but she can't let go, grabbing the back of his neck, longing for that explosive sensation of his lips on hers again. This time fierce, bold, breathless, and for the life of her, she can't remember any other kiss ever crossing her lips before. His hands in her hair, a gentle pull on her lower lip.

A small moan released into his mouth.

Was it hers?

This makes him smile, deepening his kiss. Holding her tighter. She can feel his heart thumping against hers, his hands trailing to her hips.

"I better take you home before I lose control," he grunts. His voice hoarse as he backs up, letting Chloe in the passenger seat.

Please don't go on that date. Just don't go.

"I..." she tries to say after regaining the complex functions of breathing and speaking again. The earlier scenic view is now dark, decorated only by the moonlight. His new Aerosmith playlist is back on. "I'm sorry I kissed you."

What the hell has gotten into her? What was she doing exactly? And is she really sorry? Because it sure doesn't feel this way.

"Well, I am *not* sorry for kissing *you*," Will admits, shaking his head gently. And despite the darkness, he clearly seems ... jovial. "Although I don't think I've ever kissed a boyfriend-ed girl before."

"Is that even a word?" she chuckles.

"It is now." He gives her a lopsided smile. "I don't mean to pray on Jimmy's downfall, but if you ever decide to leave him, I would definitely do it again."

CHAPTER 16

Taking A Stand

"I finally did it," Chloe types quickly on her phone and hits send. If there's one person in the whole entire world who will be ecstatic to hear the news, who's hated Jimmy from the first moment they met...

Valerie responds within less than a second, "What *it* are we talking about?" Of course, Val being Val, her imagination has probably ventured out further – steamy scenes with Will. In her mind, Jimmy is not even worthy of a text.

"Not exactly what you're thinking right now, sorry. But I packed up my stuff and..." She's not sure which word to use.

"HOLY. SHIT. YOU. DUMPED. THE. ASSHOLE!!!" Val shoots back. And by Val's texting rules, this gets the best-news-of-the-year award. Heck, the best-news-of-the-century award. She adds those firework and balloon effects decorated with additional "Yay!!!" and party emojis. "I would totally call you right now and scream happy screams in your ears, but I am at an army base waiting to be called for an interview. Using my phone might get frowned upon. I am pretty sure there's a sign above me that says it, but it's in Hebrew. I haven't learned all my letters yet."

Chloe chuckles. Even through written messages, she can clearly hear Val's voice. Her texts read exactly like she sounds.

"You're actually doing it! I'm so proud of you! GOOD LUCK! Call me later, don't want to ruin your first impression! Go dazzle them!"

Chloe thought she'd be broken, sad, and hurting after finally taking that final step she'd been contemplating for the past several years. But she isn't, as if every single cell of her body had already made that decision long ago. It just took her so long to actually get the memo. She feels relieved. A little sad for Jimmy, especially when his face twisted to a lost, agonized expression as he realized she was serious about it, that she had made up her mind, and nothing he could do would change that. She did plan to make her escape before he came back from NYC but decided she at least owed him the chance to explain. It was highly unlikely and probably wouldn't have changed her decision, but just in case it wasn't what it seemed. He confessed he had plans for that woman from the photos, but they never actually materialized, and not because Jimmy had a change of heart. Maybe that woman had other plans. Jimmy, of course, brought protection because *being protected is essential*, the asshole. He also said she shouldn't be mad at him for playing it safe.

Playing it safe?

Seriously?

She was beyond furious at that point. "It's your fault," he said, "that you chose to take it this way." And that wasn't the first time he had made that argument. "There are no surprises with me," is something she's heard from Jimmy time and time again. "You already know my pros and cons. At least you know what to expect."

Yes, he was right about that for sure.

He then tried to plead, apologize, even shed some tears, and promised to change, another one of those empty promises. Chloe took her suitcase and her one box of stuff. That's all she owned. Everything else was shit they'd bought together – and although Chloe had probably paid for most of it, she didn't want any of it, nothing to remind her of those past five sad years. She left her spare key on the kitchen table (she'd never found the one she lost on that rainy night). She's been taking care of the rent forever, but the contract is under Jimmy's name, so he gets to keep the apartment. Then she rolled herself out and closed the door behind her, putting that chapter to rest. Time to start over.

Admittedly, she hasn't entirely worked out the details beyond that moment of leaving. All her thoughts and energy were devoted to that one victorious moment when she broke free. Not that anyone, other than her own self, was forcing her to stay. But then, it's not like anyone was waiting for her on the other side either. She hasn't been too communicative with Will since that scandalous kiss, combined with the fact that he was going on a date with someone else, she's kind of been giving him space.

Well, more like avoiding him.

He's texted several times, sweet, caring, enticing. But her responses have been laconic and terse. Leaving Jimmy was something she had to do on her own. She owed it to herself. And although Will is her friend, her timing sucks because tonight he's going on a date, and she can't bother him with stupid rescue missions that involve crashing at his place.

But that's not the main reason why her timing sucks. If she had done it sooner, before Will's impending blind date, maybe their not-date could have been an actual date?

Nah... Better shake away her fairytale fantasies ASAP, because he's so out of her league. There's no freaking way that a guy like him could ever be interested in ... her.

"Can I crash at the studio tonight? Have a situation," she quickly texts Tania. She has the key, can spend the night there, and figure out the details tomorrow.

Tania takes some time to reply. "Sure. Everything OK? My boyfriend wouldn't mind if you stay with us for a couple days," she offers, being polite. By that time, Chloe is already off the bus, dragging her luggage toward the studio's front door.

"Thanks for the offer. I'm fine." She's actually better than ever. "The studio is good enough if that's OK with you."

Tania sends a thumbs up, and Chloe trails straight into the yoga studio. She sets her stuff in one corner, piling a few yoga mats and meditation blankets, and she's got herself an improvised bed. She changes into her sweatpants and Will's hoodie.

Yes, she hasn't given it back yet. Hasn't washed it either...

She brushes her teeth in the studio's tiny restroom, and positions herself on the pile of yoga mats. Now that the excitement of her actions starts to settle, her mind drifts off to Will and his date. It keeps her tossing and turning all night. The thought of Will going on a first date with another woman somehow bothers her far more than leaving Jimmy, despite them being together for the past five years.

How is that even possible? Why has it taken her so long to see?
Is she too late?

She gets up at the crack of dawn. The yoga room is all the way in the back, but the studio is designed in a way that fills it up with natural light. Her muscles ache from attempting to sleep on the pile of mats. She feels at ease with her decision about Jimmy, about finally being on her own. Yet a little worn down by the repeated insults of her imagination, detailing all the possible post-blind-date scenarios for Will. Spoiler – none of them end well for Chloe.

She brushes her teeth, changes into her workout clothes, pulls her hair back in a ponytail, and unlocks the front door, ready for her first class of the day. Even the coffee machine is operational this morning.

"Good morning." Will's voice carries itself with confidence throughout the studio.

Of course. She can't keep avoiding him anymore. Even if all she can think of is their first and last kiss while he's seeing someone else.

"Good morning." She walks out to the entryway to greet him, stopping mid-way as their eyes meet. She can't hide forever.

"Are we okay?" he asks, looking handsome as always in sweatpants and a hoodie, ready for his class. With her.

"We are," she says quietly, her eyes falling to the floor.

He takes a step closer. "I can't help but think you may be avoiding me. Did I make you uncomfortable?"

Is he referring to the kiss?

"If anything, I kissed you first, so *I* would be the one making *you* uncomfortable."

"I am very comfortable." His lips curve up a tad, "but I know you have a boyfriend, and if you don't want to see me again... I'll understand. You don't owe me anything." He hands her his punch card – one more class left. Wow, those ten classes sure went by fast. And now he's giving her an out.

But this is not what she wants.

"Is this what you want?" she asks.

Please say no.

"No, I don't," he says. "I don't want to lose you."

"I'm sorry for being distant," she says, handing him back his punch card." I figured I should give you some space now that you're seeing someone."

"So that's what it's all about?" He looks ... relieved?

Chloe nods, trying to chase away those images of Will with his date that have been taunting her, possessing her mind. "And... I broke up with Jimmy. I had to do it on my own." Her eyes shoot to his.

Please say it's not too late...

"Took you long enough, but I was hoping you'd say that," he muses. His eyes scan the room, honing in on the suitcase and her entire-life's-possessions box in the corner.

"C'mon, it wasn't an easy thing to do. It's not like someone is waiting for me out there, promising to love me unconditionally," she says defensively.

"I am. I do."

ALERT! Swooning risk! This man should come with a label warning for the potential side effects of being around him.

"That's not funny. Please don't tease me."

"I'm not teasing you. I mean it."

"You're seeing someone."

"That's an overstatement," he chuckles. "And you're crashing at my place tonight."

"That's very kind of you, but I have to say no. I am going to find a place of my own."

"Suit yourself, but until then, you can sleep on an actual bed, in an actual home." His gaze travels to her suitcase and back to her face. "There's a new mattress in the guest room, so this time, I may be able to sleep too," he chuckles.

"Are you sure?"

This might get awkward with his new date and all...

"Never been so sure." His lips curl, and a small smile creeps up into her face too, spreading warmth across her cheeks. Hopefully, she's not blushing again.

They move into the Pilates room to start their last class.

Better make the most of it.

Will positions himself on the reformer, hands behind his head, feet on the bar, waiting for her commands. "Coach, I was thinking..." He smiles to himself. His eyes are gleaming, reflecting the morning sun. "Maybe go out with me on a real date?"

He's joking, right?

"I don't date rich guys," she says, half-joking back.

"Is that so?" He smirks. "You only kiss them?"

"Not *them*, just you!" She slaps his arm. "I had to test a theory."

"Oh yeah? What theory?" His dimples reappear, she helplessly tries to muster her wits.

"Can't tell you."

"Okay. Then what were your findings?"

"Mmm..." She considers it. "Can't tell you that either."

"Fair." His gaze lingers, and he sits up, so their eyes are level. "Enlighten me. Why don't you date rich guys?" He doesn't look bothered by that stereotypical statement of hers.

"Two main reasons." She crosses her legs, positioning herself more comfortably. This might take a while to explain. "And these are my opinions," she warns. Will nods, giving her the green light to proceed with her propaganda. "One – people only need a certain amount of money to get by and save for rainy days. Less than that equals a struggle to survive. Too much money and they become greedy, or they stop thinking about it and take it for granted. Either way is bad." She stops to examine his interim reaction. Will looks ... well ... pensive. "And two – rich boys have a sense of entitlement. Many think they can fix everything with money. But money can't buy happiness or love or health. Plus, they'll never be able to take someone like me seriously." She pauses to take a breath. Will's intense look makes her a little breathless. "Or worse, they may even think I'm after their money."

"Alright," he says finally, "but your theory has some flaws," he challenges, still smiling.

Thank God.

"Humor me."

"I do agree partially with number one – but having something and taking it for granted are two different things. The same goes for people – why do some people take their spouses for granted while others are grateful for how lucky they are every single day of their lives?"

"That's probably a romantic movie theme." Her eyes drop to the floor.

Will brings his hand to her chin, pulling it up gently to return her gaze to him. "I know Jimmy took you for granted," he says softly. "I would never do that."

Sparks shoot through her veins, and the sensation is so intense that she has to look away again.

She likes where he's going with this.

"Now your second argument. That's quite stereotypical, Chloe Barrett," he says, his tone seeming amused but his eyes serious. "I agree, money can't buy everything – happiness, love, health – you have to make those for yourself, like you said, combined with some degree of luck. I think finding happiness and love involves some active pursuit. You have to want it, make room for it, and seize it when you finally find it."

It's interesting how Will sees things.

She had no idea.

Her well-crafted walls of prejudices seem to be cracking.

"I like the way you see it," she says finally.

"So, I hope you realize by now, I am not your typical *rich boy.*"

"You are William Allentown, which is by definition..." Hearing his full name coming out of her mouth brings a smile to his face. "Okay, I see your point, but there is one more thing you haven't been able to refute," she insists.

"What?" He frowns. "Do you feel that I don't take you seriously?" He goes on to the next concern she's just listed. Chloe shakes her head. That wouldn't be true at all. "Are you referring to your last argument?" His eyebrows crush further together. Chloe swallows hard and just nods. "I know for a fact you couldn't care less about whether or not I come from money," he says, sounding confident.

"Really?" Can he really tell?

"What car do I drive?"

"What?" She stalls. "It's ... black and..." She has been in his car several times by now but hasn't really noticed.

"Exactly, you have no idea."

"That doesn't mean anything. I'm just not into cars."

"Okay, what watch do I wear?"

"Something nice, but I don't really—"

"You preferred wearing my sports hoodie over any of the designer clothes in my closet that night when your clothes got soaked in the rain."

And she still does.

"Because it's comfortable."

And smells like him...

"And you don't like gifts with a price tag over $10."

"Still doesn't prove anything."

"You're humble, and I can see it in everything you do, the way you carry yourself, the way you interact with others."

"Just me lacking confidence, probably." She pulls a strand of hair off her face and tucks it behind her ear.

"I don't mistake the two," his left eyebrow curves up under that little scar, "and you're not lacking any confidence." Okay, he's definitely been observing her closely in these past several weeks. "And instead of using your late adoptive parents' money to fix up your life a bit, you chose to donate all of it to the Tay Sachs foundation." And he's definitely been paying attention to her confessions. "So there, I rest my case." He smiles contentedly. This leaves her quite speechless. In a good way, but still at a loss for words. "So ... a date it is?"

"Are you sure you want to go on a date with someone who's just broken up with her boyfriend?" she says when she gains her words back.

"Positive, and not *someone*. You." He smiles, positioning himself back on the reformer, awaiting further instructions from the coach. This last conversation chewed up almost half of his class time, but having a flirty discussion and teaching Pilates at the same time, let alone thinking coherently around him, is practically impossible.

"What about your blind date?" Her thoughts trail back to last night.

Did he kiss her? Did he take her home?

"It was exactly that, a blind date. I have no plans to see her again."

"Why? Was there something wrong?"

She tries to sound casual but is overwhelmed by how happy this makes her feel.

"Yes, she wasn't you."

CHAPTER 17

A Not-So-First Date

Will picks her up after work, carrying her one little box of belongings and her suitcase to his trunk. "I'm taking the day off tomorrow to look for apartments," she announces. This whole situation is so weird. She's at his penthouse, going to use his shower to get ready for their first real actual date he so eloquently talked her into. It sounds like a scene from a romantic comedy.

"Or you could move in with me instead," he offers.

Is this man for real?

"You are too kind. But no, I need to do this one on my own. Plus, you live way too far from my work and college."

"It's not that far." Will turns on the fireplace, instantly adding a touch of warmth to the large seating area.

"It's probably a thirty-minute ride without traffic. So with traffic and two different buses..."

"My office is literally a ten-minute drive from the studio. You can ride with me every day." He studies her carefully. "Or I could just get you a car." The first part sounded awfully tempting, the second part makes her flinch. No, she's already spent five years of her life relying on Jimmy for everything. She needs to get her independence back in order before dumping her dependence on someone else. Even if that someone is this incredible, gorgeous man, standing beside her.

"This will defy my $10 rule," she quips. "Okay, be honest," she says, mustering some courage but mostly deflecting, "what made you book those ten Pilates classes with me?"

"What do you think?" He returns the question. A small smile rides up his cheeks.

"Well, you did say you wanted to improve your flexibility and become my friend..."

Is she giving him a way out?

"It's true, but I had some additional reasons." His dimples appear again.

"What *additional reasons*?" she teases.

"Seeing you, talking you into going on a date with me." He smirks.

"But you knew I had a boyfriend."

"A boyfriend who wasn't treating you right. I knew it was just a matter of time. I saw it in your eyes."

"Oh, did you now?" She chuckles.

"I figured I should stick around."

And boy, she's glad he did.

"And risk being the rebound?"

Did she seriously just say it out loud?

"I'm willing to take my chances."

Apparently, she did...

"Is that a photo album?" He squints in the direction of her one single box, her life's belongings. Apparently, she's not the only one with topic changing skills.

"It is," Chloe says, and his eyes beam. She walks over and pulls the old album from the box, handing it over to him. With its wrinkly edges, one would think this has passed through generations, but with moving from one foster family to another – it has just been poorly maintained. Will, however, takes it from her hands with utmost care and tenderness, as if he's holding a precious heirloom. He situates himself on the carpet by the fireplace and lays it gently in his lap, pulling Chloe to sit beside him.

"Is that you?" His eyes rest on the first picture, a tiny baby sleeping in a girl's arms. The image only shows the lower part of the girl's face, making it hard to make out her features. But she looks young, very young. She must have been younger than Chloe is right now.

"Probably, but I can't tell for sure. That's the photo the hospital staff found with me. Maybe this was my biological mom." Chloe traces the young woman's chin. "You can skip this one." She points to a little girl in a hospital bed. "Apparently, I came with some medical issues and needed care. Child protective services had the hypothesis that my biological parents couldn't afford medical treatment, or maybe thought it was just too much for them to care for a sick kid."

"For medical problems *they* caused..." Will's jaw clenches.

"At least they had the sense to abandon me near a hospital."

Gotta look at the bright side.

Will's eyes shift from the sad photo of a helplessly weak and pale child to present-day Chloe in the flesh, his eyes full of pain and empathy. "And apparently, it wasn't an easy task to find an adoptive family for a sickly kid, at least back then, took some time. So, this is me around four years old." She shifts her hand to the next photo, her young self, dressed in old worn-out clothes. "With the latest hand-me-down fashion at foster care." Her eyes are mischievous, wild, careless, her knees all scraped from playing, climbing, fighting.

"All better here."

Will swallows hard. "My little fighter," he says, pulling Chloe closer to him, holding her tight as if trying to erase that old pain away.

"These are my fellow inmates," she jokes, showing her friends from various foster families she's had through the years. Will flips the pages gently. The view changes for the better as they reach older Chloe. "Finally, my adoptive parents to the rescue!" Chloe announces, her eyes glimmering. "Meet Susie and Joseph Barrett," she says with a smile. "Holden and Thomas," she points at two separate old photos of little babies, "their late biological children. They would have been my older brothers, only they died before I had a chance to meet them."

"Tay Sachs," Will remembers. "I admire your courage Chloe, your strength and your kindness, after everything you've been through, donating everything you had to help find a cure for this disease." And these words, coming out of him, win Will a big hug and a forever special place in her heart. Finally, someone who understands.

Jimmy thought what she did was just purely stupid, and he had quite the vocabulary to go along with it.

They flip through the pages together, going through her teenage years, high school, another foster family, photos with Valerie, and a photo with Jimmy that makes her cringe, his hand propped around her like she's some kind of tool.

"You never smile in any of these photos," Will takes notice. This is the first time she's forced to give it some thought.

How has she not noticed it before?

"I wasn't a happy person," she admits.

"When did it change?" he asks.

Is he alluding to the possibility that it's no longer so?

Chloe considers this for a moment, realizing she's just used the past tense. "Maybe when you showed up."

Their first official date is very much like their first non-date a few nights before, except for the getting ready part, which happens under one roof – Will in his bathroom, Chloe in his other bathroom. They go to another nice restaurant Chloe hasn't been to before, much less known of its existence, and have long conversations about themselves, their dreams, and their aspirations.

"Tell me about the business you're going to start after you graduate," he asks. Chloe likes the sound of certainty in his voice. As if he has no doubt it's going to happen.

And now that Jimmy is not around anymore, mansplaining what she can and cannot do, maybe she should start getting rid of her doubts too.

"It's going to be a health studio for Pilates and yoga, combined with nutrition consultation, all in one place. There are many people who want to change their life for the better and improve their health and nutrition, but just don't know how to do it or even where to start. I want to help them find their way, change their mindset, equip them with the right knowledge to make informed decisions. Like how to make sense of nutrition fact labels, and how to choose the right products. That the choice to be healthier and eat wholesome, nutritious food can actually be fun, and taste good, not a punishment. That putting in some more effort upfront can improve our health in the long run and spare us from the pain and sickness and slew of medications that come as a package deal with a list of side effects that, in turn, require more medications.... The vicious cycle." She stops to look at Will, but he encourages her to proceed. Talking about it makes her perk up. "And this may not be a very business-y thing to do, but it's not going to cost a fortune. People who want to change their life should be able to do it regardless of their financial situation. I will make sure of that. Being sick and paying for medications is so much more expensive than preventing it in the first place. I wish the government would shift the efforts from treating to preventing... But until that happens, I'll do what's in my small power to make a difference in at least some people's lives."

"Don't ever underestimate your power," Will says. "And if you agree, I would love to do what I can to support it. I'll make donations to fund those clients who can't afford to pay but truly want to improve their health."

"A philanthropist. You have a good heart."

"No, you're the one with the good heart. When can you get your nutritionist license?"

"It may very well be by the end of this year if I can cram all my remaining courses in the next semester. Thanks to your lottery ticket, I can afford it now."

"*Your* lottery ticket, remember?" he chuckles.

"Now eat your veggies," she points to his plate, "and I'm going to focus on my mashed potatoes."

"I have something for you," Chloe says when they're back in Will's penthouse. "I almost forgot about it." She bends over to her backpack, pulls out a wrapped rectangular package, and hands it to him with a smile. Will closes the door behind him, beaming, accepting the box and gently unwrapping it.

"You got me a notebook?" His face lights up.

"To help you get back to writing," Chloe says. He considers that. "Oh wait, I got you a pen too." She searches through her bag again but can't find that pen she had in mind, so she pulls out another. "Used pens are the best to get that inspiration going," she laughs.

Will seems to like that. He steps closer, his gaze holding hers. "Thank you," he says. "I think I may have found a new source of inspiration." He pulls her into him and presses a small, gentle kiss on her lips, sending tiny electrical pulses through her spine. Then he pulls away, searching her eyes for confirmation. It's in her hands now, her body aching for his touch, and this time it's not the wine or any temporary moment of insanity.

She closes the distance between them, no longer afraid to get too close. Their bodies are tight together, reliving their first hug, and she's dazzled by how it all still feels like a first. Their chests rise and fall in unison with every hitched breath, faster until they are both breathless. She can feel his heart thumping against hers. His scent of soap and bergamot cologne washes over her, drawing her in. She lets her lips just lightly touch his in an unspoken approval before he takes control, kissing her deeply.

His eyes are bright as they find hers again. "I've been wanting to hold you for so long," he says. "So close ... like this."

She can only say the same, although she's never been willing to admit it. She's been trying to hold back, but her body already took over a while ago, venturing for Will's proximity and warmth.

She can feel his body itching for hers, his hands roaming across the fabric of her dress, her hands sliding beneath his shirt, touching his warm skin, his chest that won't give. Will's breaths quicken as she unbuttons his shirt, her hands hungry, almost out of control, making her tremble as she pushes the soft fabric off him, revealing the impressive set of abs and pecs she's been glimpsing throughout all those Pilates classes.

She turns around, letting him unzip her dress. His hands are gentle and caring as he pulls up her hair, kissing her nape, her skin sizzling under his touch. Her dress falls to the floor, her back against his front, cuddling into him. His hands deftly slide off her bra, capping her breasts, planting small kisses in a trail, making her groan. He turns her around, marveling at the sight of her almost-naked body.

"You are breathtaking," he whispers, biting his lower lip, his eyes exuding desire.

No one has ever looked at her like this before.

No one has ever made her feel so wanted.

No one has ever rendered her, Chloe Barrett, speechless...

At a loss for words or any remaining patience, Chloe resorts to unbuckling his belt, ridding him of his slacks. Feeling him so close makes her body quiver with excitement. Her back arches for him as his lips make their way to her breasts, sucking, nibbling gently, making her knees give in. Will senses that and slides his hands to her thighs, picking her up so effortlessly, letting her wrap herself around his waist.

"Take me somewhere," she whispers, her body enflamed by his touch.

"Bedroom?" he groans between her kisses, his voice thick and coarse. She has to take a break from ravishing his mouth to nod. Her heart is beating so fast she may explode. She blinks, and they're in his bed, under his soft sheets, all tangled up and intertwined, separated by the thin fabric of her underwear and his boxers. His hard length pulsing against her core, her body grinding against him possessively, steam radiating from her skin. His hot kisses explore her body, slowly descending, leaving no spot untouched. Will pulls the last piece of fabric off her, spreading her thighs, letting his tongue explore her body, letting her moans guide him. Her body curves and arches when his tongue circles her clit. His finger gently slides inside her, then another, making her groan loudly, awakening that G-spot she'd heard about but never actually believed existed, driving her wild. And wilder... She's never felt this way before, not with Jimmy, not with anyone.

"Come here," she demands. "I want you inside of me." She pushes off his boxers with her feet, pulling him up against her body. Will reaches a hand to his nightstand.

"I'm on the pill," she whispers into his ear, commanding his hands back to stroking her.

He stops to look into her eyes, guiding the tip of his length into her ever so slowly. "You're so wet," he rumbles, circling her entry, thrusting gently, then pulling away, sucking the breath out of her with every move. She wants more, but he seems to enjoy taunting her. She arches herself toward him, pulling against him, squirming, begging. Her moans get stronger, heavier as he gives in and drives into her, deeper, stronger, finally leveled, filling her completely, pumping, pulsing, throbbing. His rhythm is in sync with hers, their bodies perfectly tuned, electrical currents riding through her veins, consuming her. Their bodies are on fire, shivering, contracting, climaxing together until they collapse, breathless. Will wraps her with his body, curling her into him, whispering the sweetest words her mind won't even process. A grin is etched on his face. And this moment right here, feeling cherished, and loved, is something she never even knew she needed. But now that she knows she never wants it to stop.

CHAPTER 18

On Her Own

When Chloe awakes, Will is right there, his deep, warm gaze studying her, hand gently brushing her curls off her face.

"Good morning," he says softly. The room is filled with the crisp light of a wintery morning, his eyes gleaming with sunlight. Chloe has been lying there with her eyes closed for a while, afraid to let go, preparing herself for the possibility that last night was just a dream, her best dream.

Please don't let it be a dream.

PLEASE DON'T LET IT BE A DREAM.

She keeps repeating that wish in her head like a mantra. Then she runs through some pessimistic scenarios, with the excuse of being realistic, in which *last-night-Will-Allentown* would be different from *morning-Will-Allentown* once the carriage turned back into a pumpkin.

But not all fantasies end like that, do they?

How would she know? Not a single one of her fantasies had reached that level of bliss as this.

Finally, after summoning some great degree of courage, she eventually decides it's time to open her eyes slowly. Her heart is beating fast, fluttering, preparing for that moment of realization – but that's before. Before she sees him looking at her. Before she hears his voice and feels his hand in her hair. Before she feels his arms pulling her into him, welcoming her into that perfectly shaped space curved just for her. She wraps herself around him, needing him closer. Still naked. Feeling his morning self.

Will smiles lazily, a little breathless. "You're so warm," he says, planting small kisses on her lips, her neck, pulling her over him, letting her hands explore, allowing her body to shift and take him in.

"I was hoping last night wasn't a dream," she whispers gently in his ear as he pulls her tighter into him.

"If this is a dream, I promise to chase you relentlessly until it comes true," he says contently, a smile spread across his face. She slides and squirms with him inside of her, making him groan gently into her neck. His voice rumbles through her as he picks up the pace beneath her body, his hands caressing her skin, cupping her back side, their bodies moving in perfect tandem, again and again. She's shaking and shivering, explosions going through every inch of her body. She can feel him pulsing, sending her through the edge. She contracts fiercely around him as he pulls her hips tighter, making that last deep thrust, exhaling sharply and calling her name, before they both collapse into the pillows.

"You're going to make me fall for you, Chloe Barrett. Better watch out," he whispers in her ear, breathless, making her grin. His eyes a mixture of playfulness and ... admiration? This makes her blush.

"Oh, *I* need to watch out?" She manages to keep her voice in control, sounding flirty.

Did he really mean what he just said?

"Oh yes, you do." He grins and tickles her, making her giggle.

"And why is that?"

"I may want to keep you here, just to myself." His grin looks raw and childish.

She could look at his beautiful face for the rest of her life.

"And even worse," he says once they're both able to breathe again. "I'll want you to meet my parents,"

Did he just say parents?!

They've been friends for several months now, getting to know each other pretty well, possibly ... falling...? She has to park that thought away. There's never a good time to get her heart broken, but on all possible time scales, now is by far less than ideal. And although it's been a while since Will came into her life and took her by storm, they've only been officially dating for ... twenty-four hours? Not even. And she's just escaped a long and quite – she dares realize – destructive relationship with Jimmy.

"Sorry, didn't mean to scare you," Will reacts to her deteriorating articulation. Or is it the helpless look that must be smeared all over her face? But his eyes are honest and genuine.

Maybe she can let go? Maybe she doesn't have to hold back anymore?

"It takes more than that to scare me." She finally finds her voice.

"Good," he says, smiling, pulling them off the bed. "Because I'm starving."

Sydney Bell, a young real estate agent recommended by Valerie, meets Chloe at the parking lot of the small shopping center closest to the studio, where Will dropped her off on his way to work. His offer that they both call in sick and spend the rest of the day in bed was extraordinarily enticing, but involved canceling too many Pilates classes, some apartment showings with the realtor, and an evening class. He also tried to talk her out of rushing to find a new place, again.

Still a tempting idea, now more than ever.

But Chloe is quite fixed on her decision to do things right this time. She moved in with Jimmy on a whim the minute she was old enough to break out of that last foster home. Any option seemed plausible at the time, even if it meant replacing her lack of freedom and lack of support system with a dubious sort of freedom and questionable sort of support. Had she had a little more time or options, she probably would have dated Jimmy first to assess whether they were a reasonable fit. Because somewhere deep inside, she had her reservations. Ignoring the signs back then with Jimmy was a sport she played on a professional level. Not that she has the same concerns about Will. If anything, these signs are telling her to let go of what's holding her back and seize the moment. But jumping from her past dark adventure straight into even the brightest one just doesn't seem like the best recipe for success. There's too much at stake this time because, unlike then, she really wants it to work. And although Will Allentown has proclaimed himself as *not-your-typical-rich-boy*, she sure as hell doesn't want to feel like he's taking on any sort of financial savior role here, not even in the slightest. She has to do it for herself, and she has to do it her way.

"It's a pleasure to meet you." Sydney holds out a soft, perfectly manicured hand and shakes hers. She's clad in a white dress suit with high heels, hair and makeup meticulously done. It must cost a fortune just to get herself out the door in the morning. She represents everything Chloe isn't, and then more.

I'll want you to meet my parents. Will's words echo in her head. Who is she kidding? She can never be one of *them,* dress like them, look like them, spend all that money and energy on clothes or makeup. For Chloe, sitting in a hair salon for more than ten minutes is pure torture. *Simple* is her middle name, and she's very much proud of it.

"Chloe Barrett." Chloe greets her with a smile, situating herself in Sydney's BMW. She did make a mental note to check out cars after being clueless about which car Will owned that other night, a funny thing that he actually likes about her. But while Will does not give out that flashy ostentatious vibe, Sydney totally does.

"I have a few apartments in mind," Sydney says excitedly as she pulls out of the parking lot. "All around this area, like you've requested." She says it with a smile, although her tone does seem to shift slightly when referring to this lowly part of town.

"Perfect." Chloe feels that spark of new beginnings, ignoring her realtor's geographical disdain.

"Do you want to look at one bedroom apartments only, or two as well?"

"One bedroom is more than enough for me." She smiles politely. She had mentioned that before... Val's recommendations are usually spot-on, but not so much this time.

The car enters a small parking lot and parks by a two-story apartment building. "Prices here start around $1,400, depending on the amenities and area. This unit is in the lower price range, about 550 square feet, one bedroom, one bath," Sydney says, stepping out of the car and striding confidently toward the little building on her stilettos. Chloe's toes hurt just watching.

They climb up the stairs. Chloe looks around while Sydney opens the lockbox. There are several other apartments on that floor, color peeling off their entrances, revealing about three or four past shade selections – brown, red, green? It's all topped off with the last coat, where they went with some weird shade of gray. Sydney fusses with the lock until the door finally creaks open into a reasonably sized living room. They walk around the apartment, which seems like it has been freshly painted, making the air feel heavy. The carpets are in decent shape, and there's a tiny kitchen shoved in the corner, a minuscule bathroom, and a bedroom. The space could probably use some updating, but the windows are large, letting in the glow of daylight. Chloe really doesn't need anything more.

Sydney's face grimaces at the sight of the peeling wallpaper that has seen better days. "I apologize," she says, looking embarrassed. "I have much nicer properties to show you. Looking at it in the daylight, it's not in the condition I was aiming for..."

"This is great, actually." Chloe smiles, "Quaint," she offers. "And I like how bright this place is." God knows she's lived in far worse-looking places before. "And the location is perfect. I could walk to the town center."

"Walk?" Sydney's eyebrows collide. "it's about a mile."

"Yep." Chloe perks up – this may not be considered a walking distance for some, but for her, it definitely is.

Although she would probably die if she attempted to do it in Sydney's heels.

"We could try to negotiate down the rate," Sydney suggests, "but before you make up your mind, I have a few more properties I'd love to show you."

Chloe considers that for a moment, but her mind is made up already. It almost seems like Sydney will be disappointed if she turns down the offer to see more. It appears that she has a whole day planned for them already.

"Okay," Chloe finally says, and within minutes, because Sydney cannot get out of there fast enough, they're out the door, on their way to the next.

This time it's a brand-new building, higher rise. "There's a gym and a pool, and even a clubhouse," Sydney marvels. "It was built

just a couple of years ago, so all the apartments are new and modern." They enter the lobby, and are greeted by large plants in heavy
terracotta pots and a seating area. "I know! Nice, right?" Sydney
gestures toward the space, looking more comfortable in the current
setting, making her way to the elevator, which is a major upgrade
considering her heels. Although, to Sydney's defense, she hasn't
made a single complaint or showed any sign of discomfort on the
stilettos front.

She must be one of those who never get blisters or warts.

They go up the elevator to the fifth floor and into a shiny-looking
hallway that leads to the first apartment. The doors are naturally
painted wooden colors. No need to fuss with the lock either. Sydney
enters first, and Chloe quickly follows into a very nice, modern
apartment with an open kitchen design, a large living room with
a fireplace. There's a large bedroom with a small sitting area that
could be a perfect space for studying. "This one is in the higher price
range," Sydney says, still with her enthusiastic voice. "It's $2,200 and
in a great neighborhood."

Chloe feels a drip of disappointment. "That's a little over my
budget," Chloe reminds her realtor and herself. "It's beautiful, but
I think the first option was more than I needed."

Sydney nods but insists on showing a few more apartments "in the
mid-range," is the term she uses – somewhere lower than $2,000 but
higher than $1,400. Chloe plays along, but conservatively enough,
she has her mind set on the first property they've seen. It had plenty
of natural light, is near all the main bus routes, walking distance
from the town center – what more could she ask for? It may not win
the finest-looking-property-of-the-year award, but Chloe can make
it a home and is confident she can pay the rent and still afford food
and necessities.

"How fast could I sign and move in?" she asks when Sydney finally takes her back to the parking lot near the studio.

"You'll need a credit and background check, so I am guessing a few days to a week?" The last part of her sentence changes into a question once she sees the disappointment on Chloe's face. The apartment she had shared with Jimmy was under his name. She didn't think it could take so long to close the deal and move in.

"That's okay," Chloe responds, not looking to expand on this topic.

Yoga mats here she comes.

"Great, so I'm going to call them and negotiate that price. I will email you soon with some paperwork."

"Perfect, thank you, Sydney." Chloe shakes her hand and walks out the door, her head spinning. Will has been incredible, but she wouldn't want to impose. A few more nights at the Pilates studio won't be that bad. She's managed with much less.

"How was army day?" Chloe asks her best friend, rushing into the bus on her way to class.

"It was exhausting. So many questions and tests. So serious," Val replies, looking straight at her through the phone, munching on something that looks delicious. "But being around all those soldiers made me feel ... awe. I loved it!" Her face is gleaming. "They said I'll get some options in the mail, see what they think would fit me the most."

"I'm so proud of you!"

"Thank you!" Val smiles and examines Chloe's face closely through the phone. "Now, how was your hot date yesterday? You look... Are those... Holy shit, Clo! You got laid!"

"You are funny," Chloe chuckles, feeling herself blushing. "What are you eating there? Looks tasty."

A poor attempt to divert the conversation.

"They're called burekas. They're flaky and filled with feta cheese, and taste heavenly!" Val takes another bite. "And stop trying to change the subject. You did! I can see it in your eyes!" Yes, Val knows Chloe *that* well. "But what are you looking so worried for?"

Can she see that too? Of course she can.

"I think we're going a little too fast. He said he wanted me to meet his parents."

"That's a good thing, you goof!"

"I don't belong in their world. They're probably rich and fancy. I'm not like them – I'm a stray."

"Oh, c'mon! And by the way, I don't want to hear you use that word ever again. They're going to love you! Just like Will does!" Valerie's confidence is infectious despite not even meeting Will in person. "Oh shoot." She stops in her tracks, still chewing on her burekas, though. "Alon is picking me up in five minutes, and I'm not even dressed yet!"

"Alon, as in the new hot guy you met last week?"

"YES! Second date! Can you believe it? Me?" Val never goes on second dates. This is way too long-term for her liking.

"And all it took was flying across the world to meet an Israeli guy," Chloe teases. "Go! Call me tomorrow. Love you!"

Chloe slides her cell phone into her back pocket and steps into the classroom on time for once, plopping herself into the seat next to Niki, who gives her a lopsided smile.

"How's lover boy?" Ever since the panel night, Niki has taken some interest in Chloe's love life. Or maybe it's just an easy conversation starter.

"He's good." Chloe decides she better keep it low profile until she figures out where this is going. *'I'll want you to meet my parents.'*

Will's words still echo in her head. Probably not going to get too far once they meet her.

"You look ... glowing," Niki says with an obviously envious look. "And you're not denying it anymore," she adds mischievously.

"Ah ... thanks?" Chloe manages, sounding more like a question than a response. Up until now, she and Niki haven't really exchanged more than a couple of sentences at once, mostly related to school-work, nothing too personal. So coming out with a whole statement about breaking up with Jimmy and starting something with Will feels a bit too over the top. Chloe resolves to keep quiet, and is saved by the instructor, who interrupts the chatter and begins teaching.

When the class ends, Chloe shoves her stuff into her backpack and throws it over her shoulder. Wrapped in her jacket, she exits the building alongside her classmates.

"Need a ride home?" Niki asks, for the first time since they've become classmates. "You live in the area, right?"

"I do... Did." It occurs to Chloe that she hasn't figured out her plans for tonight. Spending the night at the Pilates studio without telling Will might look ridiculous. Although they've texted back and forth quite a lot today, and he even called her during her lunch break to ask how the home hunting was going, they haven't really spoken about tonight. And even if she did want to get herself back to that pile of yoga mats, she left all of her stuff at his place. Niki's puzzled look reminds her she's still awaiting the second part of the sentence.

"I'm moving to a new place, actually," she says, although that does not answer the question.

"Well, I live in Gaithersburg if that helps."

"Thanks, but that's okay, I just need to figure out which bus to take," Chloe says, summoning her phone from her back pocket.

"I don't think you're going to need a bus," Niki says, smiling to herself, that bit of jealousy still laced across her facial features.

"What?" Clueless, Chloe follows Niki's gaze into the dark parking lot, spotting a guy leaning against one of the vehicles. She squints.

Her guy?

"Well then, see you next week," Niki says and disappears into her car, turning her head once to stare at them as Chloe steps closer and gets pulled into Will's arms for a sizzling kiss.

"Hey," he says, his scent and warmth wrapping her into him.

"Hey," she answers, trying to get her breathing straight. "You didn't have to come pick me up."

"I wanted to." He grins, looking handsome as always. He's still in his business attire – probably came straight from work. "Although it would have been easier if you gave me your schedule. I had to google your class hours," he says smugly.

"Very resourceful of you," she laughs, and he pulls her closer into him – if that was even possible.

"Hungry?" he asks.

"Famished!" she replies, which is not unusual. She's always trying to maximize her work time, and forgetting to eat has become a routine. Not in the morning, though – that almost-passing-out experience was a grand enough hint to make sure she kept her blood pressure up during the earlier part of the day.

"How tired are you? Is driving down to the city out of the question?" His boyish smile is too adorable. He's impossible to say no to. Walking out of class, she was a bit tired, but seeing Will wiped it all away.

"Sounds amazing," she says. Right now, she's on a never-ending burst of renewable energy sources, and tomorrow is the weekend!

"I couldn't stop thinking about you all day," Will says when the car pulls out of the parking lot. "About last night... And this morn-ing." He gives her a happy look before returning his gaze to the road.

"Mmm..." Chloe finds herself humming in agreement, watching his smile extend, dimples making an appearance. "I had some trou-ble focusing today, too." She runs her fingers gently on his arm, and once her hand reaches his palm, he seizes it, interlacing their fingers. Extreme's "More Than Words" is playing on the radio. "I love this song!" she says enthusiastically. "Even though it's not Aerosmith, of course."

"It's my favorite song." Will sounds almost surprised, raising the volume from the steering wheel.

"It may sound naive, but as a teenager, I used to dream about love like the one in this song." She digs up some old memories.

"Why naive?" he asks, and she shrugs, unsure how to phrase her depressing past-life realizations without ruining the vibe. But he gets it, and instead of asking further, he just joins in on the song and sings along, his eyes trailing to hers almost as if he's trying to make a point. And Will, Chloe finds, can certainly sing!

"A s'mores place?" Chloe chirps as they enter the outdoor patio of the restaurant. The place is spotted with little firepit tables and chairs, each taken by a couple or small party, making s'mores, sipping hot drinks from mugs. If she had to come up with her own idea of the ideal after-hours hang-out, it would definitely be this cute little place.

"I had a feeling you'd like it." Will smirks.

"*Like it* is an understatement," she laughs.

"Outside or inside?" the hostess asks.

"Outside." They state the obvious option in unison. Turning

down the opportunity to make their own s'mores by the fire is not an option, thirty-seven degrees or not. They are shown to a small firepit table in the corner, lined with two lounge chairs, which Will brings close together before they sit down, not leaving even a remote possibility for her to stay out of his reach. The warming fire, combined with the playful lights of the flames on his face, inflict some violent assaults on her heart, and although she's not cold – not when she's as close to Will and the fire – it still makes her hands shiver. Excitement runs through her veins.

"Are you cold? We could go inside," Will offers. Nothing escapes him when it comes to Chloe, but she shakes her head, beaming, shifting in her seat a bit to bury herself in his warmth, wrapped in his arms and his scent, shielded from the world.

"That's better." She nuzzles him, letting this big smile spread across her face.

They order some food: a s'mores kit for two, and hot chocolates, which come in large mugs covered with a load of whipping cream. They chat through the night, drinking, kissing; all the secret ingredients to a perfect evening.

"William? William Allentown?" A surprised female voice shakes them out of their safe haven.

Will turns his head reluctantly, a little puzzled. Chloe sits up and turns her head in the same direction.

"Sydney?" she asks, surprised. Her very polished, ostentatious real estate agent has made an appearance.

"Chloe?" Judging by Sydney's voice and the drop of her jaw, she's even more surprised.

So, she knows Will, maybe not as well as Chloe, *hopefully*, as she used his full first *and* last name. But from the look on her face and the bite to her tone, Sydney doesn't seem too pleased to find him and Chloe huddled together, hands and lips and all. Her face scrunches. This might be the only less attractive look Chloe has seen Sydney display, but Sydney shakes it off skillfully and snaps back a professional smile, forced for sure, but even a trained observer would not be able to tell the difference. Sydney is a savvy smiler in all situations, as she had probably been trained to be from an early age.

"What are you doing here?" Sydney may sound like she meant to ask them both, but her eyes are fixed on Will, studying him. Her gaze dips to his chest and then to his arm as he wraps it warmly and protectively around Chloe, clearly sensing the discomfort.

"Having a night out with Chloe," he says, his voice unfazed. "I see you two know each other?"

"Yes, it's a funny story, actually," Sydney says but then remembers Chloe is a client, and her eyes shift to Chloe for permission.

Not so funny, really.

"Sydney is my real estate agent. We've spent our entire morning together," Chloe takes over, having nothing to hide.

"You should have told me you were seeing ... uh... William. This can... This could speed up the process." Sydney's voice wavers a bit as she tries to collect her thoughts.

"I didn't know you two knew each other," Chloe says simply. Too many thoughts are going through her head at once, making her dizzy.

Is that jealousy creeping up on her?

"Well, now we know," Sydney grabs back her put-together self and wishes them a *lovely* evening, not before she mentions that she met Will's mom for coffee the day before, letting her eyes rest on Will briefly, then disappears inside the restaurant.

"Your ex?" Chloe isn't sure what response would ease the nerve-wracking feeling happening inside her at the moment.

"No, not my ex," Will says dryly. "My mom's recent attempt at matchmaking," he explains. "The blind date," he reminds her – as if Chloe needs any reminders.

The blind date that kept her up all night.

The blind date that made her realize that not doing anything was actually worse than doing something.

The blind date that opened her eyes and showed her that she definitely had a lot to lose.

And losing Will was not an option.

"Looks like she would have loved to see you again." Chloe just has to make her observation known.

Is that possessiveness spilling out of her?

"She's very nice, but not my type." He turns to look at Chloe, his lips curving up to a smug smile when he notices her expression. "And as I said, she wasn't you." A glimpse of them dancing at the party flashes through her mind, those moments by the firepit on Georgia's patio, talking, laughing. Their Pilates classes, last night, this morning...

"But I still had a boyfriend." Chloe tries to line up the facts, again.

"You did." He nods. "Jimmy was a slight delay in plans, I'll give him that, but that didn't change the big picture."

"Which was?"

"That I had to make you mine." Will lets out that adorable smile of his. A smile no one in the entire world could possibly refuse.

The entire world being her.

"And just so you know, I'm never letting you go."

"Is that a threat or a promise?" she teases.

He laughs and pulls her in closer. "Both."

CHAPTER 19

Home Sweet Home

Running into Sydney Bell while wrapped in Will's arms definitely sped up the process of getting her rental documents approved and her contract signed. Most likely, it wasn't so much for Sydney's desire to help as it was her desire to ensure Chloe moved out of Will's apartment as soon as legally possible.

Always nice to know your real estate agent has your best interests in mind...

But since the place was chosen before any sort of perceived conflict of interest, and perhaps not wanting to seem too dramatic, Chloe lets that part go, signs the contract and is now happily holding the keys to her new apartment.

"I thought William would join you for your first home walk-through." Sydney sounds disappointed when they meet.

Was that even a thing, or was she trying to assess the depth of their relationship?

Get another glimpse at her man?

"He's at work. He'll come later." Chloe pulls out her nicest smile possible. She is certainly able to do these kinds of things alone. Will can come visit, but this is *her* place. She's perfectly capable and has, in fact, for most of her life, done everything on her own.

"Wonderful!" Sydney snaps back into her realtor shoes – or extremely high heels, for the sake of accuracy. "Congratulations on your new home!" she says in a celebratory tone, and hands Chloe a small cellophane-wrapped chocolate and wine basket from the back of her shiny BMW.

Chloe thanks her profusely, because as a real estate agent, Sydney was great.

As an ex-blind date of Will's, not so much though.

"My pleasure!" Sydney smiles again and then casually adds, "I assume I'll see you soon at the Allentowns' for dinner, yes?"

'*I'll want you to meet my parents.*'

But what would Sydney be doing there?

"I assume so," Chloe replies, not letting her confusion spill out.

"Wonderful," Sydney says again, although it doesn't seem like she's feeling too wonderful. Then she turns back, climbs into her fancy car, and drives away.

It takes Chloe a climb of stairs, some messing with her new apartment's lock, a cup of rusty tap water, and a few splashes of the same water on her face to untangle some of the knots in her stomach and bring her pulse one notch down.

What just happened there? What is Sydney up to? What is Will's mother's grand plan? Do his parents even know about her? And why in the world has she let herself become so attached to a guy she only met a few months ago, to the point that she even cares about all this?

He did indeed threat-promise that he'd never let her go... But can she use that as her excuse?

Chloe decides to resort to running, and luckily she's already in her Pilates clothes, so she takes herself outside, locks the door to her new apartment, puts her earphones in, presses play on her decompression playlist on her phone, and she's off, headed to the closest trail. She runs as fast and for as long of a stretch as she can, letting the large trees and nature sounds wash her overwhelming thoughts away, stupefied by how much all of this bothers her. Her – who never cares about what others think. Who would never fight over a guy's attention, who's never actually felt jealous before, not even when she found Jimmy's empty pack of condoms. Yes, it made her angry, made her feel like a fool for trusting Jimmy, for spending five years of her life with him, for letting him belittle her for so long until she had started believing it herself.

But jealousy?

That's one of those things that other people feel. Her breath is becoming labored, her heart beating too fast, a pain in her side, her sign to slow down. She stops near one of the large trees, letting herself fold forward, trying to catch her breath. Her phone buzzes in her pocket, reminding her of the furniture delivery she was supposed to wait for, still amazed that they were able to deliver so quickly.

Will offered to join her for furniture shopping and suggested a few stores with price ranges that made her flinch. The last thing she wanted was for him to pay for her new home shopping. They settled on IKEA – clean, simple design, and budget-friendly. Will insisted on coming along, turning a boring trip to IKEA into anything but. Will pushed the cart by her side, Chloe jumping from item to item, and they insisted on trying out all beds and mattresses and honed in on the one that made them laugh out loud, which had nothing to do with the mattress or bed, and everything to do with that moment they created, together. Will was sharing a memory of his mom walking in on his high-school-self and his first girlfriend. Objectively, it was probably not at all funny, but the way he told it made Chloe laugh so hard he had to kiss her quiet before cracking up himself.

"Do you prefer to write at a desk or in a cozy corner?" she'd asked as they reached the home office area.

"Me? I guess a desk, don't you?" Surprise decorated his gaze.

"I prefer to write lying down on the carpet." Face down on her belly actually, propped on her elbows. *"That's the only way for me to keep focused when I need to study."*

"Interesting." He smiled fondly, as if this was a top-desired quality. *"I usually sit at my desk at work, so I guess—"*

"I don't mean at work. I mean creative writing, your stories."

"Last time I did that," his smile then was nostalgic, *and oh so endearing, "was far too long ago, and actually not near a desk, probably outside or in some corner."*

"So, a cozy corner then." Chloe smiled, picked up a few large cushions, and loaded them onto the cart.

"What are we doing again?" His left eyebrow creased under his little scar.

"You'll see," she just answered and moved to the next area.

They picked up a small dining table, four chairs, a bookshelf, and a comfy sectional sofa. Chloe had always wanted one in that blue-gray color combination, but Jimmy had always objected for some unknown reason, so copying the item location into her little IKEA paper was her little moment of triumph. Then a little white coffee table, some mugs, glasses, plates, kitchen supplies, pots, and pans. A few hours later, she was several hundred dollar poorer – she had to wrestle Will at the cash register to prevent him from taking care of the bill. She did cave, though, into letting him organize the furniture shipping to her apartment.

This explains why the delivery guy is at her door so expeditiously. Time to turn around. Her place, although far from feeling like home yet, awaits.

By early evening, the new apartment is almost completely organized. Turns out Will included assembly with her IKEA delivery, which is not usually done on the same day, but today it was. And so, within less than an hour, all her new furniture is put together, freeing Chloe to clean up, organize the kitchen supplies in the closet, and unpack her belongings. And it's not too long before her new apartment starts to morph into a habitable space.

Now, to give it a final personalized touch: in the corner of the small living room, by the window, she lays out the large cushions, making that cozy corner she envisioned back at the IKEA trip. She makes a quick stop to shower, puts on her favorite jeans and Will's hoodie – she has no plans to return it but has finally washed it, now that she has the luxury of going straight to the source. She gently brushes her curls with her fingers, just in time to open the door for Will, handsome as he is, rocking his just-came-from-work look. He pulls her by her waist for a kiss, one hand hiding something behind his back.

"I hope it's not flowers." She smiles, scrunching her nose, letting him in.

"I know you better than that," he chuckles and hands her a color- fully wrapped package, closing the door behind him. She opens the wrapper – she can't really remember the last time a guy had given her anything.

Soft fuzzy fur peeks out of the wrapper as she pulls it out to observe. A stuffed animal that looks a little like... "You got me a cat-bunny?! My favorite made-up animal!"

And her favorite, although never-actually-received-one-un- til-this-very-moment gift!

He remembered. Double remembered.

She leaps into him with a squeal, legs wrapping his waist. "Where did you find it?"

"I have my sources." He smiles, wrapping his hands around her thighs, a big smile across his face. "I like your hoodie," he quips.

"You mean *your* hoodie," she giggles.

"Yes, I like my hoodie on you. Now, you need to tell me how you came up with the cat-bunny invention," he says, his eyes beaming.

"It's from a Hebrew kids' book. Valerie was trying to learn Hebrew before going to Israel, so I got to be her guinea pig. I have no idea what the story was about because her Hebrew was not... Let's just say *was not*, at the time, but the girl in the book had a stuffed animal that looked—" Chloe picks up the soft little cat-bunny to observe the wonder, "just like this little guy, and I thought it was the most adorable thing."

"I am glad you like it," he says, reaching to her neck for a deep inhale. "I missed you." His voice vibrates through her body, and she turns her head to meet his lips, devouring him just because she can.

"Do you want a mini tour?" she offers, lowering her feet back to the floor before her body might take over and drag him to her bedroom, remembering she used to have manners. "This entire place could probably fit into your kitchen," she laughs.

"A tour sounds great." He takes her hand and looks around, actually impressed.

"Most important spot first." She pulls him toward the corner by the large window.

"A cozy corner. You weren't joking." Will smiles, marveling at the new space.

"I don't joke around important stuff." Her eyes climb to his. "For you, in case you feel like writing, much better than a desk, I promise."

"Hmmm," he just says, his lips curling into a happy smile, his eyes appreciative, grateful. It's a new kind of look she hasn't seen before, not on Will, not on anyone.

She tags on his hand to continue the tour – the tiny bedroom, bathroom, kitchen, "I love it!" he says after the grand tour is complete. "You make it feel like a home." He leans in to kiss her again, this time deeper, pulling her tight against him.

"I've been waiting all day to do this," Chloe says, loosening his tie, untucking his dress shirt, letting her hands slide across his chest.

His breath hitches as his hands slide gently beneath her hoodie, searching for her skin, making her release a small happy sound as she nuzzles his neck. "Need to check out the new bedroom," he says in a low husky voice, sweeping her up.

A couple of hours later, they're in the tiny kitchen, their sides touching lightly. Will's on the sunny side up, making their eggs. Chloe's chopping some vegetables, not forgetting the olive oil and lemon squeeze. If Will makes a point of remembering all her favorite things, she should remember his too. Will is singing along to Queen's "Killer Queen" playing from one of his playlists. The music stops abruptly, as it does when a text or call comes in, followed by that incoming call. He's had work calls later in the evening before, usually from Avery, but this one has a different ringtone.

"It's my mother," Will announces, his face unreadable. He wipes his hands on a paper towel and, in a reluctant motion, takes the phone to his ear.

"Hi, Mom," he says casually, but there's a slight tension in his tone. Chloe can sense it right away, and gestures toward the bedroom to offer some privacy, but he shakes his head and leans on the kitchen counter. "I'm fine. How are you doing?"

Chloe tries her best not to tune into their conversation, especially since she can only hear one side anyway, but his out-of-the-ordinary body language fascinates her. "No, I'm at Chloe's," he says. She likes the way her name rolls out on his tongue. "You and Dad may get to meet her on Friday." His eyes shoot to Chloe for approval. "If she agrees."

She manages a soft affirmative nod, trying to hide the stream of thoughts.

Why would Will want her at that dinner when he knows Sydney would be there?

"You invited Sydney Bell?! Why would you do that?" He runs a hand through his hair, letting out a frustrated sigh.

Guess he didn't know...

"Can you cancel? You don't need to play matchmaker anymore, Mom," he says, throwing his hands in the air. His eyes search for Chloe, turning softer as he comes closer to take her hand. "I don't know, I'll let you know. I need to go." He ends the call and puts down the phone. Freddie Mercury's voice eases back into the atmosphere. Chloe goes back to the salad, trying to mind her own business.

"So, apparently, my mom decided to invite Sydney to dinner next Friday," he announces with a defeated look. "She said this was before she knew the blind date was not going to go any further and before she knew about us."

She likes the sound of 'us' coming from him.

"Admittedly, things have shifted quite rapidly since your blind date with Sydney, so your mom's invite to Sydney was sort of legit, as awkward as this is," Chloe offers.

At least Will had nothing to do with it.

"I asked her to cancel, but she said that would be rude. Now that it's done, she can't uninvite her." Will lets out an exasperated sigh.

"She has some business plans to work with Sydney, and I get that she wants to keep their professional relationship on good terms, but this is ridiculous."

"Something is burning." Chloe reacts to a strange smell hitting her nose. Some dark smoke fills up the pan.

"Sorry, I got distracted," Will says apologetically, throwing the burnt egg into the trash and cleaning the pan to restart. "We can let them have their dinner with Sydney on Friday without us," he adds, his face uneasy. "I'm not going to drag you into my mother's soap opera."

"Soap opera sounds about right," Chloe chuckles, "but we can still go." She would love to pass on the opportunity for a head-to-head competition with Sydney – just the thought of it makes her mind spin – but the idea of disappointing his parents... "Or you could go without me, and I'll join you next time." This option makes her heart shudder.

Jealous much?

But at least it doesn't require a giant leap out of her comfort zone.

"You think?!" He stretches his arm and pulls her by the hoodie until she's back in her favorite spot – tight against him. "I am not going to this dinner without you," he protests.

"O-kay," she stretches the word, "then we go together."

Let the games begin.

It seems that Will likes her tiny old apartment more than he likes his own. Chloe didn't think anything special of giving him a key. It just seemed natural. He gave her one to his place too, so it was nothing eventful, just key swapping, just in case. She hasn't actually used her copy since Will insists on dropping her off in the morning and picking her up from wherever – Pilates, Claudia's, or college – every night on his way back from work, even if he doesn't really need to stay at work as late. And despite being perfectly capable of taking the bus, Chloe definitely doesn't mind the company. It also seems unbearable to spend their nights and weekends apart, so they either end up at his place or hers, more often hers.

"It just feels like home here," Will says one night, "so much more than my apartment." In a way, she agrees. His apartment, although larger, prettier, and in a much better location, has little accents of modern design that set a cooler tone. Her place feels ... cozy, mainly because it's so small, and has come to feel like home, especially with Will in it.

And that's not even the best part. In the past few days, to her delight, she's been finding him at that newly created pillowed corner, with his notebook open and a pen in hand ... writing!

"You're writing again!" she says excitedly one night, after counting at least three consecutive occasions before formalizing her observation.

Will looks up from his notebook, a spark of happiness in his eyes. "I am," he admits, considering it for a moment. "I am," he repeats, processing the words as he speaks, as if realizing for the first time that this may be more than a one-off. He rewards her with a gorgeous grin across his face, the kind that summons his dimples.

"Does this mean you're getting your inspiration back?" A wave of exhilaration unfurls through her.

Will nods, putting his notebook and pen aside. "Come here, you!" He pulls her in for a hug. "Being around you," his fingers stroke her face gently, elevating her gaze, eyes gleaming, "you make me want to write again," he says.

Her? Will must be mistaken... This certainly has nothing to do with her.

CHAPTER 20

The Dinner

"Just to give you a heads up," Chloe says as she twirls around, spinning the hem of a teal-colored nightgown. "I am not very good with parents." She shoots him a half-joking half-apologetic look, but his eyes are too focused on the way the dress hugs her body, a mischievous smile spread across his face. "I'm being serious here." She stops her twirling, meeting his eyes.

"You're great with people, your Pilates clients adore you, Georgia adores you, I adore you. I don't see any issue here," Will says, obviously not too concerned about what his parents may have to say about her.

"What do you think about the dress?" The closer they get to Friday, the more certain she is that this head-to-head game with Sydney is an apocalypse waiting to happen. When she'd learned that Will's mom was expecting him to wear a suit and tie for dinner, she opened her closet in an attempt to figure out what to wear to this epic dinner.

Will's "I got you," response ended at some fancy rich people boutique with price tags that made Chloe nearly faint.

"No way," was her plea to take it down a notch, which brought them to the current designer boutique, which is still quite pricey, but not to the point of her passing out.

"You look beautiful." He smiles, noticing her mixed feelings. "You don't like it?"

"I like the dress, but... I don't feel like me in it," Chloe says, going back into the fitting room where all the other offerings hang neatly, waiting for her to try them on. After sliding into so many dresses, her mind feels dizzy, on the brink of overstimulation. She looks through the colors, and fabrics, trying to wrap her head around the idea of looking fancy.

Her, fancy? It's an oxymoron.

She tries on a black cocktail dress that looks simple but classy, happy to see that the face looking back at her from the mirror is still hers.

"I like this one," she approves and walks out of the fitting room.

"Wow!" Will gets up from the upholstered chair and walks toward her, spinning her with his arm to the rhythm of the soft music playing through the speakers. "Do you feel more comfortable in this one?"

"Yes, I definitely do," she says. "Is it... enough?"

"It's perfect." Will can't resist pulling her into him for a hug. "But I know where this mind of yours is going, so if you ask me, jeans and a T-shirt are more than enough."

He has gotten to know her pretty well.

"Right. Coming from the man who's going to wear a suit and tie?"

"Years of obeying my mother's requirements."

Well, nice to know, but no way she'll show up in jeans when he's all fancy, and certainly not when Miss-dress-code Sydney is the guest of honor.

She sways back into the fitting room to revert to her familiar self, putting on her jeans and sweater and tying her Dr. Martens boots while standing up. When she emerges, it appears Will has already paid, and not just for the black dress, but also the teal one. The bustling sales associate walks out of the fitting room with the dresses Chloe left behind, wrapping them neatly and handing them to Will enthusiastically, letting her eyes skim him over once... Twice... To that her man thankfully seems completely immune.

"I was going to pay for it!" Chloe protests.

"I already feel bad enough for dragging you to a dinner with my mother's failed ex-matchmaking attempt," he quips with an inno-cent-looking smile that makes Chloe pull him by his collar and steal a little kiss under the scrutinizing eyes of the lady behind the register.

Maybe she can let it slide this time.

"Next stop is getting something nice for your parents." She can't come empty handed. She recalls the outrageous flower bouquets and gifts at Georgia's house. Indeed, that was his aunt's 60th birthday, but they have to bring something at least. Sydney surely will.

"You don't have to." Will smiles, but she gives him an insistent look. She's not going to let him charm his way out of this one. His eyebrow curves up a tad under his little scar. "What do you have in mind?"

"I have no idea."

But Sydney probably has plenty of ideas.

"What do people normally get them?" And by people, she means people like *them.* "What do they like?"

"Chocolate? Wine? Flowers?" Will shrugs. "I haven't paid much attention."

"So, wine and chocolate it is," Chloe seals it. She doesn't like getting flowers, so giving them would be hypocritical. Will's smile indicates he's following her logic.

Conveniently enough, there's a lofty little place right down the street that sells both. They choose a big box of chocolate truffles and two bottles of what seems like good wine. Both get boxed and wrapped meticulously and presented to them with matching bows. Chloe has to smother a laugh; she's not sure why she finds it so funny, but this, of course, does not escape Will's fond eyes. And once they're out of the store, arms entwined, they both start laughing, maybe a little too loud, making a few heads in the crowd turn.

Chloe comes out of the shower, does her hair and makeup, and slides into the black dress and heels, feeling like a fancy version of ... possibly herself.

It's still you, she attempts a reminder while trying to forget the price tag of the dress. She pulls out a little necklace from her drawer and matching earrings Susie and Joseph gave her for her birthday. The set wasn't expensive, but it is pretty, matches her dress, and reminds her of a time she had a family of her own.

"You look dazzling!" Will whistles as he walks into the little bedroom, stopping for a moment to take her in, admiring her, then puts down his notebook. He's been writing for the past couple of hours, like he's done almost every day for a while now, making Chloe crazy proud. Stepping behind her, he gently takes the necklace and closes the clasp for her, leaving small little kisses on her nape. She muffles a soft moan as he wraps her into him, so warm and comforting. She turns around to face him, inhaling his scent and taking in his perfectly tailored suit and his damp hair, which is combed back. He looks handsome and so perfect.

"Ready?" he asks, taking her hand.

"Ready," she says, trying to hide those little anxious palpitations scorching inside her. She can't quite decipher whether it's meeting his parents or having to spend this evening side-by-side with Sydney Bell.

Or perhaps the additive effect of both.

She pulls on her jacket, preparing for the cold wind to embrace her as they step outside, down the outdoor stairs, letting the breeze cool her face a bit.

"Tell me about your day," Will says softly once they're seated in his car, trying to help her unwind. She tries to think about the past several hours, but it all seems like a blur. Will had dropped her off at the studio on his way to work.

"I taught four Pilates classes, two yoga classes."

Barely ate anything – stress does that to her.

Then she came home. "I submitted my statistics homework," she offers. "Watching you write inspired me to finally finish it." Thinking about his writing is totally her new soft spot. "I love that you're writing again!" She glances at him. His eyes are focused on driving, but his lips curve up to a grin. "How was your day?"

"Had lunch with Avery today," he says. "He's working on a new suburban development that combines both residential and retail spaces, just a few miles north of here."

"You don't sound too excited," she can't help noticing.

"I mean, the idea is appealing, it's a great area with lots of potential, but…" He runs a hand through his hair, letting it fall perfectly to his forehead. The combed-back look didn't last long. Chloe likes it either way, but the current at-ease look makes her more comfortable. "Don't get me wrong, I like Avery, and I like what I do. I just wish I could spend more time writing and less time doing … that kind of work."

She gets it. She's seen the passion in Will's eyes when he writes or even when he just holds his notebook. "So go for it, go back to writing," she says. "I read somewhere that you only need to devote one to two hours a day to writing, and that keeping a day job could actually enhance creativity."

"You're reading writers' advice now?" he asks contently.

"Maybe." She smirks.

"I like how supportive you are of this hobby of mine." He takes her hand in his, lacing their fingers together.

"I don't think it's a hobby. It's part of who you are," she says with certainty as he pulls her hand to his lips, resting a soft kiss on her knuckles.

The drive to his parents' house stretches through posh little restaurant areas and golf courses. She can tell they're getting close by the change in his posture, his motions become almost instinctive, natural, and although this place makes her stutter, for him – it's home, where he grew up, where he probably feels at ease.

He parks his car in the large circular driveway facing a huge colonial-style mansion.

"Relax," he says with a smile, kissing her hand again. "You're amazing, and they are going to love you." He pulls out the gifts with the matching bows and takes her hand in his, sending confidence back to her bloodstream. Together they walk up the large driveway and through the front door.

An elegant-looking woman, perhaps in her fifties, gracefully strides toward them, her makeup and hair professionally done. "William," she says, giving him a small, reserved hug.

"Mom." Will lowers his head and presses a kiss to her cheek. He hands her the matching bowed gifts, and she nods politely.

A man in a pressed tailored suit appears behind her, looking like an older version of Will. He's almost the same height, with the same-colored dark eyes, only lacking the vitality and spark Will possesses.

What ever happened that made him lose that?

The ritual of handshaking and polite hugs repeats. Butterflies swarm Chloe's stomach, her chest feels winded, her mind is helplessly searching for her confidence. Will steps back to Chloe and takes her hand, bringing back the color to her face,

"I'd like you to meet Chloe Barrett," he says in a celebratory tone. "Chloe, meet my mom, Aline and my dad, Maxwell."

"It's a pleasure to meet you both," Chloe says politely, her voice quieter than she intended. She holds out a hand to his mom first.

"Pleasure to meet you too, Chloe." Aline Allentown takes Chloe's hand in a polite lukewarm shake, her hand laced with large sparkling jewelry, nails meticulously done, her eyes critically observing her son's latest pick.

"Pleasure to finally meet you." His dad comes closer and takes her hand, breaking the ice-cold encounter by a bit. His handshake is confident and warm. "Both my sister and my son rave about you," he says earnestly. Chloe smiles, a little relieved, and his gaze softens, chasing away some of the churn inflicted by Will's mom. "Please come on in," he says with a smile. She can even spot the slight appearance of dimples. "Make yourself comfortable."

Will takes her coat into a large closet and quickly reappears by her side, wrapping his arm protectively around her.

"Your dad is nice," she whispers when his parents are out of sight. Fifty percent success is better than none.

The Allentown residence is elegant and stylish, with sophisticated decor and expansive artwork. Nothing flashy or ostentatious, although it does remind her of strolling through a museum, with its marble floors and high ceilings.

Will shows her around the large spaces. The abundance of white and cool colors gives it somewhat of a clinical feel. Chloe tries to imagine his parents leisurely watching TV in their fancy clothes. Is this a special Friday night thing, or do they walk around their home in formal attire on an ordinary day? She makes a mental note to ask Will later.

Their tour ends at the kitchen, where several men and women in black dress shirts and pants, clad with white aprons, are busy cooking and plating. The oldest in the group – a woman perhaps in her sixties – turns her head to them, and when she spots Will, a big smile spreads across her face.

"Here is my boy!" she says joyfully.

"Sveta!" Will returns a smile just as big, and Sveta pulls him in for the warmest bear hug, a total contradiction to the polite greeting exchange Chloe just witnessed between Will and his parents. "Sveta, I'd like you to meet Chloe," he says, and before Chloe has a chance to hold out her hand, Sveta pulls her into her arms for a bear hug of her own. It's the kind of embrace that perhaps only some lucky few get from their parental figures, a hug that spreads unconditional love without a single word, the kind of hug Chloe has seen in movies and read about in books. And here, just for being with Will, she has just gotten one for herself.

"Sveta has been with my family since I was a little kid," Will explains once the hug is over.

"I was his nanny," Sveta says with a bold accent, rubbing his cheek.

"More like my second mom." He smiles fondly. "And I finally get to meet the girl that makes you happy," she exclaims blissfully and blows Chloe an air kiss. Then she murmurs something in a different language to Will, her eyes shooting toward the dining room. Will chuckles.

"She says the ice queen is already here," he whispers to Chloe. Chloe meets Sveta's eyes, and Sveta nods at the translation.

The ice queen being her latest and greatest real estate agent? So apparently, Sveta doesn't like Sydney. That makes the two of them.

They walk into the formal dining room, although the *family* dining room was not lacking any formality. Will's dad is at the head of the table, looking bored and disconnected but nods politely. Will's mom is sitting to his right, wholly engaged in a conversation with the ice queen beside her. Chloe likes the new descriptive name. It seems to do her justice. The ice queen, also known as Sydney Bell, looks as fancy and posh as ever; her just-spent-five-hours-at-a-hair-salon hair-do extends above her head in a stylish look, not a hair out of place. Her skin is so golden – it must be the result of extra hours in one of those UV sunbed places or a very sunny vacation. Either way, she looks gorgeous and ... wealthy. She's wearing an icy blue dress, living up to her new nickname, with generous cleavage that would have made Jimmy proud.

"Chloe!" Sydney greets her with a big plastic smile that's so fake Chloe wants to throw up.

"Sydney!" Chloe matches the energy but tries to ensure hers doesn't come out synthetic.

There, she can fake it better.

"And here is William." Sydney gets up to hug him, making sure her cleavage rubs onto his chest. Chloe's heart falls to her stomach, the impending burning sensation in her ears building its way up.

Jealousy is for the weak. Yet she can't help herself.

Will takes a step back and wraps his arm around Chloe's waist, not leaving any room for misunderstandings. Sydney's eyes narrow at the edges as they hone in on Chloe's.

And it doesn't make it easier that Sydney knows where she lives.

Will pulls out a chair across from Sydney, and Chloe takes a seat, his hand on her shoulder, not breaking contact until she's settled. He then takes the chair between Chloe and his dad, facing his mom. Two of the younger staff members step in with appetizers and drinks. Chloe was planning to hold off the wine, since this dinner is complicated as it is, and she needs to stay focused, but a glass is poured for her too. Maybe this would help ease up the tension.

Will's mom takes her neatly folded linen napkin from the table, opens it, does some kind of sophisticated folding maneuver, and gently smooths it over her lap. Sydney follows just as skillfully. Chloe should probably do the same. She unties her napkin, but then, feeling Aline's and Sydney's watchful eyes on her, she resorts to simply stretching it over her lap, not sure how to imitate those polished moves. They all pick up their wine glasses, and Chloe follows. Aline's eyes narrow onto Chloe's grip.

Is she holding the wine glass wrong?

Chloe looks carefully at how Sydney has hers and tries to reassess quickly, but her fingers seem too sticky to be gently relocated. She feels out of place, an outsider, thrown back at once to the wild child she once was, that child who no one wanted. Until Susie and Joseph came to her rescue. She wishes she could see them again, talk to them, ask for their advice. She should have expanded her Google search to proper rich people's dinner etiquette when she looked up the gift thing. The observant man by her side seems to sense her distress, giving her a reassuring look. He probably has no idea it revolves around such a minuscule topic as table manners or lack thereof. Yet he puts a calm hand on her napkin-clad thigh, sending some good vibes her way, reminding her body that a proper cardiac cycle should include both contraction and relaxation – that is, if she wants to make it through this evening.

"My sister has been raving about your Pilates classes." Maxwell turns to Chloe with an epic conversation starter.

"Georgia is my best client!" Chloe returns a compliment and makes a mental note to thank him immensely one day.

"Chloe is a phenomenal coach!" Will agrees, sending a proud

smile her way.

"How would you know, William?" Sydney tries to break that chain of flattery. "You probably have no idea what Pilates even is." She attempts a teasing smile toward Will, but his eyes are still focused on Chloe.

"He's *successfully* graduated from a ten-class session just recently," Chloe says proudly.

"Interesting," Sydney offers politely, biting at her surprise.

"And enjoyed every moment of it," Will says triumphantly. His palm finds Chloe's, sending some warmth through her fingers. Sydney eyes them like a hawk.

"Georgia tells me I should try it myself," Maxwell says, smiling. "She says her back pains disappeared completely since she'd started."

"I am a big proponent," Chloe agrees.

"And what do you like to do for fun?" Maxwell's attempt at unwinding her doesn't go unappreciated. His head tilts slightly toward her with a friendly smile. She can definitely trace back Will's superb genetics there.

"I study health science," she says cautiously, Jimmy's spiteful comments still fresh in her mind. "I hope one day to make it my career."

"I like that," Maxwell approves, giving her his undivided attention.

"Not my idea of fun," Sydney says quietly to Aline, who gives her a private nod. "Fun is spending your weekends traveling." Her eyes light up as her voice picks up to hijack the conversation. Chloe doesn't mind. The focus on her was far too stressful anyway. "I just came back from a week in Monte Carlo. There's an investment property there that may pique your interest." She looks to Maxwell for confirmation, but when that lands a modest failure, she digresses. "It's gorgeous! Have you been?" Her glare turns to Chloe.

"No," Chloe says simply. To be honest, she's not even sure where this place even is, but she makes a wild guess that it was on the sunny side when Sydney visited.

"Oh, you should. It's a dream!" she offers. If it was on it at all, visiting a non-US location right now would probably be at the very bottom of Chloe's bucket list, all things considered, especially with the cost of airfare. There are so many things she would rather do if she had that kind of money and time – like taking her college courses full-time, reducing her hours at Cynthia's to be able to properly study for her exams, and maybe interning as a nutritionist.

"Have you traveled anywhere interesting?" Aline seems to like this direction of conversation better. Chloe tries to dig deep into her memory. She hasn't ventured out too far from the area. New York was probably the farthest when Susie was screening for a clinical trial. Unfortunately, she had too many pre-existing conditions to qualify, so that memory really only brings about pain.

"Not too much," she answers. Then decides she has to at least try to hold some conversation. "But my best friend Valerie is in Israel now, and I hear it's incredible. The food is amazing, and the weather is great." Thinking of Valerie brings back some of her spark, and she can feel the color returning to her face, her heart slowly fixing its pace, working on that relaxation part of breathing.

"Yes, Israel is wonderful! We went on a trip to Nazareth and Jerusalem many years ago," Aline clasps her hands, looking at her husband, who nods enthusiastically, "Maxwell! We should go again, maybe take Sydney."

As the daughter they never had? Or imposing as a daughter-in-law?

Maxwell's disapproving gaze turns to Aline, as he raises a wondrous brow.

"OMG, I would love that!" Sydney says to Aline, her confidence jumping to the roof. "Oh, and William," she refocuses her attention, batting her eyelashes, "we should have a tennis match."

A tennis match. Chloe would love to challenge her to a match... Tennis shoes are optional.

"Yes, William! It's been a while since you've joined your father and me for a brunch at the club," Aline offers. Her gaze fixes on Will, starting an entire mother-son wordless exchange. The woman has some impressive abilities. Will returns a somewhat exasperated look.

"Darling, how is work?" His mother skillfully shifts gears, clearly getting that hint.

"Going well," he sighs, "Avery has been dreaming up a new development," he adds, sounding somewhat enthusiastic. "I'm also writing again." There's some spite in his tone. Aline's eyes narrow to a glare that runs from Will's face to her husband and then to Chloe, evidently displeased with this unexpected resurrection of an all-time discouraged activity. Her eyes move to her husband again, who seems to be a thousand miles away.

So much for support.

"Writing? Contracts, you mean?" Sydney interjects.

"That too," Will smirks, "but I meant creative writing, fiction."

"Oh," she says, looking a little nauseated.

"You don't like to read?" Chloe offers.

Discovering imperfections in Sydney gives her some unexpected pleasure.

"Contracts, yes, of course. Fiction? Not really. Luckily, it's just a hobby," she says to Will as if to notify him that he's still a worthy candidate for her. "So, I'm sure you don't spend too much time on that ... hobby."

"Oh, he would have loved to spend all his time on that hobby. He used to lose himself for hours on end, writing away, that's why we insisted that he stopped." Aline jumps in as if this was a terribly negative trait she had to disclose in a contract. "His grandfather and his ideas..."

"Mom!" Will interjects, his jaw clenches a tad.

"For people who possess creative skills," Chloe has to interfere, she can't keep quiet any longer, "putting them to use is not a hobby – it's a necessity," she says, surprised by the passion in her voice.

Aline gives her a sharp glare, clearly unsettled by Chloe's daring disagreement. Maxwell remains distant, but Will – a smile stretches across his face, his eyes bright and wide, clearly enjoying the exchange.

He leans in closer. "Thank you," he says softly, sending delicious rumbles through her. The little hairs on the back of her neck stand to attention.

"Sorry William, I'm with your mother on this," Sydney says, interrupting the moment as if anyone asked for her opinion. She then starts a side conversation with Aline on any other possible topic, clearly not interested to learn more about Will's fondness for writing or for Chloe.

More food is served, putting a much-needed hold on the chatter and giving Chloe some breathing room. She looks down at the heavily polished silverware, trying to figure out which fork she's supposed to start with. Her eyes study Will's hand, following his movements, which he probably notices as he leans over for a small kiss on her cheek.

"Relax, you're incredible," he whispers, lightly flicking his finger over one of the forks. But this doesn't make her feel better. She's too busy noticing her elbows leaning on the table; she's the only one, so she quickly removes them. Her fork creates a screeching noise on the plate, making both Aline's and Sydney's face grimace in unison. If she didn't know better, she'd think they were related. A perfect pair.

"What do your parents do, Chloe?" Sydney tries to bring back the table conversation or expose her? A bad idea either way.

"My adoptive parents were teachers, but unfortunately, both have passed away," Chloe says matter-of-factly.

"Oh, I am so sorry," Sydney says contritely. Her hand covers her mouth, and her eyes show ... pity.

"Oh, poor girl!" Aline joins in on the pitifulness parade.

"That's okay, thank you." Chloe offers a smile. "I'm lucky to have had such wonderful adoptive parents, even if only for a short time. Plus, being a foster kid is how I met my best friend Valerie." She tries to put on a positive twist, winning a warm, supportive glance from Will's dad. Will wraps an arm around her, giving her an apologetic look.

The dinner stretches on, and Sydney moves into an empty dialogue of sorts with Aline, pulling in Maxwell and Will once in a while. Chloe tunes them out for the most part, picking up parts where Sydney tries to talk Will into meeting her with various lame excuses, mostly work-related. Will politely and skillfully steers away. Dessert is served, and Chloe can't count the seconds fast enough.

When dinner is finally over, they move into the living room, and she stops by the kitchen to breathe again.

"You make my Will happy." Sveta appears by her side, rubbing a rough hand on her arm. "Don't let her get to you," she whispers. Chloe is not sure whether she's referring to Aline, Sydney, or both.

"I'd much rather be here with you," Chloe says.

"Just like my Will," Sveta winks at her. "He always wanted to help me cook and clean when his parents were entertaining." Her heavy accent makes her sound rugged, but her eyes are beaming when she talks about Will. "Mrs. Allentown would always get so upset." She laughs fondly as Will appears beside her.

"Sveta, don't tell all my secrets." He grins sheepishly, his dimples appearing in all their glory. He pulls Chloe closer to him.

Sveta says something in a different language, a content smile on her face. "She says you have good eyes," Will translates, planting a small kiss on Chloe's temple.

Chloe says a bashful "Thank you" directed at Sveta, hoping her cheeks are not as pink as they feel. "Was it Russian?" she tries to guess.

"It is. Sveta is from Russia," Will confirms. "She spoke mostly Russian to me when I was little, and I'm so glad she did, because it became our secret language," he laughs, a mischievous smile across his face.

"His parents don't speak it," Sveta explains conspiratorially. She then fires a few more sentences in Russian and Will smiles in agreement. Chloe waits for the translation.

"She likes you," he says softly, "and she says it's enough torture for one night." Chloe smothers her laugh, secretly thanking Sveta.

They say their goodbyes politely, replicating the earlier ritual almost exactly. Maxwell offers a suppressed smile, as if afraid to get in trouble with the two ladies standing beside him. Aline's face stays cool as ever. Sydney is the only one looking more than pleased, especially with the overly friendly hug she throws at Will.

"Give me a call when you're up for that tennis match," she adds, her heels so high she can practically reach his cheek and very obviously takes a sniff-full of this Will's scent of his, making Chloe's blood pressure go dangerously high. Will takes a step back and pulls Chloe into him. Nothing escapes his radar.

"Don't even bother yourself with thoughts about Sydney," Will says when they're in the warmth of his car and away from the north pole of his parents.

A total mind reader...

"Of all my mom's attempts at matchmaking in the past..." He looks up, as if counting. "Five years, Sydney is by far the worst." He chuckles.

"But she's so beautiful and polished."

And wealthy, and composed, and gets along with his parents. And could easily fit into his world. Chloe is none of those things.

"*You* are beautiful. Sydney is flashy and overstated. I'm sure she'd make some guy happy one day, but that's definitely not me."

As long as he can help it, but for his mom, this seems like a done deal, and Chloe is just a bump in the road.

Chloe lets out a cynical laugh.

"What, you don't think I mean it?" His head turns to look at her, but she rolls her eyes. "Did you see the look on her face when we mentioned the writing? For her, it's all about money and making more money. If it's not – she's not interested."

"I did notice it," Chloe admits. "She looked horrified just hearing the word *writing*." She brings her eyes back to Will, which wins her his dimples, summoning back her confidence. "I mean… If you like someone, wouldn't you want them to do things that make them happy?"

"If you like them, and are not too self-centered, then yes," Will agrees, "but for some people – like my mother and probably Sydney – we are all just side characters in their Oscar-winning script. And then again – money."

"You know how I feel about it," Chloe says, a darker shade to her tone.

"I do. That's one of the many things I *love* about you Miss $10-upper-limit-on-gifts." He smirks. "How you stood up for me in there, for my writing, it meant the world to me."

And the way that makes her feel is something new entirely. Unknown to humankind.

Or at least unknown to Chloe.

Will takes her hand, letting their fingers interlace. Warmth trickles up her arm and spreads to her heart.

"You're welcome," she musters.

Did he just say – LOVE?

"Did you really mean it? Do you think writing is a necessity for me?" he asks.

"I know it is."

CHAPTER 21

Rights and Wrongs

"So, how is it going with Alon?" Chloe takes her lame excuse of a lunch break to catch up with Valerie. She has exactly twenty-five minutes before the next round of customers rolls into the studio for a Pilates class, and although she loves teaching Pilates and cares a great deal about her clients, today has been a crazy back-to-back kind of day. She hasn't even had a chance to take a break to pee. Well, she does now.

"Amazing," Val says dreamily. "Are you seriously peeing right now?"

"Sorry, crazy day at the studio today." Chloe's apology blends into the sound of Val's infectious laugh.

"But it's not *ALONE*," Val protests. "The name ends at the N; it's a blunt stop – A-LON," She goes slower this time. "Don't round the O." It does sound different in Chloe's ear, but she's not sure she can repeat it with the same proficiency.

"I'll need to practice it. So, is there going to be another date?" That's a rare thing for Valerie.

"We've practically been on one extended date for the past couple of weeks." There's that dreamy tone again, making Chloe all warm and fuzzy.

"Look at you spending more than a couple hours with a guy! Val, I am really proud of you! I promise I'll learn how to pronounce his name properly for your wedding."

"Okay, let's not read too much into it. Too much pressure." Valerie fusses with something in the background that sounds like a plastic bag, and then starts chewing. "You haven't told me, how was meet-the-parents-night? In the past few weeks, you've been talking about anything but." Val is a master of all digressions. "*That* bad?" she asks when Chloe just sighs on the other side.

"His dad is nice but has to hide it to not piss off Will's mom, so he mostly just seems withdrawn." Maxwell's somber eyes flicker through her memory. "His mom is ... controlling." That's the nicest thing she can say while trying to find the right superlative for something she hasn't quite been able to thoroughly analyze.

"Uh-oh... What is she up to?"

"She's been trying to match Will up with high-class, next-level attractive women for a few years now. Her latest and greatest attended the dinner." A thought crosses her mind – did Will want her to meet his parents just to get them off his back? She can't think of any other reason. Why would he want them to meet someone like her who couldn't possibly impress them?

"You're kidding, right?!" Val shakes her out of her downward path.

"It was that real estate agent, Sydney Bell, and she is gorgeous. It felt like a head-to-head competition, and I was clearly losing that battle."

"Losing? Are you nuts? She may be all posh and fancy, but she's no competition, I'm sure Will would back me up on this one. And by the way, you have my permission to kill me later for recommending her as an agent."

"They had already blind-dated once, and he said she wasn't his type. So I may not need to take you up on the second part."

'She wasn't you' he said, to be precise.

"You see? Told you – nothing to worry about. But why was she at the dinner?"

"His mother had apparently invited her before she knew about me, and could not *uninvite* her, I guess. She was obviously the crowd's favorite." Chloe sighs again. "Val, I am not *her* on so many levels, I could never be."

"And you shouldn't be! You're perfect just the way you are. If you start acting like that real estate agent, I'm going to disown you." Val's confidence is inspiring.

"Maybe... But being around her in that setting only emphasized how much I didn't belong there and probably never will. I don't even know how to hold my fork properly, or my wine glass, how to participate in hideous small talk, how to hold a conversation with them..."

"Who cares about that shit?!" Another encouraging confidence-boosting attempt from Val.

"Will's parents clearly did. His mom was studying me like a hawk, exchanging contemptuous looks with Sydney."

"And what did Will think of all that?" Val deftly switches to a more significant question.

"He clearly wasn't pleased with their treatment. He was being quite protective, making sure I was comfortable, trying to break the giant iceberg that lodged itself on that dinner table." Chloe's heart does a small squeeze, spreading some warmth through her veins. "And to his defense, he made sure Sydney knew he was very much with me."

Thinking back to the past few weeks after the family dinner – Will has just been his ridiculously gorgeous self. They've practically been inseparable. Every single moment not at work they've spent together, at either hers or his place, chatting, laughing, cooking, eating, kissing, making out, making love... She's not sure why she used the *L* word, but somehow it feels that way. It's a light-year's difference from her miserable, lonely relationship with Jimmy.

They've also been spending time fantasizing about her future health studio she's planning to open after graduation and discussing plot twists in the story he's been writing, and boy... Will possess a hard-core writer's wild imagination. She can't wait to read his novel.

Being with Will, she could do that every second of every minute of every hour of every day, for the rest of her life.

And worse, she can't imagine herself ever being apart from him.

But that dinner, was that what he was expecting when he wanted her to meet his parents? Is that life as usual at the Allentown household? Or was it a result of their interaction with her? Were they expecting to meet someone like Sydney? Or had they been given a crash course on her backstory? His mom looked like she was about to have a coronary when Sydney deviously started a conversation about Chloe's dead parents, so either Aline was not prepared to talk about it or had no idea. And Will may very well be immune to his parents – he was completely unalarmed and unfazed, while this whole thing threw Chloe to a new kind of whirlwind. And why the hell did her little insecure foster-kid-self have to make her appearance at that dinner? Will must have felt something, because his hand had barely left her side the entire night, his eyes kept searching for her confirmation that she was okay.

"Okay." Val's voice shakes her out of her trance. "Did you hear any embarrassing childhood stories at least?" Typical Val, trying to give nightmares a positive spin.

Chloe's serious face turns into a small smile as she tries to dig up some of that. "The only point of sanity there is Sveta, their household manager. She was Will's nanny, thank God. He calls her his second mom. If not for her, he would have been brought up to be just as crazy as the rest of them. She's Russian and apparently taught Will some of it when he was little, almost like their own secret language," she chuckles. "Watching him communicate in a different language was kind of hot."

"Yes, tell me about it!" Val says smugly. Of course, she'd surrounded herself with Hebrew-speaking men for a reason. "So, they bitch about his parents right in front of them?" She cackles. "Hilarious!"

"Something like that." Chloe can't help but let her guard down. "Sveta calls Sydney '*the ice queen.*' I think his mom is probably the ice queen. Sydney could be the ice princess. They are quite the pair."

"Sounds fitting," Val giggles in the background.

"Shoot, I gotta go," Chloe hisses in alarm. "Looks like I have a mystery visitor."

Even before the shiny black SUV pulls over by the studio and a fancy-serious-looking driver walks out, approaching the back passenger door, Chloe already knows who the mystery visitor is. Mrs. Aline Allentown, in the flesh, steps out of the vehicle, clutching her expensive purse, a severe look on her face. Judging by her fancy attire and hair, it's improbable that the reason behind her visit has to do with working out. Her stride is determined, as if running a tight agenda, which she probably is. The driver opens the door to the studio for her, lets her in, and then steps back out. She doesn't turn her head to thank him, her eyes focused on the path ahead.

Dammit. This can't be good.

Chloe gets up and approaches the door, feeling more like herself in her natural backdrop and yoga outfit despite the *you-are-in-trouble* air.

"Good morning, Mrs. Allentown." Chloe gathers every bit of confidence she can muster and holds out her hand, remembering she hasn't actually received a pass to use her first name. It had only, and probably mistakenly, been assumed. Will's mom takes it and offers an ice-cold, business-like shake.

This is not a friendly visit.

"What brings you here? Would you like to try a class?" Chloe quickly looks at her watch. "Our next one starts in fifteen minutes," she offers with a smile. While Chloe is not sure about the former, she is confident that the answer to the latter would be a hard no. Yet she tries anyway. This is a Pilates studio, after all, and an excellent opportunity to set a time limit for this fine encounter.

"Hello, Chloe," Aline says in a sharp cold voice that makes the tiny hairs on Chloe's skin shiver. "I am here for other business."

Yes, of course, she wouldn't expect any less of her.

"Please, sit," Chloe gestures to the chairs in the rest area. "Can I offer you something to drink?" There's only water really, the coffee machine broke again, but it sounds good to offer. Chloe would bet a million dollars she doesn't have that it's going to be a hard no.

Aline looks at the chair below her, then at the water tank. A tamed glare of disgust crosses her face for a second, then disappears quickly, a result of years of practice, before she says, "Thank you, this is fine." She chooses to remain standing. "I am here with a proposition." Her words cautiously selected.

"A proposition?" Chloe's voice comes out confused, a true representation of everything going through her mind right now, unlike Aline – she's never had the urge, nor the skills, to pretend otherwise.

"Yes, but first I need to ask," the ice queen raises a manicured eyebrow, "what is the nature of your connection with William?" If looks could freeze, Chloe would be covered with frostbite by now.

"We are..." Chloe rubs her arm, they haven't really gone into formal definitions, and she definitely wouldn't want to pressure Will into anything he wasn't ready for.

Is that a tricky question?

"We are together," is the most diplomatic thing she can say at this point, since this is a conversation she should instead be having with Will, preferably without his mom present. Hopefully her nervous teeth chattering isn't too apparent.

Her highness sighs, clearly displeased, choosing her words carefully. "William is at a point in his life where he needs to start taking his life more seriously."

What exactly does she mean by that?

"Mrs. Allentown, please let me clarify. I never said my intentions were not serious."

Double negative, really?

Aline's eyes narrow. "Then this is a bigger concern," she says coldly.

Dammit, she just can't quite get anything right with this woman. Didn't she just say she wanted serious?

"Being an Allentown comes with certain obligations and responsibilities. William is my only child; he has been brought up this way, and he is expected to oblige." The words come out of her mouth as if all of it should be completely clear and known to Chloe.

Well, a spoiler. It isn't.

"Since meeting *you*," says the ice queen, a sullen tone creeps onto that last word, "he has been losing his focus, works fewer hours, spends a great deal of his time on frivolous ... activities."

Is she talking about writing? Or the time he spends with Chloe?

"And has even reverted back to indulging in writing."

So frivolous activities equal his time with Chloe. It's not a shocker that Aline would view it as such.

Yet... Ouch.

Aline's face shows nothing but disdain, as if Chloe is a bad influence. As if writing or spending his time together with a girl who has it bad for him is like falling into a terrible addiction, losing oneself to alcohol or drugs.

"Mrs. Allentown, let me assure you, Will still works over sixty hours a week. He puts a great deal of effort into his work and takes it very seriously." Someone has to make sure his mom has her facts right. "As for writing – doing what you love is important. Writing is what makes Will happy." Chloe has chosen not to touch on the time they spend together. Perhaps ignoring that will make his mother steer clear of it.

"I don't recall asking for your opinion." Aline dismisses Chloe's little pep talk. "Sixty hours a week is not enough when his father will be retiring soon, and he will be taking over the entire business." Aline stops to admire the impact of her words, but Chloe is clearly not impressed. "And spending the rest of his free time with you means he is not emotionally available to pursue a serious relationship with someone more fitting."

"Excuse me?!"

Now, this is beyond offensive.

"More fitting?" Chloe tries to keep a calm front, but inside, her blood is simmering.

"I'm sure you are aware..." Aline looks her up and down like an appraiser evaluating total-loss car damage. "William comes from a certain class. As I said, there are certain expectations from the woman who will be chosen to stand behind him."

Have they gone back in time to the eighteenth century, and Chloe just somehow missed the memo?

"Mrs. Allentown, with all due respect, I find your comments very offensive." Chloe takes a deep breath. "But aside from that, your son is a grown man. Don't you think he is capable and should be making his own decisions?"

"It is my responsibility as his mother to guide him and make sure he doesn't make decisions that would have grave consequences."

Grave consequences? Seriously? This woman has completely lost her mind. And perspective. But on second thought, maybe she never actually had either.

And speaking of guidance, this sounds more like forcing his decisions rather than guiding him.

"Sydney Bell has graciously agreed to give him another chance. She can see the potential in a marriage relationship with him, but in order for this to happen—"

"I am very sorry to interject." Chloe tries to pull the same attitude and tone Will's mom is using. "It was my understanding that they had one blind date." The mere thought of it makes her sick to her stomach. "And Will was not interested. In addition, he is currently not available, as he is seeing *me.*"

"Which brings us back to my proposition to you." Aline recovers quickly.

Great, so Chloe has just walked herself right into it.

"I thought *this* would dissolve. But it appears to be persistent." She emphasizes her nouns like she's talking about a fungal infection. "You will stop seeing my son, move on with your life, free him up to move on with his."

"And why would I do that exactly?"

"Yes, of course, it's all about money for you." Aline's glare narrows into contempt. "I will make sure it will be worth your while. You'll make a nice exit for yourself. This should get you settled comfortably."

A nice exit? Has she just regarded her son as a start-up?

Aline pulls out a pre-written check from her opulent-looking purse. Her lips are tight together in a narrow line, accentuating each and every wrinkle she tries to conceal.

"You're buying him out? Seriously? Not everything is about money!" Chloe says.

"Everything is about money when enough money is involved," Aline says with a painful degree of certainty.

"Will is not even interested in Sydney." Chloe feels her fists clenching, her nails cutting into her skin.

"He will eventually come to his senses. You will be doing the right thing for the both of you."

"What if I say no?"

"You don't want to do that. William has a lot to lose, including his finances, his title, his business, his inheritance, his parents... I'm sure you don't want to be the one responsible for all this." Her voice is severe but unwavering. Would it be so easy for a mother to obliterate her own son from her life? Was it the same for Chloe's biological parents?

"Why would you do such a thing to your own son?!" Chloe wants to shout and protest, to try to change her mind, tell her how she really feels, but Aline releases a scold and turns her head toward the door.

She's losing this battle.

Their conversation ends abruptly when the first client of the next Pilates class walks into the studio. The ice queen just drops the check on the counter and says quietly in a cold, sharp, yet extremely collected voice that makes Chloe shrivel, "Remember, William has a lot to lose if you refuse to cooperate. I want you out of my son's life in the next 24 hours, and make sure you keep our little arrangement and this entire conversation strictly confidential."

And before Chloe has a chance to give her glossy eyes a blink, her ice majesty disappears into the car, and her driver drives away.

"We need to talk," is the text Chloe manages to send to Will after teaching the most difficult Pilates class on earth. This may have been a beginner class, but her head was spinning, heart pounding, her entire body quivering from the longest fifteen minutes of her life spent with Aline Allentown. She's rapped in too many feelings at once, her neurons helplessly misfiring in all different directions. She has no idea what to do or what to say to Will, but they *have to* talk.

"Uh-oh," Will texts back before she even has a chance to take a breath. "Everything OK?"

She can't lie because, literally, *everything is not okay*, not a single thing is okay right now. But she also doesn't want Will to spend his entire day worrying. She should have waited with this text, but somehow felt she needed to, at the very least, give him a heads up before...

"Can we meet for coffee later?" She tries to get the conversation into a neutral place where she won't get tempted to lose control and back off on whatever plan her mind and heart are battling right now. Because nothing feels right about what she has to do. There are no winners here, only losers – well, except for the ice queen, of course. Whatever choice Chloe makes is doomed to have casualties. One thing is for sure – she's spent most of her life without a family of her own. She can't be the one responsible for Will losing his.

Her eyes travel back to the screen, where Will has not responded to her lame coffee message. A quick glance at the schedule board shows her that apparently her last class for the day has been canceled. She sighs, partly relieved – at least she doesn't have to pretend to not be falling apart for another hour.

Chloe walks to the back room of the studio and leans into the corner, letting her back slide down the wall until she feels the hardwood floor beneath her, her head cradled into her knees. An all-too-familiar position, but the feeling is new, a new and very unwelcome kind of low. The cold sensation of the wall against her thin yoga top does nothing to ease her heartbeat or her pain, but the room is dark and isolated, and maybe she could, at some point, form some coherent thoughts. What should she say to Will? His mom made it very clear that this conversation should stay confidential. But saying anything outside of the truth would be a lie, and Chloe may be many things, but she's not a liar. She has to let him go, for the sake of keeping his life intact, for the sake of keeping his family. A bright future with Sydney, Aline's happy ending. The thought of it makes her sick to her stomach, and her blood shoots to her ears. Spending time with Will almost made her forget that people like her don't get to have happy endings.

They just don't.

And the more she thinks about it, something else starts to simmer and burn in her chest, and it's probably called *tomorrow...* The day after Will.

Addicted much?

She would do anything, risk everything for just one more hug, one more kiss, one more day with Will, but it's not her future that is on the line here. And besides, *one more* is not even remotely enough, nor several – heck, when it comes to Will, a lifetime is not enough.

Is that how it feels to be in love?

She thought she had been in love with Jimmy, but this... This is nothing like anything she has felt before, not even close.

And, of course, Will drops everything and summons his addictive self before Chloe within less than fifteen minutes, because he read the guide to the ridiculously perfect addictive man of the galaxy, or actually wrote it. He kneels before her, on the hardwood floor, with his pressed suit and all, pulling her weeping self out of that little corner and into his arms as if trying to chase all her demons away.

If he only knew.

And for a moment, she lets herself forget everything, lets herself believe there's a way for them to come through.

"Chloe." Will's baritone voice is filled with concern. "What's wrong?" His hand gently caresses her cheek, his eyes so unbelievably worried.

"I don't even know where to start," she says, and her voice betrays her.

Well, that's just great – she hasn't even said anything and already can barely speak.

"Try the beginning," he says softly.

"Okay." She takes a quivery breath. "What would you do if you were forced to make a decision that would break your heart... But you knew was the right thing to do?" She hears herself say, her voice wavering.

Will studies her for a long moment. "*Forced* to me means that it is not really a decision," he says. "And if it breaks your heart, it can't possibly be the right thing to do." His hands reach out to her, gently unwinding the fists she wasn't aware she was clenching.

"You make it sound so easy," she says, trying to make that lump in her throat go away.

"Chloe, tell me what's going on. Are you in trouble?" His gaze is alarmed. Her throat tightens, and she shakes her head. She can't bring herself to speak. "Did I do something wrong?" His hands find her shoulders, turning her to face him.

"No, of course not!"

Great, now he's blaming himself.

"Does it have anything to do with Jimmy?" he asks warily, his jaw tightening. "Whatever it is, I can make it go away." His eyes narrow. Chloe shakes her head, wishing it was a Jimmy-related issue. She's already adept at dealing with his assholeness. "Okay, help me out here," he asks, looking clueless and frustrated. Then something shifts in his gaze, a painful realization. "Does it have anything to do with the dinner at my parents'?"

She can't shake her head now because, in a twisted way, it does. She tries to think of a diplomatic thing to say, but her pause clearly registers.

"It does," he concludes without asking her to confirm. "I'm sorry I dragged you into this family mess." His eyes soften, and a gentle hand slides a curl off her face and tucks it behind her ear. Little speckles fill her field of vision. She tries to blink the tears away.

How can she ever let him go?

"I'm sorry," he says again. "Whatever it is, we can work through it."

"We can't," she finally manages. "Our worlds are so different... *I am* different." A traitorous tear escapes her eye. "You have to understand, where I come from, I can't possibly fit into your kind of life. And it's not fair to you, because I... I have nothing to lose."

Yes, except for a heart.

"And you," she continues, "you have everything to lose."

"What are you talking about?!" Will gets up and pulls her into his arms. His warmth is impossible to resist. "Do *I* make you feel like this?" He wipes away her tears gently.

Their happy moments surround her, wash through her. Making s'mores, laughing, watching movies together, chatting into the night, the way Will kisses her, hugs her, makes love to her. His special smile reserved just for her. "No, you don't," she admits.

He makes her feel like she belongs. He makes her feel like home. Loved.

"My parents made you feel this way?" He lets go of her and paces up and down the studio, trying to come up with a rebuttal. Something catches his eye as he walks by the counter. He stops and turns in his place, his eyes narrow as he picks up a piece of paper, an unfamiliar tremor to his hand.

The check. The completely forgotten, insulting, pride-smashing piece of paper.

Will's expression changes to incredulous, then stunned. Pain fills his eyes. "I see," he says quietly, collecting himself. He shoots her a glare, a side of him she hasn't seen before. His eyes are suddenly empty, as if all his memories of her have been wiped entirely. As if he doesn't know who she is anymore. "The right thing to do." He releases a sad, cynical laugh. A creeping darkness takes over the space between them.

"No, Will, you don't understand." She tries to take a step closer, to start at the beginning this time, something she should have done *before* he saw the check.

But he takes a step back, deepening the abyss before them. "I understand perfectly," he holds out his hand as if to mentally push her away – from him, from his heart.

"You think I took it?! Seriously?!" The insult is unbearable, paralyzing, worse than any insult thrown her way in her lifetime, and God knows there have been many. Anger fills her lungs, burning through her throat. She can feel her blood pulsing through her veins, simmering in her head, filling her ears, her hands clench up. She can no longer assemble any form of speech. She can't breathe.

"Let me make this *forced* decision easier for you." Will slams the check back into the counter and walks out, leaving a bitter gust of wind behind him.

CHAPTER 22

Sadly Ever After?

It all still feels the same when Chloe opens her eyes again. Dark, raw, oozing, burning... It's been a whole week without Will, and it still feels impossible. An entire week in which she hasn't gathered the strength to leave her apartment, not even for groceries. The mere thought of taking those few little steps from her bedroom to the kitchen is unbearable. She has constantly been struggling to avoid that empty cozy corner where Will used to write. Or any other space, for that matter, because every square inch brings up memories of Will. Even her linens still bear that addictive smell of him.

The only thing Chloe was capable of doing after feeding that vicious check into the shredder was falling apart. She canceled all of her classes at the studio and her shifts at Claudia's for the week, because going outside or having any kind of interaction with the world requires an immense amount of effort. The thought of picking herself up from her bed is an insurmountable task. Her cell phone has been turned off and shoved into the drawer of her nightstand. The vain hopes for his messages, the useless wishes for his calls, the longing for his voice ... they were just all too painful.

He's not going to call you – you fool, he hates your guts, he hates you. He thinks you chose money over him, and why wouldn't he? The check was right in front of him, and you had your chance to speak up, but you blew it.

She has to shut her thoughts down.

Aline's valuation of what she views as her son's freedom was set to a whopping three million dollars. As if any amount of money could fix a broken heart. *'Everything is about money when enough money is involved,'* her highness had said.

Sorry to break it to you, Mrs. Allentown, but she begs to differ. There is no amount of money in the world that would make this poison any less toxic or make its flavor any less bitter.

Chloe hates how the look on Will's face made her feel. She hates Aline Allentown for thinking she would choose money over her son. She hates Will for thinking she would even consider taking that money. If Chloe could transform back into that moment, she would tell him everything: the conversation with his mom, Aline's plans for him and his future with Sydney, about the grave potential of all he could lose if she didn't walk away. She would tell him all about that stupid check and her plans of shredding it to pieces once she could pick herself up from shuddering on the floor in the corner because the thought of losing Will made her lose *herself*.

But she had missed her single chance of doing things the right way. She didn't want him to know about his mom's shitty proposition, about Aline's willingness to obliterate her own son from her life. Chloe tried to spare him from the pain of that conversation but ended up hurting him more.

In this new nightmare reality, her nights mix and merge with the days. Everything seems like a big, long mess. She's utterly and officially lost track of what time or day it is.

She keeps replaying that moment over and over again, with different outcomes. In her head, she tells Will everything from the beginning while she still can. She tells him she loves him, and she lets him choose. In each possible scenario playing in her mind, Will always chooses her but loses his family, which doesn't make her feel even remotely better. The more she thinks about it, she realizes that nothing could have led to a better outcome – at least this way, she is the only one suffering.

What would Susie tell her now if she was still alive? Despite dealing with so much loss, she always had these inspirational thoughts about life. Joseph and Susie Barrett somehow managed to pick themselves up and go back to life after losing Holden, and then again three years later, after losing Thomas. That was before Chloe came into their lives. *'You just put one foot in front of the other,'* Susie used to say. *'First, you go through the motions, and then eventually, you'll be able to pour a portion of yourself into it. Until it becomes a new normal. Although there's nothing really normal about it.'* Susie's laugh comes into life in Chloe's head, part ironic, part sad, but always with an impressive degree of acceptance and courage.

And with that, Chloe decides to get up and go back to living. Because that's all she knows.

Time to stop feeling sorry for herself. It's pathetic.

Chloe drags herself into the shower. Her week-old unwashed hair requires a great degree of shampoo scrubbing, until foam starts to fill up the tiled floor. The hot water helps her aching muscles relax and give her pounding heart a short break. She wraps herself in a towel and walks into her bedroom, taking off the linens in determined motions, putting them in the laundry in an attempt to shed off all traces of Will. She puts on a workout outfit. She hasn't canceled her classes for this week. Returning to work and keeping busy is probably the best thing she could do for herself right now. She walks to the kitchen for a quick coffee – no milk, because that ran out a few days ago – and some leftover stale toast with peanut butter. Her fridge is begging for a refill ASAP. She pulls her hair into a messy bun above her head and puts her jacket and sneakers on, feeling a little more like ... a person. She takes a deep breath which shuts on itself midway as she notices Will's notebook resting on the little coffee table.

Shoot.

She picks it up. Her heart is pounding as she gently puts it in her backpack, making a mental note to give it to Georgia after class today. Will's parents and his bride-to-be might not be that supportive of his creative side, but Georgia, being the incredibly encouraging figure she is, must be.

Chloe walks out the door, finally, for the first time in a week, letting the crisp fresh air brush her face. Sad and alone may not feel so good, but it sure as hell feels familiar, which makes it surprisingly ... comfortable.

Chloe steps into the bus, greeted by her favorite bus driver's smile.

"Al!" She's surprised at how good it feels to see a friendly face again.

"Haven't seen you in a while," he says, his gaze narrows at the sight of her eyes. "Girl, you don't look too good." Even her bus driver notices.

"Yeah, I had a rough week." She sighs and drops in the seat behind him, her backpack resting on her lap, protecting Will's precious notebook inside.

"Sorry to hear," Al says. "Whatever it is, I'm sure you and your special someone will work it out."

"How do you know it has to do with a special someone?" A ghost of a smile travels to her lips.

"Oh, it's written all over your face." Al gives her his reassuring, knowing look through the head mirror.

"Oh boy." It hurts to smile again, as if she's forgotten how to use those muscles, but albeit sad, it does win him a genuine smile.

"Sometimes you just need to *let it love*, you know?"

"Let it what?" She raises an eyebrow. Romantic Al, who knew?

"Don't give me that look." Al laughs through the mirror. "I've been driving this same line for a few years now. I've seen people sad and happy before. Past few months – you had a different kind of happy on you, the best kind," he says, sending a quick smile her way through the mirror again. "But today, I see a new kind of sad, which only means one thing." He halts his speech as more people step into the bus. Chloe sits a little straighter, impatiently awaiting the next part. She wasn't aware of how observant Al was. And she definitely was not aware she was letting her feelings show.

"And what is that, Dr. Phil?" she quips.

"It can only mean one thing." Al pauses for a more dramatic effect. "LOVE."

As the women start trickling into the studio, Chloe marks another milestone – she's still mentally absent, but at least physically there. Quiet music is playing in the background. Chloe had to ditch the depressing playlist she's been playing all week for something more subtle.

"Chloe! You're back!" Joan gives her a warm hug. "We've missed you! Tania said you were sick? How are you feeling?"

She did tell Tania she wasn't feeling well, which was a massive understatement.

She's helplessly battling a broken heart.

"I wasn't feeling well, but I'm much better now." From understatement to severe overstatement. "Thank you for asking." She gives Joan a smile.

"Oh, dear!" Georgia storms inside, taking off her coat. She grabs Chloe by her arm and pulls her into the back of the studio. "I am sorry to say, but you look terrible," she whispers, "and Will looks like he's been hit by a semi-trailer. No, a full trailer would be more accurate. From madly in love to... For goodness' sake." She cups Chloe's cheeks, studying her gravely. "Would someone tell me what is going on?!"

"I don't think I can," Chloe says quietly, pulling her cheeks back. "You should really be speaking to Will about it." Chloe pulls the notebook from her backpack. Holding it carefully, she hands it over to Georgia. "Would you give this to Will? I didn't realize he had left it at my place. I hope he won't stop writing, now that..."

"Yes, of course." Georgia takes it off her hands in the same delicacy it was given to her and carefully puts it in her purse. "Now that, what?" She tries to understand.

"Just now..." Chloe is unsure what else she can say. Whether there's anything she is *allowed* to say. Aline made it loud and clear – she was to keep it strictly confidential.

Or else what?

Georgia nods, pulling her in for a bear hug. Chloe has to swallow hard to rid of the lump forming in her throat and blink some traitorous tears away, but Georgia takes notice, offering a fond squeeze to her arm. "I'm here if you need anything," she says, and together they walk back out to the main room.

"Thank you," Chloe mouths, as the studio is now full of her favorite clients, waiting to start the class, counting on Chloe to help make their day even better. An insurmountable task, considering she can barely help herself, but she'll do her best.

"Good morning, ladies," she says into the mic, giving her best attempt at an energized voice. She has a glimpse of Will untangling the mic's cord off that bare inch of her skin the first time he walked into the studio. Chloe has to battle her memory back. "Let's start with a full-body warm-up." She tries to control the shiver in her voice. She takes the ladies through the moves, the stretches, the highs and lows of the workout. But Will seems to be everywhere. *'I have ten hours to convince you to be my friend,'* he said on that first class, not knowing he'd already had her at their first s'more.

Chloe stops at the grocery store on her way back home. She hasn't completed her nutritionist training, but she's pretty sure that subsisting on dry toast, chips, and milk-less coffee is probably not sustainable, even if you add some protein bars to the mix. She grabs the smallest cart from the entrance. A smaller shopping cart helps ensure she doesn't buy more than she can carry, a habit she developed once Jimmy stopped joining her for grocery shopping, which actually occurred quite quickly in their miserable relationship.

The store is almost empty, aside from a few teenagers in the candy aisle. The non-nutritionist side of her picks up a gallon of milk and a box of Frosted Flakes. Drowning her sorrow into sugary cereal might as well be the answer to tonight's gloomy mood. Ice cream has never been her go-to comfort food, and she doesn't feel like making mashed potatoes right now. She might need to reconsider switching her favorite food.

"This has to be a sign." She hears an all-too-familiar voice from behind her, making her jump out of her own skin, which is ridiculous because one can't really expect to be entirely alone in a grocery store.

"Hi, Jimmy." She turns reluctantly toward the voice, knowing he's going to frown at the sight of the sugary pleasures decorating her cart.

"You don't look too happy to see me." How observant of him. On the already-empty list of people she would want to see right now, his name would have been crossed out at least twice with a red marker.

"Sorry, I'm ... uh..."

"Still getting over the breakup?" This seems to make his smile wider.

Does he know about her and Will?

"Understandable, I'm still struggling with it myself,"

Oh, he means that breakup.

"No, I moved on, Jimmy."

"Fuck, that hurts," he says. "I still miss you. And I'm sorry I was such a dick to you. I've changed, you know?"

Sounds extremely doubtable, but... "Good for you."

"And just so you know, I'm not seeing Stacy anymore."

"Ah, Stacy? So that's what that boyfriend snatcher's name is?" she says spitefully. "Too bad. She looked hot, the way you like them."

"Still feisty as always," he says slyly, letting his eyes give her a slow once-over before they travel into her cart. "I see you're not taking your own nutritional advice?"

Why is he still annoying?

"Just so you know, my nutritional advice includes not taking anything to the extreme. I hope you have a nice evening," she says sarcastically, turning away.

"Wait, sorry, I was just joking. Christ. Want to grab something to eat? For old times' sake?"

"Not really," she says from behind her shoulder, going back to filling her cart with more junk food, and this time on purpose.

"Coffee? I'm a changed man, I promise, I'm not going to try anything." She turns her head to him, her body still facing the other direction. "Unless you're up for more..." He attempts to look enticing.

Five years. She spent five years of her life with the man. Everything about him is so familiar, yet every neuron in her forlorn brain and every cell in her body has Will etched all over it. She's a lost cause. Maybe coffee wouldn't be such a bad idea. At the very least, it will be a distraction from her current pitiful situation. Maybe she needs closure.

"Coffee, fifteen minutes." She points to the little in-store coffee shop. "Then I'm going home."

"I can give you a ride home." Jimmy jumps to seize the opportunity.

"Alone. Going home alone," she clarifies, "and no, thank you, I don't need a ride."

"Fine, suit yourself." He shrugs.

"But let me finish my grocery shopping first."

"Can I come with?"

"No, you can wait at the coffee place. Let me shop in peace."

"Damn." He smirks, biting his lip, but obeys, letting her do just that.

Chloe finishes going through her grocery list. When Jimmy is no longer in sight, she shelves back that load of junk food she took just to spite him. Then she gets herself through the self-checkout register, bagging her stuff, aware of Jimmy's eyes watching her every move. She puts her bags in the cart and rolls them toward the little coffee area, where Jimmy is already sipping from his cup.

"Got you some tea," he says, gesturing proudly to a second cup on the table.

"Thank you," she says before realizing. "Tea?! Since when do I drink tea?" Has he not been paying attention for the past five years? She wouldn't be caught drinking tea even when sick.

"I dunno." Jimmy shrugs. "It seemed like something you would drink," he says, unbothered.

Seriously?

"Whatever." She sits across from him, pushing the teacup in his direction.

Of course, he wouldn't offer to get her something else instead.

She shouldn't be drinking caffeine at this time of night anyway – that is, if she has any plans of attempting to sleep.

"So, from the way you're still dressed, I can assume you're not seeing anyone," Jimmy starts.

Took him long enough.

"How can you tell?" Her shoulders slump, knowing what he's going to say.

So much for changing.

"Still not showing off that cleavage of yours, still no makeup, not a bit of effort."

"You are aware that I teach Pilates for a living?"

"Fully aware." He nods. "So the answer is no?"

"No *what*?"

"No new special someone in your life?"

"There is ... was," she admits.

But still is in her heart. And now forever will.

"Oh." Jimmy looks surprised but then slaps on his sly smile again. "*Was...* That means you're up for grabs again."

"No!" He always has this way of making things sound so ... romantic.

"Did you not just say '*was*?'"

"Jimmy, what do you want exactly?" she sighs. This conversation is draining her last bit of energy. Getting on her nerves has just reached a new record.

"I want you back. I've made a mistake."

"*A mistake?!* A chain of unfortunate mistakes!"

Were these mistakes, though? Or merely the symptoms of his shiny personality?

"Okay, a chain of unfortunate mistakes. I need you to give me another shot." His tone doesn't even sound honest.

"Not going to happen, Jimmy. I'm sure there's someone special for you out there, but it's definitely not me."

"How can you say that? We had something special between us."

"Something special?" *Is he for real now?!* "You barely even know me."

"Are you fucking with me now? I know you better than you know yourself," he says smugly. "Surely better than whoever you were fooling around with."

"I wasn't *fooling around!*" she protests.

She was falling in love.

"Whatever. Was it that rich boy, Allentown?" His brows smash together in their typical move when he tries to piece information together.

"Will." Just saying his name makes those butterflies come to life again.

And they are swarming...

"Ha, yes, you went for the big bucks." If humans could project the dollar sign from their eyeballs, like they do in cartoons, this would be Jimmy right now.

"Jimmy, you know I don't care about money. In fact, if he wasn't an Allentown, we would probably still be together right now," she says grimly.

"How's that? Money got to his head?"

"No. He's not like the rest of them," she tries to explain. In front of her, Jimmy perks up at the prospect of money, making her nauseated. "But his mom tried to buy his way out."

"Heck yeah!" Jimmy rises for an enthusiastic high-five but folds back when he realizes Chloe is less than a worthy partner here. "How much?" He sits back expectantly as if waiting for the good news about his new fortune.

"It doesn't matter."

"There's so much we can do with that money!" He grins.

"*We*, Jimmy? There's no *we* anymore. And you definitely don't know me at all if you think I took that money!"

"You didn't?!" His brows crush together to a chastising frown. He slaps his forehead and shakes his head in grave disappointment. "Of course you didn't."

"I fed it to the shredder, where it belongs!" she exclaims.

"I always knew you were stupid, but this is new-level stupid. Chloe."

"You know, I don't think the new Jimmy is so different from the old Jimmy."

"I mean, honey..." He shakes off his berating frown. "Money is money."

"Can we stop talking about money?"

"O-kay," he says reluctantly while attempting a deep breath. Not thinking about money is clearly difficult for him, especially knowing there was an uncashed check out there. "You are definitely better off without him," he says with certainty.

"And you conclude that on what basis?" Chloe crosses her arms tightly on her chest.

"Because now we can get back together. You've played around, checked what's out there. Now it's time to come home." He smirks.

"I wasn't playing around!" This is another unique talent of Jimmy's – pushing all her buttons at once. "And don't flatter yourself too much. I'm never going back together with you."

"At least I love you for who you are, and I'm here," he tries.

"You can't possibly love me for who I am. You've spent the entire time we were together criticizing me, trying to change me, mold me into whatever it was you thought I should be."

"I was trying to help you become a better version of yourself," he insists, as he did for the past five years.

"By whose standards?" This is getting exhausting. "And besides, you barely even know who I am."

"Are you going to drink that?" He points to the untouched cup of tea.

"This is a perfect example. We were together for five years! Have you ever seen me drink tea?!" Her voice comes out louder than called for. Some heads turn to look at them.

"Jesus Christ, Chloe! Relax! It's just tea." He pulls the cup toward him and takes a sip, wrinkling his nose. "What? I already paid for it, might as well drink it." He takes another sip and wrinkles his nose again. "So why do you think I barely know you?" He brings up a clueless gaze. "I know you better than you know yourself," he says snidely. "Challenge me."

"Okay," Chloe sighs. "Simple question – what's my favorite gift?"

"Easy!" He chuckles. "Flowers."

"*Really?* Since when?"

"I dunno... All girls like flowers."

So, it was a generic guess?

"I don't."

Of course, he wouldn't know.

"Okay, that was a tricky question. Hit me again."

"What's my favorite food?"

Jimmy scratches his head. "Pizza?"

"No."

"Favorite book? Favorite game?"

"C'mon Chloe, you know I don't dig that spare-time kind of shit. Ask me something more meaningful."

"Okay, what am I studying right now and why?"

"Some science bullshit, I don't know. And why? God knows. You have all those unrealistic aspirations. I've lost track already."

"Lost track? I've only had one professional dream since graduating high school. And it hasn't changed one bit." And somehow, she still finds herself surprised by how clueless Jimmy really is about her. "And by the way, you were a shitty boyfriend."

"Yeah? Why's that? Humor me, please," he says with a snark.

"You cheated on me."

"I was going to, but I didn't." His tone is unwavering. "So it doesn't count."

"Right, you get the best-boyfriend-of-the-year award for that."

"Thank you." He pretends to bow.

Such a bright sense of humor...

"You let the guy you call best friend, fucking Trevor, harass me over and over." Her voice raises again.

"You never said," he rebuts, "and lower your voice. People are looking," he says between gritted teeth.

"I did! Many times, actually!" She ignores his last remark, setting her voice free. "You said I was leading him on, that it was my fault!" She can't help the incredulous tone to her voice.

"Well, kind of, yes," he admits.

"Where were you when he was coming on to me outside the bathroom at your birthday party? I really needed you back there. Why do you think I left early?"

But Will was there for her.

"You seemed moody from the outset," he tries to recall. "Forget about Trevor. He's just playing around. What else?"

"Whatever," she sighs. "You took all my college savings without permission!"

"Pfft... Please, you can't be serious with this college fantasy of yours. I was taking care of our financial stability."

"Stability?"

This is getting better by the minute.

"Remind me what you're doing now? Do you still work at selling poison to people who are trying to lose weight?"

"Uh... Not anymore actually."

Of course not. Jimmy keeping a job for longer than a couple weeks? Unheard of.

"But I'm interviewing and will take care of our financial future. You could stay home and do whatever. Clean, cook, take care of the kids," he snickers.

"What kids? Do you think I'd want to raise kids with you? And who said I wanted to stay home? I happen to enjoy working, and I'm not planning to throw away my dreams."

"What dreams? Seriously, you have no touch with reality. Do you really think you could make something out of yourself? You and I, we're those stray dogs no one wanted, remember? I swear to God, Chloe, you hanging out with this rich boy fucked with your head." Jimmy's invalidating face reappears, his chastising tone – it's all too familiar, but she doesn't have to take this anymore.

"Even a stray dog like me is allowed to dream, Jimmy!" Chloe raises up from her chair, pressing a finger to his chest. "I will never forget where I came from," the voice coming out of her is confident and unwavering, "but that doesn't mean I can't change my trajectory, and the first step is to get you out of my life."

A few bystanders supportive clapping sound in the background. "Hell yeah, girl!" someone says.

And with that, she turns away, takes her grocery bags, and leaves.

Coming back to an empty apartment has its pros, especially when looking for some peace and quiet. But for some reason, at this moment, Chloe can only think of the cons. She's not a cup-half-empty kind of person usually, but she just can't help it right now. Or maybe her cup is just completely empty.

Standing up to Jimmy felt pretty damn good, especially watching how his expression changed in front of her, from that confident prick he is to surprised, almost pitiful. It was long overdue.

But after dragging her grocery bags on the bus, dropping her bananas and tampon box to roll on the floor under the watchful eyes of late-night passengers, when the driver had to make a sudden stop due to an annoying stoplight that changed from green to red without warning, then struggling with all those bags up the stairs to her apartment, searching for the keys in the dark, dropping her belongings ... again, just an unfortunate collection of *ugh* moments ... It made her wonder:

1. What was she thinking, getting so much stuff at once? Well, the fridge had reached an all-time low...

2. What in the world was she thinking, talking to Jimmy like that? The only person who had actually interacted with her face-to-face for more than a small talk in the past week. Could she really live up to everything she'd just said? That surprised look on him ... and here she starts doubting herself...

Just go through the motions, she reminds herself. Hopefully, the rest will follow. This must be true until proven otherwise.

She puts the milk, yogurt, and cheese in the fridge, bananas on the counter, and the rest in the pantry. Unlike Will's walk-in pantry, hers sums up to a tiny cupboard, but it's more than enough for just one person. Yep, better get used to it – cooking for one, shopping for one, no plus-one for parties or work outings. Yes, one might say this is temporary – until someone new comes into her life – but this adds another question to her daily list:

3. Why does it feel so unbelievably impossible?

Chloe gets into the shower, dropping her clothes into the laundry basket – yes, laundry for one – it will probably take her a while to fill up her entire washing machine. She might need to get more clothes and underwear to last her in between washes. These wicked little adjustments. And she's not into self-torture, but when she spots Will's hoodie folded neatly in her closet, she just can't help but put it on. This, combined with spending the last few days hugging the little cat-bunny stuffed animal Will gave her, brings about the last question on her daily collection of wonderings:

4. Is she really willing to let Will go without a fight?

Another night and almost another day that she manages to pull through, but for some reason, she doesn't feel better, just numb-er.

She gets off the bus and makes her usual run into class, almost as late as always, dropping her backpack to the floor and slumping into the seat next to Niki.

"You look like shit," Niki offers, an incredulous look on her face. This doesn't even come close to how she feels, so it's probably an understatement. "Troubles in paradise?"

"Something like that," Chloe says quietly, her eyes focused on an invisible artifact on her desk.

"You two looked like forever. What happened?"

"Life, I guess."

That pessimistic outlook right there, making an appearance again. It's becoming a new common theme.

"So, are you saying he's available now?" Is Niki praying on her downfall?

Will is probably happily engaged to Sydney by now. And if he's not happy about it, his mom and Sydney undoubtedly are.

"No," she just says, "he's off-limits."

"He was here last week, you know?"

"Who?"

"Your prince charming. He came looking for you, waited in the parking lot like always, only you never showed up to class."

"He did?" The annoying butterflies show up again.

"I told him you ditched class," Niki says. "He looked like shit, by the way. What did you do to him?"

"Believe me, you don't want to know."

Will came for her?

Chloe counts the minutes until class is done. Words go in one ear and out the other without attempting any interaction with her brain in between. Just empty words, empty minutes, empty hours, empty days; it's just one day of a full empty week that will probably extend into an empty month. A black hole, sucking everything into the void – it might as well take Chloe along too.

Class ends, eventually, after a long, torturous hour. Chloe picks up her stuff quietly and makes her usual way to the bus, stealing glances at the parking lot along the way.

Is she hoping he'll be there? Trying to add some more torture?

But he isn't. She takes the first bus to her neighborhood, even though this one stops farther away from her apartment. Walking outside, jacketless, into the cold night feels better than getting into her empty home. She's just grateful to be feeling something other than longing. But even the long walk comes to an end eventually as she reaches her apartment complex.

She looks up to her window, already dreading the moment she'll have to walk into her dark, lonely apartment, eat her dinner alone, and see that cozy corner where Will liked to sit and write. Once upon a time, when she still lived in Fairytale village.

The only thing Chloe looks forward to is putting Will's hoodie back on after her shower, smelling him on her again, and hugging that little cat-bunny he gave her. Pathetic is her new name . But then...

Chloe's heart stops beating for a second, and the blood drains from her face, or maybe just shoots itself directly into her stomach where the butterfly flutter is going wild, as she realizes the lights in her living room are on – and she knows for a fact she didn't leave them on this morning. Something is definitely off. Either Will came to pick up the last of his stuff – after all, he still has a key – or someone has broken in. Given the consequences and the potential collateral damage of seeing Will in the flesh again, dealing with a burglar is her preference now.

She quietly pulls out her keys and sets them in between each of her fingers – that one Krav Maga class Val made her take taught her how to weaponize her fist for a more powerful punch when self-defense is called for. Chloe's never actually put that training to use, so whether she could do it is questionable. She should probably call the police, but she's feeling too numb, combined with hopeless bravery and some curiosity. She opens the front door quietly, carefully, fists clenched.

CHAPTER 23

Snapping Out

"Val?! What are you doing here?" This may not have been one of the options, but it's by far the finest one.

"Are you kidding me?!" Val looks mad, smoke almost literally coming out of her ears. "You haven't been returning my calls or my texts for over a week!" She pulls Chloe in by her coat and shuts the door. "I thought you were mad, then I thought you were dead, then I spoke with Will, who, by the way, is completely clueless and broken for something I bet he had nothing to do with! I'm still trying to figure out why you wouldn't talk to him either!" She throws her hands in the air almost violently but then grabs the shocked Chloe and pulls her into a bear hug. "I'm still mad at you," she shouts in her ear, "but thank fuck you're okay!"

It takes Chloe a few seconds to snap out of her shock. "Val! I missed you so much!" Her hands rise to reciprocate the hug, and she just can't help the tears that seem to now burst out of her like a fountain. "When did you ... how did you..." There are too many questions she can't quite articulate in between her sobbing. That quickly turns into a silly two-person sobbing, as sobbing tends to be contagious.

When they finally calm down, her best friend explains. "Will flew me over," Val says as she ravenously unwraps an old granola bar from Chloe's snack closet. "He said you wouldn't answer his calls, that you haven't shown up to work or school." Val stops to chew. "And that he respects the fact that you don't want to speak to him. But he got worried when I told him you weren't answering *my* calls either, you fool! And I say this with love."

"You spoke to *Will?*" It's like a magic word. Just putting it on her lips again makes her hopeful. "He tried to call me?"

"Yes, stupid, he's worried, and he's angry too, but he wouldn't tell me why, so he asked how soon I can get away, and I was like – *why do you ask*?"

"Wait, Will flew you all the way from Israel to here?! Like bought you a plane ticket?"

"Uh-huh." Val nods her head vigorously while taking another mouthful of her granola bar. "He had his admin book me a flight for the next day, first-class! Holy shit, I felt like I was on a fucking vacation! I was in a private booth – did you know those seats recline to completely flat beds? They give you a pillow and a comforter, but I couldn't waste all that good time sleeping. I binge-watched the entire new series of *Manifest*." She stops to laugh. "Probably shouldn't watch that when you're physically on a plane." Val walks up and grabs another granola bar from the kitchen and shoves another bite in her mouth. "He even had someone pick me up from the airport, like his own driver with a suit and all. Ruby, the sweetest guy. He even had a sign with my name on it, then he carried my bags to a black Tesla X that had a mini-fridge inside." Valerie speaks so fast and enthusiastically that the granola bar flies out of her hand and lands on the other side of the carpet.

"Will did all that?" Chloe's still trying to process all the newly discovered information.

"Yes, Will, and he sent the key to your apartment with his driver, who dropped me off here to wait for you, and since you're still not answering my calls—"

"My phone!" Chloe slaps her hand to her forehead with the recollection of that little device she deposited in her drawer a week ago... She gets up and pulls her abandoned cell phone out of the drawer. "I turned it off the day Will and I... I couldn't handle the anticipation of a call or a text. I didn't really think he would, anyway." She waves the phone to Valerie as proof.

"*Give me that!*" Val snatches it away and turns it on. "What about me? Will is not the only person in the world who might call you, you know?"

"You're right." It does seem kind of stupid now. "I only meant to do it for a few days..." The week's worth of accumulated messages start trickling in violently. Chloe reaches for her phone, but Valerie moves it farther away.

"Why didn't you call me? We tell each other everything, always. And this..." Val studies her worriedly. "This looks like a big thing. And you're not getting your phone back until you talk to me! Not that you even need it." Val jumps from enthusiasm to frustration at the speed of light.

"I'm sorry. I couldn't bring myself to talk about it." Chloe raises up slowly. "And I was afraid you'd talk me out of my decision."

"Okay, so now we're at the part where you keep your ass right here." Val pulls her back down to the couch. "And I am not letting you get up until you tell me all about this shitshow."

"Wait, how did you find Will in the first place?" So many questions are attacking Chloe's brain right now.

"Dr. Google," Valerie says with a raised eyebrow, "I googled

William Allentown. He's *handsome*, by the way! I found his office address and phone number, called, told his admin I'm his girlfriend's best friend and that this was an emergency, and he got on the line faster than 911."

"Emergency? He probably freaked out!"

"*He* freaked out?! I was already freaking out! Which on its own is an emergency!"

"Thank you for doing all this for me." Chloe's tears are flowing again, and Val jumps into another hug in response, this time huddling Chloe to one side so they can share the couch. "You're probably exhausted after the long trip," Chloe says, resting her head on Val's shoulder.

"Are you kidding me? The flight alone was like a full-on vacation." Val smirks. "By the way, in case you didn't notice, this guy is crazy in love with you. You should have heard how worried he sounded and how his voice made these little shifts every time he said your name." Valerie pulls her phone out. "That reminds me. I need to report back," she says, opening Will's last message. Turning her screen away from Chloe, she texts something.

"What are you texting him? Can I see?"

"No!" Val snaps and turns the screen farther away from Chloe.

"Okay. Tell him I say thank you and that I'm sorry for making him worry."

"You'll tell him yourself," Val insists, "face to face."

"I don't think it's a good—"

"Did I stutter?" Valerie interjects, her fingers still typing something. Then she stops for a beat. The phone buzzes within seconds. "Okay, now that your boyfriend can breathe again—"

"What did he say?"

"He's relieved. What do you think? But he's still angry and broken. What did you do to him?" Val stands up. "I'm still starving. Do you have anything to eat that's actually food?"

"Sure, I just went grocery shopping yesterday." Chloe gets up to open the fridge.

"No, I mean actual food, not the green stuff. You're eating way too much lettuce – It's not good for you." Val scrunches her nose, making Chloe laugh.

"I finished all the frosted flakes last night. Sorry."

"Okay then, we're ordering pizza and ice cream," Val announces.

"Fine, can I go change?" Chloe asks and turns toward the bedroom.

"You have three minutes, then get your tiny ass back here and tell me everything," Val calls out after her. "By the way, I like your new place."

"I'm so glad you're here!" Chloe calls out from the bedroom. She hadn't realized, until Val appeared in her living room, how much she missed her.

One hour, an entire tray of pizza and a bottle of Coke later, they're sitting on her carpet, nibbling on some chocolate ice cream.

"Okay." Val summarizes Chloe's long monologue. "So the real problem is the ice queen, and to a lesser extent, but still a partner in crime, I'm guessing, is her evil twin, I mean, wanna be daughter-in-law, the ice princess," she says with a spoonful of ice cream in her mouth.

"Correct." Chloe nods, taking a small bite of the ice cream. "How do you not get brain freeze from these huge bites?" She looks at Valerie as if she's a magical creature with superpowers.

"And so, you texted Will and said you needed to talk. What were you planning to tell him?" Val says, dismissing the brain freeze question as if brain freeze is a myth.

"I don't know, I was trying to come up with that part." Chloe's voice wavers as she recalls. "I thought we would meet after work, but he came within less than fifteen minutes after I texted him."

"Like someone who's madly in love would do."

"I didn't even get a chance to process everything, let alone get rid of the check. I was so shocked I forgot Aline had just left it there."

"So, he came and thought you were trying to break up with him."

"I kind of was..."

"WHAT?! Why in the world would you do that? It's not his fault that his mom is a controlling basket case freak."

"Val, you of all people should understand – you and I, growing up – we would have given anything to have a family," Chloe's throat feels tight again. She puts down her spoon. "I could not live with the possibility that he'd lose his family because of me."

"Chloe, Will is a grown man. He's perfectly capable of making his own decisions. This is not for you to decide." Val lets go of her spoon as well. Talking about family is as hard for her as it is for Chloe. Unfortunately. "You can't make such a decision for him, and besides, what if it was just a threat?"

"I didn't consider that possibility," Chloe admits, "but his mom said he'd lose everything – his inheritance, his job..."

"Well, that should be his decision to make, too."

"And there's also the part that... I don't belong in their life, and that's true. You should have seen their faces when we had dinner. I did everything wrong, from how I held my wine glass, folded my napkin, cut my food. I'll never be able to fit in there. I'm an outsider. I'll slow him down. I'll mess him up."

"Poor Will, has he made you feel this way?" Val's eyebrows smash together.

"No, of course not! Being around him is the most amazing feeling."

"So why are you punishing him?"

"Punishing?! I had to make the right choice for him. I was doing him a major favor, believe me. Giving him an out of a life with someone like me."

"Shouldn't he be the judge of that? Have you asked him what he wanted? Or do you just go about assuming what he needs?" Val gives her an incredulous look.

"He really needs someone like Sydney who would play tennis with him at the country club and have all those tedious small talks with important people."

"Oh, c'mon! Don't even go there. If he wanted Sydney, he would have pursued that bitch a long time ago, but that's not what he wants, and I bet that's also not what he needs." Val has always been the voice of optimism. Well, more accurately, her voice has always been the crazy-impossible, wild, get-you-in-trouble voice, but now ... she has a point.

"Well, his mom has already planned their entire life together, so I'm not sure—"

"I don't care for that Sydney bitch. I'm sorry I ever recommended her as a real estate agent for you. I'll make sure to give her an anonymous shitty review on, let's see – Facebook, Yelp, LinkedIn, Google... Does she have Instagram?" Val types away on her phone, spreading the word. "Now for the second part – why is he mad at you? And why are you mad at him?" Val fakes a scoff. "Kids these days."

"It's this stupid check."

"How much was it for, by the way?"

"Three."

"Thousand?"

"Million."

"Jesus!" Val's hand covers her mouth in shock.

"Let me remind you that you are part Jewish."

"Holy shit!" Valerie is deemed officially speechless, and that never happens, ever, not to Valerie.

"And he thinks I took the check."

"Well, you did have it on the counter..."

"I had other things to deal with. Like shattering—"

"How do you forget about a fucking three-million-dollar check?" Val grabs the ice cream again. "Well, never mind, that was a rhetorical question. If there's one person on earth who's capable of that, obviously that would be you." She lets out a loud guffaw. "So, he's mad because he thinks you took the check." Val pieces the info together. Chloe nods quietly. "I already know the answer, but I'll ask anyway. Did you?"

"Of course not! His mom left it there, I wasn't going to take it, and I definitely wasn't going to use it."

"Good girl, I wouldn't expect any less of you," Val says in an authoritative voice. "And you are mad at him because?" She raises an eyebrow.

"Because he should know me better than that."

"Did you tell him that?"

"I tried, but he was so pissed he turned around and left. And that made me so mad that I didn't bother chasing after him."

"And what did you do with that check?"

"Fed it to the shredder," Chloe admits in a low voice.

"Of course, you would." Val smiles. "And that's why I love you." She hugs her. "But why didn't you tell him?"

"What difference would it make? I let him go, freed him up to live his mom's idea of the perfect life, with Sydney as her daughter-in-law."

"If you say it one more time, I'll punch you," Val threatens her with the spoon in hand. "I told you already, this bitch is not for him. Get that out of this head of yours," she says and hands Chloe back her cell phone.

It's been a week without it, and Chloe didn't miss it even for a second, except for... She opens her messages and sees a trail from Will. Asking if she's all right, then saying he misses her despite being mad, apologizing for not hearing her side, asking her to answer his phone calls, saying he's worried and that *he loves her*.

He loves... Her...

But then a final last message, "*I'll have to respect the fact that you don't want to talk to me anymore. I won't bother you again, but please just let me know you're OK.*" Chloe's eyes glisten as she dwells on this last one for a bit. Should she respond? She lifts her gaze to Valerie.

"Don't you think he deserves to hear the whole story?" Val asks.

A tiny little sparkle of hope chirps in, summoning those butterflies into Chloe's stomach again, making her heart flutter, the thought of seeing Will again, talking to him, looking into his eyes again...

Will he fight for her?

"He has too much to lose." That dismal conscience of hers comes through.

"Let him be the judge of that," Valerie cuts in. "It's his decision to make, not yours. That is, if you want him, and as your best friend, I can tell you beyond doubt – *you definitely do.*"

CHAPTER 24

Snapping Back

Chloe tosses and turns all night. She can't get her brain to shut down, can't get her heart to shut up. She's grateful when the sun finally sparks those little beams into her bedroom. She gets up at once, and dizziness hits her, but she perseveres. She shoves some sugar and caffeine into her system to battle the impending hypotension, then puts on her running shoes and goes for a run. She needs to clear her head. Enough of the wallowing.

Quietly to not disturb sleepy jet-lagged Valerie, she drags herself out the door and down the stairs of her apartment building. The chilly early morning breeze burns her face, shaking her numbness away, reminding her again how good it is to feel something, anything. She takes a deep breath of that crisp air and starts running, slow at first, then faster. When her favorite trail comes into view, her mind starts to relax, and the steady beats of her soles hitting the ground help her focus again.

What does she really want? What should she do?

Spending the evening with her best friend and reading through

Will's unreciprocated messages made her realize – she can't let him go without a fight. There's too much for her to lose.

Will can stay mad at her all he wants, but at the very least, he deserves the truth. At the very least, he should be angry over things she's actually done. Not that stupid check...

What will he do? What will he say to her?

A wave of hope hits her again, but she forces it out with a shaky exhalation. She picks up her speed, letting her emotions guide the way. In the past week, she pushed away everything that could have made her feel better – her best friend, running, Will... If it weren't for him sending Valerie over, she would still be wallowing right now. She should at least thank him for that in person.

She hits the wooded part of the trail, picking up her pace, feeling her lungs burn from the cold and labored breathing, enjoying the rush of adrenaline that comes with it before turning back and heading home. Sweaty and breathless, she enters her apartment to find Valerie in the kitchen, whipping up pancakes and FaceTiming someone.

"This is Chloe." Val smiles as she sees Chloe taking off her sneakers, aiming the phone screen at her. "She's a bit crazy, going for a run when normal people sleep and it's freezing cold out. Chloe, this is Alon." Val shoots her a happy look.

"Nice to finally meet you." Chloe snatches the phone and looks into the camera, slapping on a smile, so glad her best friend has finally found someone she'd want to spend more than one night with.

"Same here," the charming stubbled guy on the other side says with a smile. Chloe turns her head to Valerie. "He's hot!" she mouths.

"I know!" Val squeals. "Now go get ready. I picked out some clothes for you," Val commands and grabs the phone back.

"Where are we going?"

"*You* are going, and you know exactly *where*." Val gives her a mischievous smile.

Yes, there's no point delaying it. She's made up her mind, and now it's time to act.

Excitement looms over Chloe, chasing away everything else, as she jumps out of the Uber, looking around the large building with the Allentown logo on its front. Valerie gave her the address and suggested she'd call Will's admin to make sure he was there, but Chloe refused, using his signature surprise method back on him. Plus, despite flying Val over to her, first class and all, and chauffeuring her over from the airport to Chloe's apartment, he's still mad at her, so giving him time to prepare may not be in her favor.

Valerie went a bit wild with her choice of clothes for Chloe – a revealing dress with matching lingerie that she dug out of the closet. It all seemed too far-fetched at this point. *She's not sure what Val had in mind...* Chloe ditched the scandalous collection for a comfy pair of jeans and a sweater – and no fancy lingerie, just her typical T-shirt bra and plain underwear. She was too worried to assume such a positive outcome. Then, equipped with Will's office address written on a sticky note by Valerie, she clambered into an Uber.

And here she is now, still standing at the entrance to the building, thinking over what to say. And it's not that she's going in without a plan. She hashed it all out repeatedly during her run, then gave it a reality check by scrutinizing it with Valerie. Her best friend, of course, had a different idea of how this would go. It involved being pushed against his office wall into what sounded like a scene taken from an erotic movie, hence the dress and lingerie...

But now that she's finally here, her plans just dissipate into the void. She definitely likes the idea of being pushed against the wall by Will, followed by that erotic scene. But given the current chain of events, she'd be lucky to have a chance to tell her side of the story. Because from where things are currently at, she can't even bring herself to answer the polite greeting of the security guard seated in the lobby.

"Can I help you?" he says with a raised eyebrow in response to the crickets...

"Uh ... yes, I'm here to see William Allentown," she finally manages. The mere act of saying his name makes her heart pound profoundly.

"Do you have a meeting scheduled?" the guy asks, looking down into his lists.

"No, it's ... a surprise." She tries for a smile, but all she can muster is some lame trace of it. She can feel the blood rush into her face.

The guy lets go of the list and stares at her for a second, as if contemplating. "Got it," he finally says, releasing a small smile and gesturing toward the elevators. "Mr. Allentown's office is on the fifth floor."

"Thanks," Chloe releases a pent-up breath and walks into the elevator, pressing the little circle next to the number five with a shaky hand.

The ride is too short, not giving Chloe nearly enough time to prepare, as the doors open into the fifth floor's lobby. She steps out on wobbly legs and walks toward the receptionist.

"Good morning." She's greeted by a shiny-white-toothed smile that belongs to a young woman sitting behind a large, heavy mahogany reception desk.

"Good morning, I'm here to see Will...iam Allentown," she stutters, unsure how he prefers to be called in his office. Other than briefly seeing Avery from afar that night at the bar on Jimmy's birthday, when Will came to her rescue and she was too shaken to be introduced, she hasn't really seen Will in his work environment. And it looks so serious in there – all business-y. A big Allentown logo covers the wall facing the elevators. The area is a combination of glass, metal, and brick walls, giving a hi-tech kind of vibe. A few people walk around, all wearing suits and ties, talking quietly and politely. She feels a bit under-dressed in her jeans.

"Is Mr. Allentown expecting you?" The woman's voice shakes her thoughts away.

"No, he doesn't know I'm here," Chloe says.

"Oh, he's out with Ms. Bell. He should be back in an hour," the woman says.

"Right."

Ms. Bell? As in Sydney Bell... Just wonderful. Of course he's dating Sydney now; his mom wouldn't waste a second, couldn't let her boy stay single for too long.

What was she thinking coming here, showing up at his workplace unannounced?

It's only been a whole entire week – admittedly, it did feel like forever. He's probably already engaged. Guess one can't escape their trajectory after all.

"Would you like to wait? I'll let him know you're here. What is your name?" the receptionist asks, picking up the phone. Chloe's brain is already forming an escape mission. A vision of Sydney showing off her giant engagement ring, gloating away, creeps into her mind. "Miss?"

"No, that's okay, I ... have to go." Chloe turns around and walks back into the elevator, abusing the little button marked with a star, mentally begging the elevator doors to shut.

"Wait, you forgot to leave your name, miss—" the receptionist calls after her as the elevator doors close. Chloe pulls out her phone and opens the Uber app, needing to get out of there as fast as she can. She presses her home address and is relieved to see that there's a driver three minutes away. At least one thing is working for her today. The elevator doors open into the entrance floor, and she sprints through the lobby.

"The surprise didn't go as planned?" the security guard calls after her.

"Not really," she says without turning her head. She steps outside, trying to get her breathing back into a life-sustaining tempo, letting the wind cool off her blood-shot face. Rodrigo, her 4.98-star driver in a red Passat, pulls over at the curb. She has about three hours to get her thoughts straight, then two Pilates classes to teach, one afternoon shift at Claudia's, and zero energy to drag herself out of the Uber and up the stairs to her apartment.

"You're jumping to conclusions!" Val's voice of reason comes to her rescue. They're sitting on the little couch, Chloe's head resting on Val's shoulder. Val is busy dipping her spoon in last night's leftover ice cream.

"What would I do without you?" Chloe lets out a small sigh. "I'm so glad you're here."

"I'm glad I'm here too," Val says modestly, "and it's all thanks to your boyfriend, who, if I may say, is madly in love with you and cannot possibly be engaged to that spoiled brat."

"*Out with Ms. Bell*, that's what that admin said, probably planning their engagement party..."

"Did she say out on a date? Or out on a meeting? There's a big difference, you know?"

''Who says *out on a meeting*? Of course, they were out on a date."

"Did-she-say-that?" Val rolls the words slowly in her mouth.

"She just said *out,* she didn't specify. She didn't need to."

"Who goes out on a date at 10 a.m.?!"

Chloe shrugs. "Brunch date?"

"In the middle of the week? You goof... Did you leave your name?"

"Of course not!" Chloe exclaims. "No one needs to know of this miserably failed attempt. I feel bad enough. Besides, you should have seen his office, big-shot Mr. Important. Everyone's so serious with their suits; it's not the place for me."

"Stop belittling yourself! It's okay to step out of your comfort zone sometimes. It's a good thing."

And Val may be right, but now is the time to move on, because Will certainly has.

"Now you're taking your best friend to lunch because I'm starving." Val concludes the conversation and gets up to throw away the empty ice cream tub. "And then I'm going to visit TJ and Elle. Did you know they moved in together?"

"I knew they'd get back together!" Chloe says contently. They were that ever-after envied couple, and when they had broken up after high school, it had felt like a fairytale gone wrong, a blow to the stomach, so hearing they're back together – that's one point to team hope.

"They have a spare bedroom, so I might stay the night."

"You can stay here with me," Chloe protests.

Val smirks. "No offense, babe, but you move way too much when you sleep."

"Honey, you look like a hot mess." Claudia examines Chloe's face carefully as she puts on her apron, ready to start her shift at the restaurant.

"Thanks, Claudia, that's actually better than how I feel," she offers. Having Valerie around has a mood-boosting effect, but moving from hopeless to hopeful and then again hopeless in the span of a week, and mostly in the past 24 hours, has been exhausting.

"Oh, no, no, no," Claudia protests fondly, then turns Chloe around to braid her hair. "This always cheers up Mia," she says, referring to her youngest daughter.

Okay but Mia is five years old...

"Who broke your heart?" Claudia asks, her hands deftly pulling and tying.

"Me, this is all on me," Chloe says. "I gave up too easily."

"Well, then you can fix it."

"I kind of tried... It's too late for that," Chloe mumbles.

"No, never too late. Now, take a look." Claudia pushes her toward the large mirror facing the kitchen. Two little braids extend from each side of her head and into a ponytail. This makes Chloe smile. Susie used to braid her hair like that. "You see? Already better." Claudia grins at her from the mirror. "Now keep this smile on and get to work." She gives her a small pat on the back and disappears into the kitchen.

The evening stretches out slowly. A few families come in for dinner, ordering the night's special, the burger, fries, and surprise – this time, the surprise is a ticket to a local high school musical show.

A few hours pass, and the place empties completely. One more hour to her shift. Chloe starts cleaning up for the night, organizing the menus in the corner, and polishing wine glasses. The little bell above the door announces another customer coming in, probably the last one for the night.

"Good evening," she hears Claudia's cheerful voice from the entrance. A familiar baritone voice floats into her ears, flooding her with so many memories, rendering her gasping for air.

She dares not turn around.

She can hear footsteps making their way to what sounds like the more isolated corner booths by the window. He has the nerve to show up here with his new girlfriend ... fiancé ... whatever she is.

"Table four." Claudia appears in front of Chloe, offering a big smile.

Right, why not rub some salt in her wounds? Might as well.

"Can you take that table, Claudia? Please?" Chloe pleads, lips on the verge of quivering.

Claudia raises both eyebrows in wonder and gently ushers Chloe to turn around. There's no sign of Sydney. Will is sitting alone by the table, that same table where he sat at that first night he came by. He's still in his work clothes, although he ditched the suit jacket, the sleeves of his dress shirt folded halfway on his forearms, his tie loosened. A rare sight. Chloe's heart flutters and falters as she walks slowly toward him, her legs about to give out any second.

Just put one foot in front of the other... The complex task of walking.

"Chloe," Will says when his eyes spot her, his tone pained. He gets up to face her, and she takes a step back, trying to remind herself that he is not hers anymore, but his scent draws her in.

Already breathless.

From up close, Will's face appears nothing like the face she's spent so many hours nuzzling. His beautiful deep eyes are now decorated with dark circles and red rims. He has several days' worth of stubble and tousled hair. This could have been a rugged, handsome kind of look on him if he didn't seem so tired, drained ... and so incredibly sad. And all she wants to do is throw her arms around him and make him smile again. Then claim him back.

But she's too late.

"What are you doing here?" she asks, trying to hide the battle going on inside of her.

"I wanted to talk."

"We have nothing to talk about."

Stay strong. Got to stay strong.

"You came to see me today," he says knowingly. Chloe gives him a confused look, or at least she feels confused, because she never actually left her name with the receptionist or the security guard.

"How do you know it was me?"

"I pieced it together." His lips curve to a sad little smile, making her heart throb in her chest. Awakening those butterflies in her stomach.

"Okay, so I did, but you've apparently moved on, and probably for the best, so..." She's about to turn away.

"Wait." He takes a step closer and grabs her arm. "*Moved on?*" The little scar above his eyebrow pinches up.

"With Sydney. The receptionist said you were *out with Sydney*. So, congrats."

"*What?!* Out, as in a walk-through at the construction site." Will releases a soft laugh. He sounds relieved. Those angry muscles in Chloe's face begin to unwind. "My parents are contracting her as the exclusive realtor for the project. She'll be working with Avery," he says, still amused by Chloe's interpretation.

"It's not funny," she protests.

So, he's not with Sydney? He hasn't moved on?

A shiny bit of hope climbs its way and settles into her heart.

"I'm still mad, but I'm certainly not moving on," Will says, gesturing for her to sit.

"I'm mad too, and I can't do this right now. I'm working." Chloe points to her apron.

Will looks up to find Claudia's watchful yet knowing eyes. Everyone seems to know everything except for Chloe herself.

Claudia looks at Chloe. "Take a break," she commands and motions her to sit.

Okay then.

Chloe sits down at the booth. Will takes a seat right next to her, turning his body to face her, blocking her escape route with this unyielding chest of his.

"So, what did you want to tell me?" he asks.

"That you need to get your facts right. If you want to be mad at me, at least be mad about something I actually did, not something I didn't do." Her voice is strong and confident to the point that it surprises her. "I also think you deserve to know the truth about this whole thing. I wanted to spare you from the pain, I didn't want you to get hurt, but I think the way it came down is hurting both of us more," she says.

Her hand gravitates to his without her mind having any say in it. The touch of his skin strikes an unexpected current up her spine. She tries to pull away, but Will's hand closes on her wrist, bringing her hand back to him. He must have felt it too, because his eyes brighten.

"By the way, thank you for flying Valerie back to me. I really missed her," Chloe chooses to say, starting with the positive twist before attempting to unload his mom's shitshow of a story.

"I was worried about you. You wouldn't answer any of my phone calls or texts. I figured you wanted nothing to do with me, and I respected that, but I also wanted to make sure you were okay. And I missed you... I *miss* you."

Gosh, she misses him too. So, so much.

"I had turned off my phone. Didn't think you'd call me, but I also ... couldn't bear the anticipation in case you did."

"Well, I did, multiple times. I also came to look for you at work, at school... I would have used my key to check up on you at home, but I was pretty sure that might be on the verge of harassment."

"Despite being mad?"

"Being mad doesn't magically erase how I feel about you, Chloe."
It doesn't?

"I'm sorry for what my mother did," he says, and she wonders how much of it he really knows. "Is that why you're mad?" he asks quietly.

"Seriously?" Disbelief spreads across her face. "I'm mad because you think I took that stupid money! Do you think I would give up everything I care about for money? I thought you knew me better, but I guess I was wrong." This makes her voice waver and her eyes glossy. She has to initiate a series of blinks to battle it. And now she's mad all over again.

Now is not the time to get emotional. It will ruin her entire façade.

"I know you didn't take the money."

"But ... wasn't that why you left?"

"At first. I was shocked and upset, realizing what my mother had done – trying to break us apart, letting money come between us... You were crying, saying you had to do the right thing although it would break your heart, taking away every ounce of hope. And then that check on the counter. But after I drove away, none of it made sense. I knew you wouldn't have taken that money, with your strict under-$10-gift rule. You flinched when I paid for the dresses, you battled me every single time I pulled out my wallet, even for a cup of coffee. Taking that check would have gone against everything you believe in."

"So why *are* you mad?" She blinks a few freshly formed tears away.

"Because you gave up on us." His gaze searches for her eyes as if looking for a sign, a signal that would indicate otherwise.

"I had no choice." She takes a deep breath before continuing. *Here goes nothing.* "Your mom threatened you'd lose everything if

I didn't walk away – your job, your inheritance, even her and your dad. Your own parents… There were times in my life I would have given anything to have a family. There is no way in hell I would knowingly make you lose yours."

Treacherous tears now escape her eyes, roll down her cheeks. Will sends a gentle hand to wipe them away, still holding her gaze. "Don't you think I should have a say in this decision?"

"I just want you to be happy."

Will gives her an incredulous look. "Do I look happy to you?!"

"No," she admits.

The truth is, she has never seen him so sad before, and it's breaking her heart.

"But the last thing I want for you," she presses on, "is to lose your family because of me."

"Chloe, I don't think you understand." He takes their entwined fingers and presses them against his chest. His heart is throbbing as fiercely as hers. "From the first moment I laid eyes on you at my aunt Georgia's party, I knew I had to make you mine." He lifts her chin gently, making her look into his eyes. "Settling for too many things I didn't like made me forget what I needed, forget who I was. You brought it all back, even my inspiration, something I thought I had lost forever." He uses his free hand to smooth a curl off her face, tucking it behind her ear. His touch brands her skin. "I know you think that not everything is about love or happiness." He pauses to study her gaze. "But to me, *everything* is about love, and *everything* is about happiness, and all of it is about you." He presses a gentle kiss to her knuckles, his eyes deep and gleaming.

"What are you saying?" she asks, as if he's speaking an entirely different language.

"I'm saying *I love you*, Chloe Barrett." His words suck the last bit of air out of her lungs in one swift motion. "Tell me you don't feel the same, and I promise I'll leave you alone."

"I can't tell you that," she manages, dumbstruck. Everything around her becomes a giant blur.

Will loves her. It was one thing reading his text. Hearing it in-person is a new thing entirely.

"Then tell me you are willing to fight for us."

"Will, I can't let you lose everything."

He. Loves. Her.

"I already lost everything when you shut me out, Chloe. I don't need any of it if I can't have you."

His words hit her so hard that all she's able to do is wrap her arms around him and sink into his chest, allowing her body to fit against that perfectly shaped space he has just for her. She lets everything go. She's so profoundly addicted to his scent, and touch, and everything Will...

It takes a while for her to gain her breath back and muster enough bravery to rip herself away from his touch. Then she sits up and says, "I promise to give a heck of a fight." She seizes his lips for a kiss, claiming him back. "But there's something I have to do first."

CHAPTER 25

Righting Wrongs

"I'm outside." Chloe sends a quick text message as she steps out of the Uber. The driver looks around in awe, taking in the expansive grounds before driving away slowly. Her phone buzzes back with three thumbs-up emojis. Looks like she has the green light to proceed. She walks up to the main entrance and rings the doorbell. Her heart is violently somersaulting for what seems like forever while she waits for the door to open. Chloe tries to inhale deeply to calm her nerves down, but all she manages is a few shallow breaths.

"My dear Chloe!" Sveta opens the door with a big smile on her face, pulling Chloe into a big, loving bear hug that blows life back into her nervous self. All it took was one short text message exchange with Georgia Allentown. When Chloe asked her for help, she wasn't sure what to expect. Being Maxwell Allentown's sister and the ice queen's sister-in-law, helping Chloe could pose some risks along the extended family tree dynamics. But Georgia has been on her side all along. After all, she was the one who introduced Chloe and Will.

"*I thought you'd never ask,*" was all Georgia had to say in response, no questions asked.

"Let me take your coat," Sveta offers, and then leads her to the informal living room. "You got this." She winks at her.

Maxwell and Aline Allentown are seated, hopefully comfortable, Georgia by their side, all ready for her to make her appearance. This time they're not in formal attire. For the Allentowns, that means expensive tailored slacks and a polo shirt or blouse, but for Chloe, it's her typical jeans, a sweater, and her favorite Dr. Martens boots. No makeup, no fancy hairstyle – just her go-to ponytail, the kind of appearance that would have made Jimmy scowl. But Jimmy is not in her life anymore. And Will ... he just likes her the way she is.

He loves her.

So here she is, taking her leap of fate. And in order to do it right, she has to be herself, and that includes the entire package – hence her Dr. Martens boots and all.

They all get up as she approaches, offering their signature cold handshakes and polite – albeit on the reserved side – greetings. But Georgia, who insisted on coming to *"balance out the atmosphere and provide moral support,"* gives Chloe a warm hug. "They're ready for you," she whispers in her ear and gestures for her to sit down beside her. Georgia's role in this grand plan included three parts:

1. Making sure Will's parents were home and in a comfortable state – this part has clearly been accomplished.

2. Lay the groundwork for a positive conversation – and judging by Georgia's facial expression, the odds are in her favor, more so than not, hopefully. But given the ice queen being ... well ... the ice queen, there's still a lot of work to be done.

3. Making sure Will is not aware of the plan and is not plan-

ning a surprise visit to his parents tonight.

"Mr. And Mrs. Allentown," Chloe says, "thank you for agreeing to see me tonight." She swallows hard. "I am here to ask for your blessing."

"I think I was very clear with my proposition. We made a deal." Aline Allentown's eyes narrow.

They're thirty minutes into the conversation, and not a lot of progress has been made. Chloe told them all about herself, about her past, about her dreams and aspirations. Aline, insistent on staying silent on her shameful proposition, has been only talking around the topic. This is the first direct mention of it, and by the slight shift in her composure and the puzzled look on Maxwell Allentown's face, it dawns on Chloe that he may not have been brought in on that degrading offer.

With a small glimpse of hope to support her rebuttal Chloe says, "I never agreed to your proposition." She pauses to stabilize her voice. "You see, money has never been a driver for me. Sure, one needs some amount of money to survive, but beyond that, money makes people blind, makes them lose track of what's truly important." A strike of realization hits Maxwell's face. Chloe continues, "The most important things in life, at least for me, no amount of money could buy."

"I have said it before and will say it again," Aline interjects. "Enough money would."

"Oh, for goodness' sake Aline, let the girl talk!" Maxwell, for the first time in the conversation, speaks up. "Please proceed, Chloe." He gives her a curt nod.

"Thank you," Chloe says formally. "My adoptive parents lost both of their boys to a genetic disease before they turned three."

"Jesus," Maxwell offers. "I am very sorry."

Georgia takes Chloe's hand quietly and gives it a supportive squeeze.

Chloe's voice loses its beat for a few seconds, but she perseveres. "No amount of money could have saved them then, and unfortunately, it wouldn't now either. Tay Sachs has no cure. And," she continues with conviction, "no amount of money could have saved my adoptive parents either. You see, they had money, but it meant nothing when each lost their battle to their illnesses. Do you think your money could have made a difference there?" Chloe takes a deep breath, preparing for another interjection from her majesty, the ice queen, but this time Aline remains quiet.

Speechless? Respectful of her husband's wishes? Of Chloe's dead family?

Chloe takes it as a sign to proceed. "Money can't buy love either. And like you – I *used to* think that not everything was about love."

"Not everything is about love. At least we can agree on one thing," Aline interrupts. Staying silent is clearly not her strong suit, especially when it comes to money or love. Or, more precisely – the over-rating of money and under-rating of love.

"Is that right?" Maxwell gives his wife a sarcastic look that makes her settle back into her seat, gracing them with momentary speechlessness. "Please proceed." He looks at Chloe again, this time offering a slight smile that brings out a ghost of resemblance to his son. This inspires a new source of energy in Chloe, helping her push through.

"I used to question whether love even existed," Chloe continues. "But your son changed everything the minute he came into my life." She exhales a pent-up breath. "I love your son, Mr. and Mrs.

Allentown, I love Will more than anything, and I can't imagine my life without him. I tried to let him go without a fight. I thought I was protecting him. I couldn't live with the thought that *I* would be responsible for him losing everything ... losing his family." Her eyes move from Aline's glare to Maxwell's confused expression.

"I'm sure my little proposal helped steer you in the right direction," Aline snares.

"It offended me greatly." Chloe returns a glare. "And surely you must know the money never left your account. I fed that check into the paper shredder, where it belonged."

"Aline, what is she talking about?" Maxwell turns to his wife, demanding an explanation.

"Oh, don't bother yourself with this nonsense," Aline responds. "It's time for you to leave, Ms. Barrett."

"Mom tried to buy me out for three million dollars."

That voice.

Aline turns her head in a sudden jerk, and her eyes widen.

Chloe's head follows. Her eyes spot Will leaning against the heavy door frame, looking determined and ... surprised.

This makes the two of them.

How long has he been standing there?

"A miserable valuation when accounting for a broken heart, don't you think?" Will's voice is unwavering.

Two! Two broken hearts.

"William, what are you doing here?" Aline's face is a mix of astonishment and pain.

Is she surprised her son is here? That he knows the truth? Or is it the broken heart that got her?

"I called him." Sveta appears behind Will, "I thought he should be part of this conversation." She says something in Russian under her breath, making Will nod.

"Mom, Dad, for almost thirty years, I've been following your lead; my hobbies, my friends, my career choice, trying to make you proud, at the cost of my own happiness. I'm grateful for everything you've done for me, but this ends here." He stops and walks over to Chloe, holding his hand out to her. She takes it triumphantly, and he pulls her up to stand beside him. His proximity has this magical effect of bringing back every ounce of her courage.

"William, it was all for your own—" his mother tries to interject, but Will signals for her to stop.

"I am not done," he says with admirable composure and conviction. "I love Chloe." His eyes shoot to hers for a brief moment, then back to his parents. "She's my best friend, my inspiration. She's everything to me. I don't want to spend a single day of my life without her, and there is nothing you can do to change that. I am not going to let you push her away. I don't need your money, you can wipe my name off any financial document for all I care, but I do ask that you accept the way I feel, accept us." He turns to Chloe, pulling her closer. "I heard you say it," he whispers. "You love me." An adorable boyish grin stretches across his face. "You mean it?"

"I do. I love you, William Allentown!" She lets her own foreign words penetrate her mind, as if love needed permission to cross the blood-brain barrier.

Maybe hers does.

But it comes out so naturally, as if loving this man is the easiest thing she's ever done.

She can hear happy claps behind them, guessing that Georgia and Sveta are the ones responsible for them, encouraging her to continue. And now that she's set these words free, she cannot stop there.

"Will, you brought to life a naive wish I had buried and forgotten years ago." Her eyes drowning in his. His warm touch surrounds her, completely shutting out the outside world. "You showed me what it's like to love and be loved. And now that I know, I don't ever want to lose you again. I don't ever want to forget what happiness feels like." A tear escapes her eye, trailing across her cheek.

Will wipes it away gently, bringing her chin up to face him, and with beaming eyes, he says, "I promise I will never let you."

"I think we have heard enough." The ice queen's voice violently pulls them back from above the clouds. Georgia, who's been a quiet observer for the most part, voices her surprise.

"We certainly have," Maxwell agrees and stands. "Son," he says. "Chloe," he adds, addressing them both, "you have our blessing." He then does something completely unexpected, a facial expression that Chloe was sure his face was not capable of producing. He smiles. A big, proud smile.

Chloe just can't help herself, and sprints over to give this new Maxwell a hug, ignoring his surprised expression. "I suppose a hug is fitting," he approves and reciprocates.

"Your acceptance means a lot to me, Dad." Will says and approaches his father for a hug, a warm hug this time, unlike those cold ritualistic hugs Chloe witnessed between them before.

"Speak for yourself, Maxwell." Aline's sullen glare still holds on to that berated look she so proudly possesses, her typical resting face.

"No, Aline, I am sorry, but this is where I draw the line," Maxwell says with praiseworthy certainty, especially since he is now on team Chloe.

"My place or your place?" Will asks when they're in the comfort of his car.

"Mine," Chloe replies, "in case your mom finds some fancy clause to evict you tomorrow morning."

"Even my mom isn't that fast," he says smugly. "Plus, she can't, it's mine."

Chloe pulls out her cell phone. "Fifty percent success," she texts Valerie.

"Look at you seeing the glass half full!" Val texts back, followed by, "You kids have the place all to yourself tonight," and a winking face emoji. "I'm staying another night at Elle and TJ's guest room. Did I mention it has its own ensuite bathroom?"

"You did, and thanks, babe," Chloe texts back.

"So now you have a broke boyfriend, possibly soon to be un-employed," Will says half-joking, half-serious. Actually, more like thirty percent joking and seventy percent serious. It turns out his dad doesn't have much say in financial matters. Nevertheless, a big, dimpled grin stretches across his face, reaching all the way to his eyes.

"Look at the bright side. You'll have plenty of time to work on your book." Chloe smiles broadly, interlacing her fingers with his. "And you've just referred to yourself as my boyfriend. I like that for me."

"Good," he says as he snatches a parking spot under her apartment complex. Perhaps calling it *their* apartment complex is now in order. "I like that for me too."

CHAPTER 26

Epilogue

"Okay, ladies, one more stretch for the day before I let you go," Chloe walks around the room, adjusting her cordless mic. She still can't believe she owns this place.

Waking up with a smile has become her new normal – that is, since she and Will moved in together.

It took Aline Allentown about a month to accept Chloe (even apologize, an almost surreal scene for any observer), primarily due to Aline coming to realize a few important facts:

1. Love does exist if you let it. Realistically speaking, Aline will not go as far as admitting it, but at least she came to peace with permitting others to experience it. And it seems to be contagious.

2. Obliterating her own son, at the age of thirty, for choosing his girl over his mom was not as straightforward as Aline had thought, especially during Christmas time. Plus, Aline's best friend Melinda is now a happy grandmoth-

er, and the clock is ticking. That could also explain why Aline didn't choke when Will broke the news about his and Chloe's ENGAGEMENT! Yes, that was Chloe's first and best trip to Florida.

3. Sydney Bell, having moved on quite quickly, has been sighted on multiple occasions with Avery, her new happy boyfriend, and Will's business partner, rendering Aline's previous matchmaking attempt rather futile.

4. Not going against her husband's wishes for once after forty years of marriage actually won Aline some points with Maxwell. Chloe isn't sure what that entails exactly, and doesn't want to know either, but this seems to be playing itself out quite well.

Chloe packs her backpack, turns off the lights, locks up the doors to her studio, and takes the elevator to the fifth floor. Her college graduation day surprise from Will was a set of keys to a Pilates and nutrition health center (and not just for women), now known as Chloe's Place, on the first floor of the Allentown building. Her very own studio, in his building. And the best part – current and past foster kids and their families are welcome free of charge, courtesy of the Allentown family.

The doors open to the fifth floor's lobby, and she walks past the empty desk belonging to the receptionist, who has already gone home for the day.

"Hey," she says as she opens the heavy door leading to Will's office.

Will lifts his gaze from his desktop, and his face lights up when he sees her. "Hey!" he says, pushing his chair away from his desk, following her with his eyes as she steps closer and lands in his lap.

"I waited all day to do this," he says, pulling her in for a kiss. "I love you! You know that?"

"I love you too," Chloe says, a little breathless from the kiss, and yes, she does know, Will makes sure of that every single day. "Ready for your big event?" she asks excitedly.

Will nods. "I just hope someone shows up," he says nervously, cupping her face with his hands.

"Are you kidding me? Your book has sold over 10,000 copies in less than three months. Something tells me this is going to be a busy book signing event." She cuddles into him, nuzzling his jaw.

"Mmmm," he groans happily, "keep doing that. I'm already feeling better." A dimpled grin appears on his face.

"I promise to do it every day for the rest of our lives," she straightens his tie, "but now, Mr. CEO, I must drag you out of here. Your parents are waiting downstairs, and we're riding together – your mom insisted."

Something happened with his parents after Will finished writing his first novel, *Let It Love*. His debut romantic comedy. The first time he let Chloe read it, she couldn't put it down. She had to read it cover to cover, twice, and could not rest until Will promised to work on a sequel. It had a similar effect on his parents, who somehow turned from dubious literature critics to his number-two and number-three fans. Not number one, of course, because that spot is reserved just for Chloe.

About Me

Emma Aiseman is my pen name, devoted to my romance writing. I live in Maryland with the loves of my life – my husband and our three amazing children (and our tiny yet mighty puppy).

I am a scientist by day – working in the biotech industry. Not because I have to keep my day job, but because I love science, and I truly believe that doing both (science and art) has a special synergistic effect. I have a PhD in biochemistry, postdoctoral fellowships in the fields of epigenetics and autoimmune disease, and have been fortunate to work with quite a few outstanding mentors who have guided me along the way. I am passionate about research and new discoveries, especially when it involves questioning central dogmas.

I am a writer by night – writing is part of who I am. I write because it makes me happy and because I just can't not write. I've been writing fiction since learning the alphabet, in different languages. During high school I worked as a teen journalist at one of the top teen magazines in Israel. I also wrote and published a children's book in Hebrew as a young adult.

The first time I picked up a romantic comedy novel (well, one might argue it picked me), that book kept me up all night, put a big smile on my face, made me blush, made me laugh, and made me wish I could read it for the first time all over again. And before I knew it, I was transported back to my bookworm phase, and feel-good romance became my favorite genre. Then came the uncontrollable itch to write something new again! So here I am.

If you enjoyed *Let it Love*, please leave a review (Amazon, Goodreads, TikTok or anywhere else). I would love to know!

Check out my website or follow me on Amazon for news about my next book.

Hope to meet again.

Sincerely,

Emma
emmaaiseman.com

Emma Aiseman
Romance Author

Acknowledgements

This whole adventure started thanks to several outstanding romantic comedy novels and story development books, which brought back the urge and the courage to pick up my pen, grab my notebook and get back to writing fiction (and then get Scrivener because my notebook became a huge mess). This book is my first romance novel and a dream come true for me. Writing it was so much fun, I enjoyed every minute of it (well, except for the part where Chloe and Will hit rock bottom, despite already knowing they would come through).

I would like to thank my husband and our three children – the loves of my life – for their love, support, encouragement, inspiration, and for putting a big smile on my face every single day!

To my parents, sisters, grandparents and extended family and close friends for your love, cheering and support. Especially my mom – who's patiently read every one of my manuscripts through the years, and always with a positive outlook. And to my grandfather for teaching me the joy of writing, and for reminding me that even short stories deserve some sort of closure.

To my story development team - Isaac, Lia, Anat, Ori and

Jonathan for the fun and thought provoking brainstorming sessions.

To my beta readers, especially Lia - for your clever comments and character development remarks!

To my editor who's made an incredible job improving the grammar, readability and flow without changing my voice.

To Mitxeran - for the illustration and cover design, I can't wait to work with you again.

And finally, to my family's puppy for patiently and persistently sitting by my side during my writing hours, even when I ran out of dog treats.

Made in United States
North Haven, CT
10 March 2024

49775172R00168